Into *the* Sunset

Into *the* Sunset

Clare Matravers

Sapphire Series Book 3

Into the Sunset
Published by Clare Matravers
New Zealand

© 2019 Clare Matravers

ISBN 978-0-473-48745-4 (Softcover)
ISBN 978-0-473-48746-1 (ePUB)
ISBN 978-0-473-48747-8 (Kindle)

Production & Typesetting:
Lizelle van Antwerpen & Andrew Killick
Castle Publishing Services
www.castlepublishing.co.nz

Cover design:
Paul Smith

PART ONE

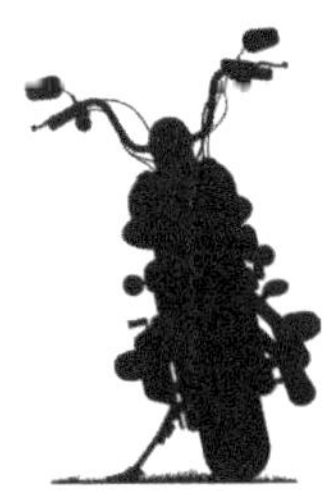

Chapter One

Summer early 2006

"Look, James, there's our baby!" Sapphire could hardly spare a glance away from the screen; she had already fallen in love with the wee blob of humanity. "We've waited so long for this." She stared harder at the indistinct image showing on the monitor. "Am I seeing things?" she asked, before looking up at the sonographer—it was worrying to watch her smile straighten into a frown. "Is there a problem?"

"Absolutely not," the woman said and smiled again. "I'm just making sure—I didn't want to get your hopes up unnecessarily. I detect two little hearts pounding away in there."

"You mean?" Saph peered at the picture again. "We're going to have—"

The sonographer turned the volume up and the sound of life filled the room. "Yes, Mr and Mrs Holden, it looks as though two babies are on their way."

"Twins? Seriously?" James sounded aghast and Saph turned her attention to him.

"Is something wrong, James?" she asked—he seemed more dismayed than happy and her joy leaked out a little.

"No, it's just a bit of a shock, that's all." James rubbed his face as though weary. "A little overwhelming."

"I did warn you," Saph said.

"Yes, you did—but I didn't think it would actually happen." Then he smiled, although it seemed to take effort. "Two babies for the price of one. Boy, are we going to be busy."

"The Lord has certainly heard our prayer." After six years of begging God for a baby, it had been tempting to give up. But at last it had happened. In abundance.

"Now we'll have to buy two of everything," James said, once they were out in the corridor. "Perhaps that overseas trip wasn't such a great idea. It cost a fortune and we're still paying it off."

"Stop being such a pessimist. We couldn't see into the future." Saph grinned. "Besides if we hadn't gone on that holiday to relax, I doubt there'd be any babies. Anyway we can't send them back." She cast a glance at her husband's gloomy face. "Don't worry, we'll manage somehow. If God gave us these precious gifts, I'm sure He'll provide for us."

Outside, Saph all but danced her way through the car park, James stumping along beside her.

"Now that I'm past the twelve-week mark," she said, "and everything looks normal, we can finally tell people our amazing news." This was so different from her first pregnancy, a shameful secret which she had only confided to a single close friend. Now she wanted to make an announcement from the rooftops.

"I can't wait—Candace can be the first to know." She stopped suddenly but James kept walking. "Oh, I've just had a horrible thought—I hope she won't feel as though she's being replaced. After all she's had eighteen years of being an only child." Saph had to stride to catch up to him.

"She'll cope," James said. "She should be mature enough by now."

It was true. Her little girl was all grown up. Saph resumed her dancing until they reached the car. It was only when they were pulling their seatbelts on that she noticed how subdued James was.

"Aren't you happy about having children?"

He hesitated as though thinking of what to say.

"Of course I am." He seemed to be choosing his words carefully. "It's just daunting, the thought of two babies at once. Especially at our time of life. Let's face it Saph, we're not exactly spring chickens anymore. Although my mother was young and energetic when she had us twins, she reckoned it was still difficult keeping up with two boys."

"Maybe ours will be girls. They tend to be a little less active."

"Even so it's going to be hard work. When Mum found out she was expecting two babies, she was thrilled—she thought we'd entertain each other. But instead we used to fight like crazy and she was kept busy trying to minimise the damage."

Saph chuckled. "Would you prefer girls, boys, or perhaps one of each?"

"I don't really mind as long as they're healthy. Thinking about twins does remind me of Darryll though …" He clenched his fists on the steering wheel. "If only I'd known back then what he was going to do …"

"Oh James, I didn't even think about that." She rubbed his arm. "I'm sorry."

But he seemed to give himself a mental shake and patted her hand as if to reassure her, before turning the ignition key.

"Best not to dwell on the past. I am happy, really." Although his words lacked sincerity, she wanted to believe him. "I'm sure everyone will be overjoyed for us. If these twins are identical, they can have great fun confusing their teachers and friends, just like we did." It was a relief to hear him laugh a little. "Sometimes even our parents found it difficult to tell us apart."

Candace stared at her mother and then her father with suspicion. The whole way through dinner her parents had hardly spoken a word; just made silent communication with gestures and meaningful glances. Their shared furtiveness which had been going on for weeks now hadn't gone unnoticed, but tonight it had ramped up big time. Even at her age, it made her uneasy, stirring up memories of the whispering that had gone on behind her back for much of the latter part of her childhood.

Until two years ago. It was the day after her sixteenth birthday when Mum had hesitantly revealed the shocking and unbelievable Big Secret. Candace had not once suspected that Saph was actually her birth mother, and Kathy, the woman she had always called 'Mum', had apparently 'adopted' her. To find out she had been deceived for all those years had been incredibly painful at the time.

But there had been an even bigger and nastier surprise in store. In an effort to find out who her father was, Candace had done some digging of her own. To her horror, she had at last uncovered the full story of her origins: Saph, with Kathy's help, had attempted to have her drunken 'mistake' aborted. The feelings of rejection had been almost overwhelming and it had taken quite some time to work through her forgiveness of the two women.

Even now the memory was still tender. Surely her parents didn't have another Big Secret they were keeping from her? Mum looked set to make an announcement and Candace braced herself.

"We've got something to tell you," Mum said.

"I guessed as much." Candace waited. Hopefully it wasn't going to be a bombshell. Perhaps they were thinking of selling the house? But no, they couldn't because it wasn't theirs to sell—when Kathy had died, she had left it in a trust for her.

"I'm pregnant!" Mum looked both pleased and nervous at the same time.

"Oh!" That was unexpected. Her parents had been married for years now with no sign of a baby, and Mum's yearning had been all but forgotten; she hadn't mentioned her dream for some time.

"I've been dying to tell you," Mum said, "for weeks, but we thought it best to wait until I was out of the danger zone. I had a scan this afternoon and was given the all clear. We wanted you to be the first to know."

It took a little while to absorb the news and to ponder how to react. How was this going to affect the family dynamics? No longer would she be an only child. What was it going to be like to have a sibling? She looked up to find her parents gazing at her.

"So when's the baby due?" she asked. Hopefully it was a safe enough question and would throw them off the track of her concern.

Her mum visibly relaxed. "So you're not upset?"

There hadn't been enough time to fully process the news and all its implications but before she could say anything, Dad spoke.

"*They* are due in July."

"They?" Candace gulped. "How many are you having?"

"Just two," Dad answered.

"Double trouble! Sorry, I mean a double blessing." Another minor bombshell, on top of the first. Although the news was still reverberating, Candace stood up and moved around the table to hug first Mum and then Dad. "Seriously, I am happy for you both," she said, trying to be. "I know it's something you've been wanting for a long time." But her father's smile looked insincere, and contrasted with her mother's obvious joy. Perhaps he wasn't as rapt with the idea as Mum clearly was.

Candace mock-pouted. "So as soon as I leave home, you replace me?"

"We couldn't replace you!" Mum looked dismayed.

"We can't have an empty nest, you know," Dad said. Again he sounded more resigned than happy.

"Naturally, we'll expect you to babysit." Mum grinned at her. "It'll be good practice for you when you have children of your own."

"Who says I'm having any?" Candace lifted her chin in defiance.

"I thought you would be having ten at least." Mum was still teasing but Candace wasn't laughing.

"Will there still be room for me here?" she asked.

"Of course." Although Mum gave her a reassuring smile, Dad didn't look so certain. "Anyway you'll be off to university before they're born, and then aren't you planning to do your great OE?"

"Is that a hint?"

"No," Mum said. But she appeared distracted and Candace was not convinced.

After Candace had excused herself, Saph noticed James's serious face.

"What's wrong?" she asked.

"Candace has got a point about the lack of space," he said. "It shouldn't be a problem having the babies sleeping in our room while they are still, well, babies but what happens when they get older and bigger?"

"Then they can go into Candace's bedroom."

"But what about Candace? When she comes back for the holidays?"

"It'll be a squeeze but we'll cope if it's just for a few days. Anyway I wouldn't be surprised if she stays on in Hamilton. And if she does eventually return to Auckland, she won't want to live with us; she'll be wanting a flat of her own."

"Might I remind you this is her flat? Or at least it will be soon."

"Oh, I'd forgotten about that." Saph grimaced.

"You don't think she'd throw her weight around and kick us out?" James asked.

Saph shook her head. "That's not Candace's style."

"Still, we need a bigger house. A house of our own."

"But can we afford it?"

In her room, Candace sat on her bed for a few minutes, still processing the implications. If she had been irresolute before about leaving home, she certainly was not now. She was being pushed, none too gently, out of the nest.

Resentment dug in. She would be coming of age in a couple of years' time—she could chuck them out of *her* unit. And then what would they do? That would teach them … but she couldn't do that to her family. She reached for her cell phone and speed dialled Tiffany.

"You'll never guess what Mum and Dad have just told me!"

Tiff too was somewhat taken aback at the news. "But aren't they, like, really old?"

"Obviously not too ancient."

"So my Johnny will be older than their kids, and yet I'm the same age as you. Weird."

"Gosh, I've just had a thought; I hope nobody thinks the babies are mine!"

Tiff pretended to sound shocked. "As if!"

"It's just as well I'm clearly single."

"And far too sweet and innocent to carry on like that." Tiff chuckled. "Watch out, this might make you all clucky. Now don't you go getting any ideas." Ignoring Candace's scornful snort, she continued sounding stern. "You need to get your degree and use that fine brain of yours. Don't waste it like I did." There was a note of wistfulness in her voice.

Chapter Two

By late afternoon most of the beach goers had left, but the occasional shout could still be heard through the open French doors of Helen's café.

"Mum, you're wanted." Saph indicated the man who was peering in.

"Are you still serving?" he asked.

"No," Helen said. "We stopped an hour ago." Obviously disappointed, the man turned away.

"I'd have thought the big 'Closed' sign on the door would be a bit of a clue," Henk muttered after the man had gone.

"It's testament to your great cooking skills, Mum," Saph said tapping a nervous rhythm on the Formica topped table. She took a sip of her ice-cold lemonade, and quietly prayed it would settle her stomach. The faint smell of barbeque smoke wafting in from outside, and the food odours lingering in the café air were not helping. She fidgeted, impatient to announce her news, but unsure of how her parents would react. They didn't seem to notice her edginess. Saph raised her eyebrows at James and he nodded slightly. She opened her mouth but Helen spoke first.

"There's some mussel chowder left over from lunch," she said. "We could have that for dinner. With crusty rolls."

Just the mention of one of her favourite dishes made Saph want to heave. A fresh sea breeze had started up and she inhaled deeply to quell the nausea, while exchanging glances with James. "Not for me, thanks. I'd better not risk it."

Helen looked insulted. "I would reheat it thoroughly."

"I'm sure you would, Mum. It's not food poisoning I'm worried about, but listeria." Her mother's expression flickered as the mental cogs began to turn. "You see, the reason we came to visit is …"—Saph reached for James's hand—"we have some news. And this time it is what you might think."

It didn't take long for Helen to click.

"You're going to have a baby!" She gaped while Henk's eyebrows lifted.

"Times two actually," James said.

"Twins!" Helen reached across the table to squeeze their hands. "Congratulations to you both!" But her delighted smile became a doubtful frown. "Babies at your age?"

"Mum, that's not very subtle."

"I mean, will you have the energy to run around after them?"

"Don't worry." Saph tried to sound breezier than she felt. "I'm fit and healthy and I'll manage. There's still plenty of life left in me yet." But judging by Helen's unease, it was obvious that wasn't all she was worried about. "Yes, I am well aware of the risks involved in having children later in life. I know there is a chance of Down syndrome."

"Are you going to be tested?"

"No, I've decided not to. Partly because of the risk of miscarriage but also, even if there are some issues, we're determined to love these babies. No matter what."

"Very wise of you to avoid seafood then." But Helen still didn't look totally convinced.

Henk grinned at James. "I don't envy you, mate. I could barely cope with one baby. Mind you she was quite a stroppy one."

Both Saph and Helen glared at him. James said nothing, just stared at the contents of his glass.

It would not be a good look to throw up in front of the boss. Saph paused to draw in some deep breaths of the hallway air, but it was musty and of little help. She peered through the open door into her Dad's old office. Even though it had been some time since he'd retired due to ill health, not much had changed and it was still a little disconcerting to see Lydia and not Dad, in the big swivel chair behind the vast desk.

With her head bent over paper work, the manager hadn't noticed her yet, so Saph tapped on the door and cleared her throat. Lydia looked up before beckoning her in.

"Are you all right?" Her boss stared at her. "You're very pale. Do you need to go home sick?"

"No." Saph felt her white face heat up as she stood in front of the desk. "I'm here to put in a request for maternity leave."

It clearly took a moment for her words to sink in. Then Lydia gave a knowing nod and lit up in a giant smile. "Now I understand your pallor. Congratulations!" Her expression dissolved into a non-serious frown. "But it feels as though you've only just come back from your overseas trip."

"Think of that as a practice run." In spite of the nausea Saph grinned. "You coped without me back then didn't you?"

"Only just." Lydia grimaced. "And certainly not as efficiently. I was overjoyed to see you return. Now it seems I'll have to wave you good-bye again. How far along are you?"

"Only three months gone. Anyway I'm not resigning just yet. Apart from a bit of nausea and tiredness, I don't feel too bad at all. I should be able to work at least until the end of May, so that will give you plenty of time to find a replacement. Even after that I could help out remotely via phone and email if necessary."

"You won't have time! A baby will keep you on your toes."

"And two even more so."

"Seriously?" Lydia sighed. "In that case I guess you won't be coming back again for ages, if ever. At least not to work. You're not going to be easy to replace. First your father retires and now you." She smiled. "The business is in danger of going belly up without a Nord here."

"You won't even notice I'm gone." But Saph was pleased with the compliment.

Lydia snorted her derision. "Can you think of someone who could step up to take your place?"

"Just about any staff member in the office should be able to do the job."

Lydia looked doubtful. "But not as well as you."

"What about the original office manager?" Saph asked. "Perhaps Dianne might like her old job back. She was super efficient."

"You are joking aren't you? She may have been brilliant at the job but she had no people skills. And I could do without the dramas amongst the office staff. Remember how she left without giving notice?"

Saph chuckled. "She looked so embarrassed after accusing me of having an affair with the manager—only to find out he was my father."

Lydia let out an unladylike guffaw before recovering her dignity. "Mind you, she was certainly efficient. Perhaps I should consider—"

"Sorry, Lydia, I have to go." With her hand over her mouth, Saph made a dash for the nearest bathroom.

Rather than switching on the kitchen light, Saph left the fridge door open. She jumped at the flood of sudden brightness and turned to see James blinking sleepy eyes at her.

"I was trying not to disturb you," she said.

"What's that you're eating?" He looked horrified. "Really? Sardines and ice-cream?"

"Just be grateful it's not something more exotic," Saph said as she resumed filling her bowl, "or I might be sending you down to the nearest service station ..." She paused to lick the salty-sweet spoon. "... in the middle of the night."

James pulled a face. "I hope the ice-cream doesn't taste fishy."

"No chance of that—there's none left." Saph grinned. "And we're out of sardines too."

Chapter Three

"Thanks for coming to see me off." Candace gave Tiffany a hug, made awkward by young Johnny on his mother's hip. She gently patted the infant's chubby face. "You be a good boy for your mum, young lad." He solemnly regarded her over the fist in his mouth.

"Now who will I get to babysit?" Tiff asked, pretending to sulk. "Since my star childminder is so inconsiderately going away?" Her pout became a smile and there was a twinkle in her eye. "Make sure you have a wonderful time down there but you behave yourself, girl." Even though Dad was absorbed in packing the boot and Mum was already in the car, Tiff still lowered her voice. "I know what uni students get up to. You don't want to end up a young mother like me."

Candace shook her head hard. "No chance of that. I'm giving the opposite sex a wide berth, at least while I concentrate on my studies." She leaned over to whisper in her friend's ear. "Please keep an eye on Greg."

"For sure. We'll invite him round for dinner now and then." Tiff grinned. "It might be the only decent meal the man gets."

"He probably has lots of single women who would love to cook for him." Candace put on a brave smile, hoping her words weren't true. It was selfish to expect the love of her life to wait and pine for her for years, but the thought of him finding anyone else while she was away, was unbearable. "I'd better not keep Mum and Dad waiting."

"Have you got everything?" her mother asked as Candace shoe-horned herself into the back.

"Yes Mum." Candace's resigned sigh was exaggerated.

"Just as well." Dad climbed into the driver's seat. "I doubt we could fit a single sheet of paper in, sideways. Candace, we might have to leave you behind."

"I wish you would," Mum said in a low voice. "I can't believe my baby girl is off to uni." She shook her head.

"I'm not a kid anymore, Mum." Candace rolled her eyes.

"Yes, as you keep reminding us. But it only seems five minutes since you were …"

Saph stared out the windscreen, sweet memories of Candace as a child causing a nostalgic tear to well up. And there were regrets too—for missing out on the babyhood and early years of the daughter she had believed to be dead.

Another memory surfaced unbidden, one that Saph longed to blot out: of her own foolish behaviour the day after she had arrived in Hamilton. Drinking herself into a haze at her first ever student party had been a completely stupid thing to do. But regrets were pointless; the past was set in shatterproof glass. And if she hadn't made this drunken error of judgement, there would be no Candace. As always, God had brought something wonderful out of something bad. *Lord, please look after my daughter.*

James interrupted her thoughts. "Can you text Mum and tell her we should be at the Hamilton lake café by eleven-thirty?"

She dabbed the tear away. There would be plenty more later. "Should we make our big announcement to your parents before or after lunch? I'm sure they'll be thrilled to hear our news."

There was no reply from James. Perhaps he was concentrating on his driving.

After a final wave to Tiff and Johnny, Candace kept her eyes on them until they were stick figures in the distance. Then she sat back as Dad steered the car through the familiar local streets. But at the motorway on-ramp, where the overhead sign pointed to Hamilton, it finally hit her; she was leaving home.

It was all becoming real, far too real. Her childhood was being left behind along with all that was predictable, comfortable and safe. To hide the threatening tears, she turned to gaze at the unexciting industrial landscape sliding past, and mentally farewelled the only home she had ever known.

Was it too late to change her mind? *Dad, please, please, please take the next off-ramp and return me to the familiar.* But oblivious to her unspoken request, he kept on driving.

She didn't have to go. There was a perfectly good university in this city—she could study here instead. Then she could get in touch with Greg and tell him she wasn't leaving after all, maybe ask him about that date he'd wanted to take her out on last year, when he'd claimed to be in love with her. She loved him too—but she had never told him that. Instead, she had given him the brush off, telling him how she longed to spread her cramped wings and experience the big wide world.

Okay, so Hamilton wasn't exactly the world but it was at least a launching pad to fly from. And with a teaching qualification, she could fulfil her long-held dream of travelling and working around the globe. As she planned to be away for years, she had set him free and made it clear he wasn't to hanker after her—although secretly she wished he would.

Since then she hadn't seen much of him. She had been too busy with exams and then a holiday job, to go to the youth group that he led or to help out in his soup kitchen. Presumably he was busy too. Or was he deliberately avoiding her at church? Sometimes it felt like it.

She missed him like crazy but if she stayed here to study, he would be a distraction. A clean break was for the best. At least that's what she told herself. She had to be brave and unselfish. Maybe after she had finished her training and travelling and if they were both still single …

No, she couldn't ask Dad to turn back. It would be too cowardly and embarrassing. She needed to get out of her comfort zone and be stretched. And out of the unit before it became too cramped with the arrival of the new babies. That alone was motivation enough to fledge.

Anyway she was an adult now, ready to make her own way in the world. And giving into fear was entirely the wrong attitude. It was just a momentary wobble in her confidence. She gave herself a little shake. This was an adventure; that was the best way to think of it. She was no coward and God would go with her. Her whole future lay before her. She was going to meet new people, make friends and have a whole lot of interesting experiences. Excitement began to replace fear.

Saph led the others into the café and spotted James's parents already seated at a table, gazing out the window as they sipped coffee. It was her mother-in-law who first turned to see them. Marion alerted Len with a nudge and they both stood up. During the round of hugs, Saph was careful to avoid pressing her slight bump against them so as not to give the game away prematurely.

"You'd better eat up large now," James said to Candace as they all waited in the rapidly growing queue to select their lunch. "It might be the last decent meal you'll have for some time. University hostels don't have a great reputation for their grub."

"Don't tease her," Saph said. "I'm sure it's of a decent quality these days." But Candace seemed either too nervous or too excited to take much interest in the food. Saph made up for it, by filling her tray. Back at the table, she noticed Marion eyeing it with surprise.

"Are you eating for two?" her mother-in-law asked, her eyes darting from Saph's face to her waistline and back again.

"Can I tell them?" Saph mouthed at James as they sat down. He nodded.

"No," she said with a tentative grin, "for three actually." She waited for her comment to sink in.

"You're pregnant?" Marion looked a little taken aback. "With twins?"

"Yes, that's right," James said, "I'm going to be a dad. Again. At least I think so …" They would never know for sure whether it was him or Darryll who was Candace's father.

Len shook their hands and beamed at them but his wife turned to stare out the picture window for a minute. Saph felt for her. Surely this must remind her of the twins she had raised, only to have Darryll commit suicide as a young man.

Then Marion seemed to rally. "I did wonder." Although it looked a little forced, she managed a smile. "I thought you seemed … well … rounder than the last time I saw you." She reached across the table to grasp both their hands. "That is wonderful news. And if you need any advice on having twins, I can certainly help you out. Although it's been many years since I had to raise children." Again Saph observed the wistful expression. "Do you know what you're having?"

"No, we want it to be a surprise."

Over lunch Saph noticed how quiet Candace was as she sat picking at the little food she had. Too much talk about babies perhaps or was the girl thinking about the start of her new life?

"We'd better get going soon," James said, glancing at the café clock. "We still have to install Candace in the hostel, say our farewells and then beat the motorway traffic home."

"Good-bye Mum," Candace said, as they embraced on the pavement outside the hostel. She clenched her jaw, determined not to cry. Her mother clung wordlessly to her as though she would never let go. And part of her didn't want to let go of Mum either—she represented all that was familiar and safe, the self pep talk in the car nearly forgotten—until she felt her mother's expanded girth. It was a reminder she was about to become surplus to requirements and she disentangled herself. Suddenly she couldn't wait for her parents to leave.

"We really need to get going, Saph." Dad sounded impatient. "If you want to avoid the traffic. And I'm sure Candace can't wait to see the back of us." Although he grinned at her, he looked as though he too was putting on a brave face for her benefit.

"But she's never left home before," Mum said. "I want to put off our departure until the last minute."

"Hamilton's not that far from Auckland," Dad said. "We can always come and visit. That is if Candace wants to be seen with us." He put a hand on her shoulder. "You're going to be fine, kiddo."

Instead of her usual indignant reaction to the nickname, Candace allowed her father to give her a brief hug, before he turned and opened the car door for his wife. Mum climbed into the passenger seat, dabbing at her face with a tissue.

In spite of the feelings of rejection, it was still not easy saying good-bye and Candace had to flick away a sneaky tear of her own. Then with Mum calling farewells and waving frantically out the window, they disappeared around a corner, taking Candace's childhood with them.

But at last she had made it out of the nest. Now she stood on the threshold of a sparkling new and exciting chapter of her life. Turning her back on the past, with the unfamiliar key in her hand, she marched through the foyer and up the stairs to her future.

It was fun, if a little disconcerting settling in, finding her way around the hostel and campus and making new friends. Only occasionally in the wee small hours of the morning, Candace would wake and experience a twinge of homesickness. But this was her new life now and she had to stop looking back.

She joined the small but thriving group of Christians in the hostel who met once a week to pray and provide crucial support to each other, in the largely atheistic university environment.

At the first meeting, one young man, Lance, seemed to take special notice of her. They got along well and it was nice to have a friend. Or did he want something more? He was out of luck there because she had made a rule for herself: no relationships while at university, at least for the first year while she tried to settle down in a new environment. Too distracting. She didn't want to get involved with anyone at the moment.

Chapter Four

"Hi Greg," Saph said to the young man's broad back. He froze in the church aisle before turning to face her. Over the last few months, she had only caught brief glimpses of him on the other side of the church, frantically mustering the youth. He always appeared to be busy. Or was he trying to keep out of her way, so as not to be reminded of Candace?

Now without a charge in sight, he looked like a morepork caught out in the daytime. His eyes grew even rounder when he glanced at Saph's waistline, before making a conscious effort to look at her face. She chuckled at his gentleman-like attitude.

"Yes, I am pregnant."

"How wonderful for you," he said and his face softened into a smile. Then he seemed to reconsider. "It is a good thing isn't it?"

"What, you mean at my age?" Saph grinned at his stricken look. "It's a dream come true!" She waited for the inevitable question.

"How's Candace?" There it was but hesitantly asked. "I was hoping to catch up with her before she goes to university."

"I'm afraid you're too late, Greg. We dropped her off in Hamilton the week before last."

"Already?" Although his crestfallen expression was painful to witness, surely there was a hint of relief there too. "I've been so busy, I lost track of time." It sounded like an excuse but Saph let it lie. "I bet you miss her." He looked wistful, perhaps projecting his own feelings on to her.

"Like crazy," Saph said. "Not that we saw much of her once school finished. She worked all summer and she was out quite a lot, socialising … but somehow she's managed to leave a huge Candace-shaped hole behind."

"I fully intended to see her before she left but life has been pretty hectic …" Greg seemed on edge. "Anyway I must go now, young people to round up and all that."

Saph didn't point out there was not a youth to be seen. He started to walk off.

"Greg?"

He spun around.

"Why have you been avoiding Candace?"

His gobsmacked expression was almost laughable. He closed his gape then opened up again as though to protest but sagged instead. "Is it that obvious? Because," he said, his voice soft, "although she didn't say it in so many words, she wants space. She made it clear she wants to spread her wings and fly off to experience the big wide world, and that she's too young to settle down. And I don't want to stand in her way. She even told me not to wait for her, to find someone else." His voice lowered further still. "But I don't want to."

Saph was torn; she could see Candace's point and admired her maturity, but at the same time she was annoyed with her daughter for letting this once-in-a-lifetime man get away.

"Next time you speak to Candace," Greg said, "please tell her I said 'hi'." He turned and with shoulders slumped, walked off.

And send love—Saph filled in the blanks.

"Have you got time to talk?" Saph asked.

"I'm just about to go to a lecture." Candace's voice distorted—she must have tucked her phone against her shoulder. In the background, Saph could hear the shuffling of paper and a ring binder being opened then closed.

"I'll be quick then. I thought you might be interested to know I spoke to Greg at church yesterday, for the first time in ages." The background noises stopped. "He noticed I was pregnant, but I didn't tell him it was twins. And yes, he did ask after you." Saph answered Candace's unspoken question. "He sends his greetings."

"How is he? I barely saw him over the holidays and that was only from a distance. It was almost as though he was avoiding me." Candace sounded wistful.

"Only because he thinks you want him to. He's under the impression there's no room for him in your life."

"Mum, I'm doing what I thought would be best for him—setting him free so that he can get on with his own life. Still, it would have been nice to see him once in a while. Just as a friend."

"Anyway his excuse is he's been very busy but he reckoned he did want to catch up with you before you left. He seemed disappointed to hear you'd already gone."

"Relieved more like."

"He might not say it but I'm sure he misses you, Candace. Don't let this one get away."

There was the sound of a door opening and shutting and then the echoes of a hallway.

"Sorry Mum, I have to go."

It was a pity Mum had to ring just then and mention Greg—now it would be a struggle to concentrate on the lecture. Heartening as it was to hear he was missing her, she must stop being selfish. If she truly loved the man, she would want what was best for him. Hopefully she was it. Not just yet, but one day perhaps …

"Hey, Christian." The sneering voice interrupted Candace's thoughts. She spun round to see who had spoken. Although she had seen the formidable young woman stalking the hostel corridors in the distance, so far there had been no close encounters. Until now—she was heading towards Candace, eyes gleaming defiance in heavy dark make-up. Dressed all in black and standing at least six-foot tall in her Doc Martins, she folded her arms and blocked the way. Candace hid her gulp and sent up a quick prayer.

"Yes, I am a Christian." She drew herself up to her full height—and still had to tilt her head back to meet the girl's derisive stare. "And not ashamed to admit it. But how do you know that?"

"I've seen you and your lot going into the meeting room."

"Did you want to come along too? Everyone's welcome." It was the right thing to say but still Candace braced herself for the anticipated response.

With an arrogant look in her eyes, the girl chuckled and swore but shifted her gaze from Candace's face to some distant spot. "I'm an atheist," she said, pride and defiance in her voice.

Candace grinned, fear gone now. "So your point is?"

A scowl flickered across the heavily made-up face. Perhaps she was used to people scarpering when she confronted them, especially cheeky pip-squeaks. She shrugged. "So why would I come to a religious meeting if I don't believe in god?" Her words dripped with scorn.

"Well, He believes in you." Candace was getting a crick in her neck. "Because He created you."

Looking slightly taken aback—whether it was because of her confident attitude or her words, Candace couldn't tell—the tall woman instead glanced at her watch. "I have to go." She turned on her heel and stalked off.

Although she was running late, Candace remained where she was, gazing after the retreating figure. Had she made the girl think? Or did she genuinely need to be somewhere?

The defensive teenager was standing in the hallway a couple of days later. Her eyes narrowed when she saw Candace, and again she moved into her path.

"It's the god-botherer." She taunted Candace with a sneer. "Off to worship your non-existent god then?"

Candace had had enough. "How do you know there is no god?" she asked. "Have you been everywhere in this universe, checked in every nook and cranny for one?"

Surprise flashed across the sceptic's face before she began an exaggerated dramatic search all around.

"I can't see one," she said sounding scornful.

"You can't see the wind or electricity—or for that matter," Candace couldn't resist saying it, "the brain inside your head."

The girl glared at her. "Are you implying I don't have a brain?" Her stance became even more defensive.

"Not at all, I'm merely making a point."

"True, they are invisible. But you can see the effect of wind, electricity and"—there was a challenge in her eyes—"my brain."

"Then you can see the effect of God—all around you, in the miracle of life."

The girl snorted. "But you lot say he's good. What about all the bad stuff in this world? If he does exist and he's supposed to be good, why doesn't he prevent it from happening?"

"Because there is a devil too. And God gave us freedom of choice. It's up to us which one we follow."

With a dramatic yawn the girl sauntered off. Candace didn't go after her.

After making some enquiries, Candace found out her tormenter's name was Amanda. Only her close friends were allowed to shorten it to Manda and nobody dared call her Mandy, at least not to her face. Her room was on the ground floor of the hostel block, but it seemed she had a friend, possibly a boyfriend, on the same floor as Candace, so she was up and down the stairs on a regular basis. Candace tried to remember Amanda in her daily prayers.

Although Candace normally avoided the lower corridor to minimise the risk of another tiring confrontation, today she was in a hurry and it was a shortcut. About to tiptoe past Amanda's closed door, she froze in her tracks. A strange noise was coming from the girl's room. It sounded like deep heartfelt sobs. Surely the big tough Amanda wasn't weeping? As tempting as it was to keep walking, and pretend not to hear the audible grief, Candace couldn't. She mustered her courage and tapped on the door. The noise stopped.

"Who is it?" The husky voice sounded gruff.

"It's Candace." It was doubtful Amanda would know her name but she should recognise her voice.

"What do you want?"

"Are you all right? You sound upset."

Amanda yelled perfectly clear and rude instructions for her to go away, and Candace scarpered. Upon her return to the hostel block, she walked back along the same route. At Amanda's door, she left a little posy of flowers she had picked from the hostel garden, along with a hastily scrawled compassionate note. After a moment's hesitation she added her name and room number.

Thumping on Candace's door brought her running. She flung it open and the welcome died on her lips—it was Amanda who barged past Candace and slammed the door.

"Nice to see you." Candace did her best to sound sincere. At first Amanda stood in the middle of the room, turning to look at the posters and to sneer at the scriptures on the walls. Then, folding her arms in her usual defensive manner, she glared at Candace.

"You said in your note to come and visit for a chat. Well, I want to talk."

"Sure. Pull up a chair." Once seated and to Candace's shock, big strapping Amanda hunched over and with her head in her hands, began to sob loudly. After a pause to screw up her courage and to send up an arrow prayer, Candace reached out and rubbed the girl's back.

"What's wrong?"

"It was a year yesterday since my dad took his own life," Amanda said through her sobs. "That's why I was upset. I didn't have any flowers to put on his grave marker—until I looked outside my door to find the ones you left."

"I'm so sorry to hear that. You must have been devastated."

"I just can't go on."

Was Amanda planning to copy her dad? She needed a counsellor surely—this issue was too big for Candace to help her with. But Amanda straightened up, her thick mascara unsmudged. She flicked the hand off her back as though it was an annoying fly and laughed. Candace shrank away.

"You sucker." Amanda's tone was utterly scornful. "Yes, my dad is dead but I don't care. In fact I'm glad he's gone—he was a total …"

Candace froze, trying to blot out the obscene description, and speechless at the complete change in the young woman's attitude. How humiliating—she had been taken for a ride. Still, she had only shown Christian compassion—it was Amanda who had acted badly. The young woman unfolded her lanky frame to tower over Candace.

"Got any money? Or alcohol? No, of course a nice Christian like you wouldn't drink."

Candace pulled her wallet out of her bag. "Here's ten dollars." It was her last. Amanda snatched it off her and peered into the empty purse.

"Is that all? Can't buy much plonk with that."

"Are you going to be all right?" Candace asked, stuffing down her anger and fear, and digging deep to summon up more compassion. But without a word, the girl shoved the money into her pocket and stalked out of the room.

After Amanda had slammed the door behind her, Candace slumped on the bed, shell-shocked. But the sorrow she had heard coming from behind the hostel door the previous day must have been real—not put on for her benefit, because Amanda couldn't have known she was listening. No, it was clear Amanda had been genuinely upset about something.

Chapter Five

"Hello Candace."

She looked up from her meal to see Lance smiling at her. After placing his dinner tray on the table, he pulled up a chair and she moved over to give him some space. On previous occasions when he had sat with her at meal times, his easy-going company had been enjoyable. But today, he was monosyllabic, and seemed ill at ease. Judging by the way he toyed with his food, nervousness had depleted his normally healthy appetite.

"Is something wrong?" she asked at the same time he opened his mouth to speak.

"I was wondering …" After a hesitant start, he gained momentum. "… if you wanted to go and see a movie with me some time?"

"Sort of, like on a date, you mean?"

He nodded vigorously. As tempting as it was to accept his invitation, she must stick to her self-imposed no-dating rule. It was a shame really, the young man wasn't the ugliest she had ever seen and they did get along quite well. She could do with a break from the constant grind of study too.

"Okay," she said at length. His pensive face lit up. "But only as a friend." His expression changed to mildly grieved.

"That's better than a flat refusal I guess. How's Friday night for you? I don't have a car so we'll have to catch the bus into town."

With a big grin, he picked up his half-full tray, and left. Candace frowned at his back. He had taken her seriously about the 'just friends' thing—hadn't he?

The film was cheesier than a pizza and so lame it was practically limping—but still Candace couldn't help giggling at it with Lance. It felt good to share a laugh with someone … just like she and Greg used to whenever they were together. Oh, how she missed that man and the fun times they had shared. But releasing him had been the sensible thing to do. She was too young to become serious about anyone and she needed to try out her adult wings. Any ties would have clipped them.

They emerged from the theatre to find the evening had turned gloomy—pendulous clouds loomed, threatening rain. Lance peered at his watch in the dim light.

"That went on for longer than I thought it would. We're going to have to run."

Even though they sprinted, they reached the terminal just in time to see the bus lumbering into the distance.

"That was the last one." Lance panted and grimaced, his shoulders in a defeated slump.

"Now what do we do?" Candace asked, once she had regained her breath. "I haven't got enough money for a cab."

"Me neither," Lance said. "It looks as though we'll just have to walk. It's only a couple of kilometres back to the hostel."

"But it's getting dark and it looks as though it's going to rain."

"We'd better get cracking then. Unless you have any better suggestions?" At Lance's curtness, she clammed up. He must have sensed her hurt. "Sorry," he said in a kinder tone. "The movie was my idea so it's my fault we're in this situation. I wouldn't blame you if you never wanted to go out with me again." He gave her a direct look but Candace refused to rise to his challenge.

"Perhaps somebody from the hostel will drive past and we can hitch a lift," she said.

As they walked, they kept a hopeful eye out for a friendly motorist, but none appeared until they were crossing the bridge. A horn sounded and an arm waved out a window, but the vehicle didn't slow down.

"That looked like Nick's car." Lance frowned. "Some mate he is."

They made it half way back before the clouds finally gave up their load. Lance gallantly held his coat over her head and ended up soaked himself. Under the jacket, Candace was keenly aware of his closeness, his warmth and some masculine perfume. It would be so easy to forget her resolution right now. But she must stay strong.

At last they reached the welcome shelter of her hostel block entrance.

"This is where we say good-night," Lance said, pulling a sad face and dripping on the step.

"Thank you for a lovely evening." Candace meant it.

"What, watching a feeble movie and then having to walk home in the rain?"

"I stayed dry, more or less." She squelched her soggy shoes. "Thanks to you. You're a real gentleman and I'm sorry that you got so damp. You know, I haven't laughed so much in a long time. At the movie that is. You're great company."

It was the wrong thing to say for his face lit up.

"Shall we do it again some time?" he asked.

"Yes, why not?" She watched his grin broaden. "As long as you understand it's just a *friendship*. I'm not dating anybody for at least my first year."

Lance beamed. "See you at meal time and the group," he said. Then before she could move, he gave her a shy and rather damp peck on the cheek.

"Oy you two, cut that out!" They turned to see a man grinning at them from the shelter of the other building. After a dash through the rain, he held out his hand to Candace. "I'm Nick. And this is?" He raised his eyebrows meaningfully at Lance while shaking her hand.

Lance's blush was obvious even in the bad light. "This is my … er … friend, Candace," he said. She noticed his hesitation.

"Sorry I couldn't pick you up just now but there was nowhere to stop on the bridge." With a sly smile Nick looked at Candace. "Lance is a good guy, hang on to him."

"We're just mates," Candace said.

"That's what they all say. I'll leave you to it." Still grinning, Nick splashed away.

"I'd better go before we both dissolve." Lance sprinted the few metres to his own block before turning. "I'm looking forward to it. The next date!"

She frowned as she watched him enter the building. Hopefully he was just teasing. Surely she had made herself clear …

"Hello Candace." The voice from the shadows startled her. She turned to see who it was.

"Greg!" She moved under his large open umbrella to give him a hug but with arm outstretched to cover her, and no hint of a smile, he maintained his distance. "How nice to see you," she somehow managed to say, in spite of his pain-inducing rejection. But it was understandable—he was only trying to protect himself. She stepped back onto the hostel porch and gave him some space. "What are you doing down here?"

"I had some … er … business in Hamilton."

It was obvious he wasn't being quite truthful. "Shall I make you a coffee in the hostel lounge?" she asked. "We can talk in there."

"No, it's fine, I can see you're busy." With shoulders slumped, he walked away into the soaking dimness, leaving Candace dumbfounded at his strange behaviour.

"Don't go," she whispered into the rain. But he furled the umbrella and climbed into his car. Even after the tail lights had disappeared, she remained on the porch, staring out into the darkness.

Horrors, he must have seen her with Lance. He might even have heard what Lance had said about a date and jumped to the wrong conclusion.

Once inside the warm dry foyer, she thumbed him a text.

Lance is just a friend.

For a Friday night, the hostel was mercifully quiet. Candace climbed the stairs intent on the phone screen, willing a response.

"Look out!" Amanda shouted as they nearly collided. "Get out of my way, you pathetic little Christian." The scathing words prickled. *Turn the other cheek.*

"Sorry." Candace took a closer look at Amanda's face. Although she had rarely seen the girl smile, right now she looked thoroughly miserable and this time it was clearly genuine.

"What's wrong, Amanda?" Candace asked, clinging to the handrail for fear of being pushed down the stairs in disgust. But instead the girl sank down on one of the steps.

"What do you care?"

"You look so unhappy." Candace sat down near her, careful to leave some space for fear of attack. "Sometimes it helps to talk. Is it something to do with your dad? You said he was a complete … you-know-what."

Just for a moment, the veil lifted to reveal the fearful little girl Amanda had once been, before she had grown so tall and put on her tough mask. The next instant the mask was back and scowling.

"Yes, it is about my father." She swore. "I was telling you the truth when I said he topped himself. But I'm glad he's gone." The words were spat out. "Pity he didn't do it years ago—it would've spared us so much grief. When he was on the turps, which was pretty much every night, he abused me and Mum. I hate him!" The venom was clear.

Candace sent up a quick prayer for wisdom. "That's horrible to hear what he did to you and it's understandable how much you despise him. But hating him isn't going to help—not him—and not you either. It's just going to make you all bitter. The past is just that—past, and there's nothing you can do to change it. Don't let it spoil your future."

"Have you finished your little sermon?" Amanda looked so sour Candace leaned away for self-preservation. "Anyway what do you know?" Amanda's derision was clear. "You probably come from a safe little home raised by super-squeaky clean parents." Her face twisted as she spoke.

"Hardly!" Pain at Amanda's mocking tone made Candace blurt out her indignation. "My mother was drunk when she fell pregnant to some random guy she met at a party. Then she had me aborted. But by God's grace I survived and was raised by what I thought was my solo mother. She died when I was nine—"

"Whatever." Amanda sounded bored.

"It's a long and strange story. The upshot is my childhood was no bed of roses. I didn't have a dad of any sort until I was twelve. Just after I turned sixteen, I found out the truth of my origins. It was such a shock that I ran away from home—and nearly ended up becoming a prostitute." Did Amanda look mildly impressed? "My best friend did become a call girl. Okay, so I wasn't abused like you were but I had a lot of forgiving to do of those so-called grown-ups who didn't tell me the truth for all that time. I know how hard it is to forgive. But it's definitely worth it. For your own sake."

Without a word, Amanda rose and stalked off down the stairs. Had any of what she'd said sunk in? Candace waited until Amanda was out of sight before she headed up to her own room.

The thought-provoking evening made it a struggle to sleep, and Candace was staring into the dark when a message came through.

Am back in Auckland now. Nice to see you looking so happy tonight.

It was difficult to tell from the text whether Greg was being sarcastic or genuine.

Chapter Six

To go and see Amanda would mean making a detour. Candace glanced at her watch—she was already running late and this particular lecturer took great delight in shaming tardy students. But the urging was too strong.

Amanda's door was closed. Plagued with indecision, Candace hovered outside in the quiet hallway. Should she risk the lecturer's wrath for a false alarm? She could simply keep on walking. But a strange noise caught her heightened attention; a faint gurgling followed by retching. Something didn't sound right. Summoning up her courage, she knocked.

"Go 'way." The words were faint and slurred.

Ignoring the instruction, Candace turned the handle and found the door wasn't locked. She cracked it open and peeked in, before flinging it wide.

"Amanda! What have you done?" The smell coming from the contents of the rubbish bin and the splatters on the bed and floor was diabolical. Candace put a hand over her mouth to stop herself from gagging. The girl lay slumped on the bed, a large bottle propped up beside her; rum, judging by the little remaining liquid and the dark dribble that ran from her mouth onto the stained pillow. Each twitch of the small vial in the dangling hand scattered white tablets over the floor. Then it stopped moving, the bottle landed on the carpet and Amanda lay motionless.

Reaching for her mobile, Candace gingerly felt for a pulse.

"Don't die, stay with me," she whispered then jumped when the girl groaned and tried to feebly shake her off. Candace sprinted out into the hallway and while gulping air to settle her offended stomach, dialled emergency services.

"Do you know what she's taken?"

Holding her breath, Candace re-entered the room to retrieve the pill bottle. She read the label out loud over the phone. "It looks as though she's consumed a fair bit of alcohol to wash them down with."

"Can you move her into the recovery position? In case she throws up again."

"I can try but she's quite big."

After the voice had reassured her help was on its way, Candace disconnected. What was she going to do now? She wasn't strong enough to move the heavy body on her own. Perhaps she should go to the office to get help—but Amanda might choke while she was gone.

"What's going on here?" Candace turned to see one of Amanda's friends peering in. "Oh my …" The girl was clearly trying not to gag.

"An ambulance is coming. Can you help me get her into the recovery position?" Together they heaved and hauled Amanda onto her side. She promptly threw up on the floor, some of it spattering on Candace's shoes.

Fearing she was about to do likewise, Candace hurried over to the window, pushed it wide open and leaned out to gasp for fresh air. "Still, better out than in," she said as the friend joined her and groaned.

"I could never be a doctor. Or a nurse," she said.

"Me neither," Candace said. "Any idea why she's done this?"

The girl lowered her voice. "My guess is the black dog is breathing down her neck."

"Huh?"

"Although she's never really said as much I reckon Amanda's been suffering from depression for some time now. I can see all the symptoms. It looks as though she's finally lost all hope." The girl's bottom lip quivered and she clenched the window sill until her knuckles turned white. "I kept on at her to go and get some help but she wouldn't listen."

"Was there anything in particular that could have caused her to … er … do this?"

"There doesn't necessarily have to be a specific event to trigger it. It could be clinical depression."

"Sounds as though you know a lot about it," Candace said, trying to be understanding.

"My uncle suffered from it and I recognise the signs. Thankfully he got the help he needed. But Amanda's been down ever since her dad's … er … death last year."

"But I thought she hated him and was happy he was gone."

"That might be what she claims, but it must still have been a shock for her. Perhaps she thought he'd change, maybe even make amends. That hope died when he did."

"She said he … took his own life. Do you think he might have suffered from clinical depression too?"

"More than likely. So Amanda could have inherited the condition. Added to that she hasn't been doing too well at uni lately—although it could be a symptom rather than a cause. And not that she's said anything but I suspect she's broken up with her man as well. On top of everything else, it could be what finally pushed her over the edge."

"You could be right about that. Wasn't her boyfriend on the second level, same as me? I haven't seen her up there recently. Let's hope it's not too late for her then and she can get the help she needs." Candace leaned further out the window to listen. "Thank God, I can hear the siren."

The friend insisted on accompanying Amanda in the ambulance. After it had left, Candace stood for a while inhaling the sweet air to drown out the stench, and still trembling from the adrenalin rush. There was no point in going on to the lecture now—it was far too late and she was incapable of concentrating anyway.

She was busy wiping the mess off her shoes on the grass, when she heard a cheerful voice call her name. Lance drew alongside of her and she noticed his eyes widen at the sight of her face.

"Are you all right? You're so pale."

"I've just had to call for an ambulance—Amanda tried to top herself. It wasn't pretty."

"Oh no!" Lance looked genuinely shocked. "I heard the siren but I didn't realise it was coming here. Is she going to make it?"

"I don't know." With that her strength crumbled and she burst into tears. "Oh Lance, she could die!" He enfolded her in his arms. It felt so good to be held and comforted and it took great determination not to simply melt into his embrace. Instead she pulled away. "Sorry, this is a delayed reaction to shock."

After he had helped her back to her room, he fetched a glass of water for her. She kicked off her smelly shoes and left them by the door—she would wash them properly later. Right now she was still too traumatised. She sat on the bed and Lance handed her the glass. While she sipped, he plonked himself down next to her and began to rub her back. It was comforting. Until she felt his hot breath on her cheek and his face close to hers. His intentions were clear. She pushed him away.

"No, please don't, Lance."

"I'm sorry, Candace." He turned bright red.

"Romance is the last thing I want right now."

"Sorry," he said again and stood up. "I promise I'll behave."

"I just need a friend. I thought we'd established that."

"You can't blame a man for trying." He gave her a rueful smile. "You are gorgeous."

The compliment barely sank in.

"Manda's going to be all right!" the friend told Candace. "They pumped her stomach but it was mostly alcohol. She must have been too drunk to take enough pills to do lasting damage. So she's gone home for a couple of weeks to recover, but she'll be back terrorising the lesser mortals before we know it." She grinned. "And It's all thanks to you."

"I can't really take the credit." Candace smiled with relief. "You might find this hard to believe but I'm sure it was God who told me to go and check up on her. I very nearly ignored His prompting."

The friend's initial expression of disdain soon changed to cool regard. "Just as well you didn't."

There was a thump on the door. Candace opened up.

"Amanda!" On the verge of giving her an impulsive hug, Candace stopped short—the girl still looked far too formidable. "How are you?"

As before Amanda marched in but this time her attitude seemed less aggressive, her make-up appeared more subtle, and for once she was wearing a colour: a deep red jacket over her black clothes. "I'm fine—thanks to you." She looked at Candace with a hint of a smile. "The card you sent was pretty cool."

"I'm glad to hear you received it. It wasn't easy trying to find out your home address."

Amanda planted herself in the chair. "Mum and I did a lot of talking during the last couple of weeks when I was recovering at home." Although she looked serious, still Candace braced herself for the sneer and the scorn—but it didn't happen. Instead Amanda continued. "I've never really had a lot of respect for my mother because she didn't stand up for herself to the old man. At least not that I saw. But it turns out Mum thought he'd take it out on me even more if she did. So she was actually trying to protect me for all those years. When she heard I'd tried to, well, you know, do what I did, she reckons she was devastated."

"Of course she would be—she's your mum."

"She said she wouldn't have been able to bear it if I'd succeeded like he did. It showed me how much she cares." Amanda turned her face away and swiped at her eyes. This time the emotion appeared to be genuine.

"I'm sure there're lots of people who care for you, Amanda."

She curled her lip as though she didn't believe it. "I'm going to see a counsellor too. And I've got a prescription for some … er … pills, if you know what I mean." She stood up and pulled a ten-dollar note from her jacket pocket. "Sorry for taking your money."

"No, keep it," Candace said pushing her hand away. "It's yours."

"But I stole it from you."

"No you didn't, I gave it to you."

Amanda frowned. "But you probably need it? Aren't you a poor student like me?"

Candace shook her head. Although the cash would have been useful, the initial gesture had been more important than her finances.

Seemingly reluctant, Amanda tucked the money away again.

"Just one question—how come you saved me?"

Candace shrugged. "How could I not?"

"But I was so horrible to you."

"I didn't take it personally and I don't hold grudges. I learned how to forgive a long time ago. Besides, I would have done that for anybody. Life—your life is precious, don't throw it away."

With a shrug, Amanda moved to the door. "You really are a Christian aren't you?"

Candace smiled. "What are you going to do? Stay at uni and keep studying?"

Amanda paused in the doorway. "For sure. This has been a real wake-up call. I feel I've been given a second chance at life and I plan to make the most of it."

Perhaps it was pushing it but Candace decided to try anyway. "You're welcome to come to our Christian Fellowship meetings. Or to church."

"Not really my thing," Amanda said without a hint of a sneer. "But I will give it some thought." Then she was gone.

Candace closed the door with shaking hands. This had to be of God. Although there was little chance she would take up her invitation, big forbidding-looking Amanda was definitely softening. No more would she roam the hallways, looking for Christians to terrorise.

Candace's mobile rang at the same time as something rustled under the door—a ten-dollar note emerged. By the time she'd rushed to the door and flung it open, the hallway was empty. She snatched up the cash before it could blow away, and checked her jangling cell phone. Dad. Surely it must be the news she had been waiting for. With heart pounding from excitement and anticipation, Candace answered.

Chapter Seven

"Here's your wee boy," the nurse said, holding the baby out to Saph. She took him as though he was made of the most delicate porcelain.

"And the little girl." Another nurse gently handed her the second infant before grinning at her tentativeness. The nurses exchanged knowing smiles before leaving the room. But Saph barely noticed their amusement as she absorbed every detail of the tiny wrinkled faces.

James perched on the bed beside her and with one finger, stroked each soft cheek in turn. "Wow, I'm a daddy, I really am this time." Saph glanced up at him and was touched by his expression of awe mixed with tenderness as he stared transfixed at his brand new children.

"You know, during labour," Saph said, gazing once more at the newborns, "I couldn't care less about what sex they were—as long as they were healthy. And when it was all over, I just wanted to be left alone to sleep." She smiled at the babies. "But finally it's sunk in—there's one of each. Just right." The pain and exhaustion of the previous few hours had been all but forgotten, to be replaced with an overwhelming maternal love.

James gave Saph a sideways squeeze. "Well done you, for all that hard work," he said and kissed her on the forehead. Then he rubbed his arm muscle and winced. "You have an incredibly strong grip when you're in pain, Saph." He gave her a wry smile. "Do you still hate me?"

"Sorry James, of course I don't." In contrast to her fury hours before, she was now mellow and dripping with love. "You know I didn't mean those things I said during labour. And I apologise for nearly ripping your arm off."

"Don't worry, I won't take it personally." He returned his attention to the babies.

Contentment filled Saph and she sighed deeply with satisfaction. She couldn't take her eyes off the miniature faces. After all these years of praying and dreaming, finally she had her arms full. And fuller than she had expected. God had doubly blessed them.

"Can we come in?"

Saph looked up to see her mum and dad peering around the doorframe. She beckoned them to the bedside and James moved away to give them some space.

"Let me see the darlings!" Helen gazed at the tiny infants and beamed. "They are just beautiful," she said, gushing. "And perfect." She paused and bit her lip. "There weren't any issues were there?"

"No, they were a little on the small side, but nothing apart from that."

Henk stood on the other side of the bed and examined his grandchildren. "I guess they'll do." Although a lot less sentimental than his wife, his face lit up with a pleased smile.

"Have you thought of names for them?" Helen asked without looking up from her admiration of the babies.

"After much thought and discussion we have decided the little girl is to be called Gemma Louise…"

"And the young man is Christopher James," the proud father said.

"They're lovely names," Helen murmured.

"Speaking of grandchildren," Henk said, "where's Candace?"

"She's getting a ride up here with Mum and Dad," James said. "When I told them the babies had arrived, like you they jumped in the car immediately. They're picking up Candace on their way through Hamilton and trying to get here as fast as traffic will allow."

"Apparently Candace can't wait to see her new siblings," Saph said.

"I have to take a photo," Helen primed her camera, "of this perfect nuclear family. James, can you sit on the bed next to your dear wife?"

With pride evident in his wide grin, he put his arm around Saph and posed.

What was wrong with her? Instead of rushing into the hospital room as she'd planned to do, Candace hesitated outside and watched through the window as the camera flashed. Why, after her initial impatience and eagerness to see the babies, did she now pause?

Mum and Dad looked blissfully happy, gazing down at the tiny blanketed bundles with such love on their faces—the scene so sickly-sweet, it was almost nauseating. And as she had heard her grandmother say, this was indeed the perfect nuclear family. There was no place for her in it now. She was just the spare, the outsider, not included or wanted in the family portrait.

Bitterness stirred. Mum wouldn't have looked at her so lovingly when she was born. Candace hadn't been wanted, planned and yearned for like the twins; she was just the result of a drunken night, an accident—something to get rid of.

And rejection. Even if Mum had known her infant had survived the abortion attempt, she would have likely viewed her newborn with disgust, not affection. That is if she had looked at her at all— she might have averted her eyes so as not to love her baby.

This was silly; Candace'd had months to prepare for the birth of the twins. But it hadn't once occurred to her she would feel completely left out like this. Engrossed in the babies as they were, her parents still hadn't noticed her yet. She seriously considered turning on her heel and walking away again, reluctant to spoil the happy family scene.

But it was too late, her mother had spotted her. Mum's eyes lit up and she waved her in.

"Candace! Come and meet your siblings."

She had better get this over and done with. Putting aside the feelings of rejection and self-pity, she entered.

"Gemma and Christopher, this is your big sister, Candace," Dad said as she approached. Then he leant over to give them a conspiratorial stage whisper in their miniature ears. "You'd better be nice to her because she's going to look after you one day."

Was that the only reason she was wanted? But when Candace took her first proper peek at the babies, all the negative stuff was forgotten.

"They're beautiful. Those perfect little fingers and toes." She could scarcely bring herself to breathe around them.

"Where are my parents?" Dad asked her.

"They've just popped into the hospital shop to get a wee something for you. But I … er …. couldn't wait so I preceded them." She didn't tell them she had been standing outside the room for five minutes, wallowing in self-pity.

"Here they are now," Mum said as Grandma burst into the room and rushed over to the bedside. Candace moved out of the way, to the back of the crowd of relatives, once again on the fringe. Grandma seemed just as enamoured as Nana had been, clucking and cooing at her tiny grandchildren. Grandpa trailed in behind her, looking uncomfortable as though the hospital setting didn't agree with him.

"Look dear, the boy has got James's nose."

He peered at the baby, looked doubtful and said nothing.

"This is your Papa Bear," James murmured to the babies. To

Candace he was Grandpa but being a big round man, the new name suited him to a T.

"And that must mean this is your Mama Bear," James said as his mother tried to inhale the tiny scraps.

"They're so delicious, I could just eat them all up!" she said.

Her husband frowned at her. "Why do people say that about babies? It sounds cannibalistic to me."

The other two men in the room smirked and Candace hid her own grin. But she needn't have bothered as nobody noticed; she hovered on the outside and might as well have been invisible. After all she was merely the future babysitter.

Chapter Eight

When the automatic doors slid open, overwhelming responsibility hit Saph like the chill damp air that rushed in. And then she and James, each carrying a little baby capsule, were outside. Just moments earlier, she'd been striding along the warm corridor, eager to take her new children home. But now that she had been pushed out of the comfortable womb of the hospital into the cold, it was tempting to turn around and walk back through the double doors into the warmth again. There, she'd track down a competent nurse to help her look after these fragile miniature human beings, until such time as she felt capable. It could take years.

She paused at the top of the steps; it was like standing on the edge of a precipice beyond which was the unknown. If she stepped over, would she tumble down uncontrollably? It felt like a lifetime ago since she had arrived, barely aware of her surroundings in her labour distress. Now everything seemed to have changed somehow. It was as though she was a tiny helpless ant in a forest of long grass; the bare winter trees appeared to loom menacingly overhead through the misty drizzle, the buildings had apparently grown and even her husband seemed taller.

James had moved down a couple of steps before he turned and saw her hesitating.

"What's wrong?" he asked.

"What have we done?" She grimaced. "Do you realise we are now solely responsible for these two lives? And I barely know the first thing about looking after babies. Everything they told me in hospital—all gone." If she had expected reassurance, she was in for a rude shock.

James groaned. "I know what you mean. I was just thinking the same thing. Why don't children come with an instruction manual?"

"That's no comfort." She sighed. "Such a shame Mum had to return to her café. I really could have used her help. Not that she's super maternal herself, but she must have more clues than me."

James moved back up again and put his free arm around her. "Don't worry, we'll cope somehow." His tenderness was short lived. "Or perhaps we could leave the babies on the church steps?"

"Not funny."

"Sorry. Anyway the church doesn't have steps."

Tears threatened. Then his dark humour sank in and her chuckles turned into tension-relieving laughter. James joined in and they propped each other up as they howled together. When she caught sight of baby Gemma—only her tiny face could be seen in amongst the blankets—she stopped as a sudden surge of pride and love flowed through her.

"Wow, look what we've produced."

James too was gazing at Chris, in similar awe.

"No, we'll have to lean on God's strength and wisdom." As she said it, a surge of confidence swept through her and suddenly she was impatient to take their babies home, to start their new family life. "We'd better hurry and get these poor kids out of the cold and into the warmth of the car."

Saph looked up from the armchair where she sat feeding Gemma, to see James walk past with nose pinched and gingerly carrying a full nappy at arm's length.

"How does something so small produce so much mess and noise?" he asked, sounding nasal. Although he invariably complained loudly, he wasn't shirking his nappy changing duties. He returned to sit on the couch.

"The joys of parenthood," Saph said with a fond smile. She tip-toed past him cradling a sleepy Gemma. In their bedroom, she placed the child down beside Chris in the cot. "Thanks for changing him," she whispered to James who had followed her in. She watched from the doorway as James moved over to where the babies were sleepily fussing. To her amusement he began crooning lullabies to sooth the infants. In spite of the sleep deprivation, Saph couldn't remember feeling so happy and content.

"How am I going to cope when you start work again?" she asked him after he had crept out of the now-silent bedroom and collapsed beside her on the couch. "You're a wonderful father."

He groaned. "I'm looking forward to going back to the office for some rest. My workmates warned me parenthood is exhausting, but I didn't believe them. Until now."

All too soon it was time for James to return to work and with each passing day, Saph's contentment faded. Being left alone with the two infants was worse than she had imagined—they seemed to take it in turns to cry. At night time, it was hard to rest as Saph listened for the babies' demands. She was reluctant to disturb James in case he was too tired for work the next morning, and resentment began to grow—he was apparently able to sleep right through their racket. Annoyance enhanced by exhaustion crept up on her.

On Friday evening Saph met James at the door.

"Thank God you're home, the twins have been fussing all day," she said. Before he had even taken a step inside, she attempted to hand him his infant son. It was the classic mistake. To her dismay James ignored her and walked into the lounge to sprawl on the couch. It took a few moments for her to recover from the shock and follow him.

"Please could you take Christopher," she said, too exhausted for tears, "I've absolutely had it."

"Can't you put him in his cot or something? I've had it too."

"He'll start screaming and wake Gemma up."

But James reached for his laptop, flipped it open and stared pointedly at the screen. Too weary to fume at him, Saph stalked off to the bedroom to deposit Chris. Then with her hands over her ears to block out the wails, she went and lay on the bed. It was tempting to join in. Didn't James understand how hard it was being at home all day long with two crying babies?

The evening meal was scrappy and Saph was stiffly polite, while James barely said a word. In bed that night Saph hardly slept, and not just because of crying babies. The physical gap between James and her felt a mile-wide and she heaved silent weary sobs at the apparent cracks opening up in their marriage.

After what felt like twenty seconds of sleep, Saph woke to find it was full daylight. She dragged herself out of bed, reluctantly prepared to grapple with griping babies, dirty nappies and a grumpy husband. But when she entered the twins' bedroom, she found them merely whimpering and freshly changed.

"They're only grizzling because they need their breakfast." James was leaning against the door frame, grinning at her. "It's the one thing I can't manage but I was reluctant to disturb you. I'm sorry about last night—I was whacked. I feel so much better after a decent sleep."

"Thanks." She was too tired to say anything more or glare enviously at him. Fighting to stay awake, she fed the pair. Once she had finished, she put them back in the cot and went out to the lounge to find James had made her some toast and a cup of tea.

"You look exhausted, Hon," James said. "After you've eaten, go and catch some shut eye for a couple of hours and I'll attend to the babies if they wake up."

She didn't have to be asked twice. "Cheers," she said. "You're a Godsend."

After a weekend of catching up on sleep and a little pampering, her energy began to return and she mellowed out.

The weeks began to blur into each other with sameness. On the weekdays, although physically they were both present at the dinner table, James seemed lost in his own thoughts and Saph, almost too weary to speak, inwardly fumed over his apparent lack of interest in his offspring. When she tried to discuss the twins with him, he would only give grunted responses. After the dishes were done, he would plant himself in front of the TV, while she attended to their children in the bedroom before collapsing into bed herself. Resentment grew.

She was too tired and busy to pray, apart from the occasional frustrated arrow sent heavenwards in desperation. Her Bible had been gathering dust since the twins' birth and any formerly memorised scripture eluded her.

When the occasional visitor popped in, she would put on a brave face and pretend she was coping. The friend would be too busy cooing over the charming babies—both acting as though they had no idea how to cry—to notice the weariness on Saph's face.

By Friday evening, she would be utterly exhausted to the point of semi-seriously contemplating divorce, the tectonic plates of her marriage gaping wide. But over the weekend after James had unwound, he would play the devoted husband and father, the rifts narrowed and she would start to feel better by Sunday. Unfortunately Monday followed Sunday …

She began to dread the working week. Was this how it was going to be from now on? Would their earthquake-prone marriage survive the advent of the twins?

At last the babies had been soothed to sleep. Hardly daring to breathe, Saph crept across the nursery floor. She had to stifle a bad word when her mobile, forgotten in her pocket, rang and set them off again. As tempting as it was to throw the device across the room, she answered it.

"What?" she said, not bothering to be polite. The voice on the other end sounded intimidated.

"I'm afraid we have a problem here at work."

Tell someone who cares. She clenched her jaw against the words.

"Sorry, are you busy?" Her co-worker would never know how close she came to receiving either a roasting or icy silence. Instead Saph forced herself to take a deep breath.

The woman began to explain the issue, but the kids were making such a racket she had to repeat herself twice. Saph could hardly think straight, let alone listen and it took some time and explanation before they got the problem sorted out between them.

Before the co-worker could mention any other problems, Saph killed the phone. Now she would have to settle her bawling children again. She was thoroughly regretting her offer to be on call for her old job.

"Does Chris feel hot to you?" Saph asked, panicking. "I think he's coming down with something." She held the baby in front of James where he sat watching TV.

Barely taking his eyes off the screen, James felt the tiny forehead. "He's a little bit warm but I'm sure it's nothing to worry about." Saph stifled a frustrated scream when he tried to lean around her to see the TV.

"We need to take him to the medical centre."

He groaned. "I don't want to have to go out again. It's been a long day at work."

"Now, James!"

With a roll of his eyes, he thumbed the off-button and found the car keys. They barely spoke on the journey.

"Don't worry Mrs Holden," the doctor said with a reassuring smile. "It's just a bit of a sniffle. Keep him warm and comfortable and he'll be fine."

"Are you sure it's not something more serious?"

"Saph, he's a doctor, he knows what he's talking about." James appeared to be gritting his teeth.

"Will he pass it on to his sister? Do you want to check her just in case?"

The doctor gave Gemma what Saph considered to be a cursory examination.

"First time parents I presume?" She noticed the sympathetic glance he sent in James's direction. "They're always the worriers."

No-one seemed to be taking her seriously. Surely she should know if there was something wrong with her own child?

"First time parents to babies at any rate. We do have an older daughter, but …" Saph's glare shut James up. His friendliness towards the doctor contrasted to his chilliness towards her, and it hurt. She fumed at the male camaraderie.

"If he runs a *real* temperature …" The doctor looked hard at Saph, and the feelings of inadequacy doubled. "Bring him back in."

"I told you there was nothing to worry about," James said on the drive home. He sounded sulky. "What a waste of time and energy that was."

Saph didn't answer; she was too busy holding back tears.

Chapter Nine

"It will give me the chance to get to know my little sister and brother," Candace said, waving her parents out the door. "Off you go, you two."

When a hostel mate had offered her a lift to Auckland, she had eagerly accepted with the grand and noble idea of giving her parents a night out.

"Do you really know what you're letting yourself in for?" Mum asked, dragging her feet. In contrast Dad had virtually sprinted out the door the moment Candace had arrived. He was already unlocking the car.

"Of course I do. I used to babysit for Tiff all the time." At Candace's breezy reply, Mum looked doubtful.

"They've been fed and changed," she said, "and so they should soon go off to sleep."

"Just relax and enjoy yourselves. Don't worry about a thing."

Obviously not convinced, Mum hesitated in the driveway. Dad, holding the car door open for her, must have said something either persuasive or impatient because Mum at last climbed in.

Up until then, there hadn't been a peep out of the nursery. It was the moment her parents were out of sight the twins started performing.

"If they kick up a fuss, just leave them be," Mum had said. "They should settle down after a few minutes."

With her fingers in her ears, Candace tried to block out the griping and concentrate on her study. But after half an hour of ceaseless grizzling, she entered the low-lit room to stare helplessly at the two little tykes. She was already regretting her glib confidence.

"Surely you can't possibly be hungry or wet. Mum and Dad haven't even been gone an hour." In reply, the crying increased in volume. She couldn't simply do nothing. Perhaps a back rub would help. Ignoring her mother's advice, Candace picked Gemma up. But before she could even start patting, an earful of scream made her hastily put the child back in the cot. There the baby settled down to just fussing again.

Candace's smug reassurance to her parents about her babysitting experience was now haunting her. Young Johnny had invariably been asleep upon her arrival and had hardly made a sound the whole time his parents were out. But she hadn't told Mum that. She was out of her depth here and had no idea of what to do.

"Hey, I'm your big sister," she told the twins. They cried all the more. It was tempting to join in.

Being a Saturday night, the restaurant was filling up fast.

"It's just as well we got here early," Saph said, eyeing the crowd before turning her attention back to the menu. The waiter hovered while they made their final decisions, then with brisk politeness took their orders and strode off.

"This is nice," James said. It had been a long time since he had looked this chilled out and happy, and Saph envied him. She couldn't relax; there was too much worrying to do about the babies.

James reached across the table and took Saph's hands in his. "Alone at last. Just like old times, before the babies were born."

"You don't regret having the twins do you?" Saph asked, pulling her hands away in hurt.

James's smile vanished. "No, of course not! It's just that we hardly ever get to spend quality time together on our own."

But Saph wasn't really listening. "It's not going to be a late night is it? I'm so tired and Gemma seemed unsettled today—I hope she's not going to play up for Candace." She barely noticed James leaning back, away from her.

"Can't we talk about us for once?" he asked, in a gap in her chatter.

"I thought you'd be interested in your children's development." Saph didn't try to hide her resentment.

"But this is 'us' time. Isn't this the first night out we've had since the twins were born?" His frown became a grin. "It's good Candace is fulfilling her babysitting role already."

"You don't think she's too young and inexperienced to look after such tiny babies do you? We have kind of thrown her in at the deep end."

James rolled his eyes and shook his head, his exasperation clear. "She's old enough to be a mother herself and as she said, she's an experienced babysitter."

"But she's never looked after children so young before. Perhaps I should ring her to see if she's all right."

"She'll be fine, and anyway here are our meals." James tucked into his food while Saph continued to fret between mouthfuls.

"Do us a favour and shut up about the children for ten minutes." At his sharp words, Saph lapsed into a hurt silence.

"Well, what should we talk about then?" she asked after some indulgent sulking.

"Anything. The weather, our jobs, your parents. Or mine. What's been happening in the world lately."

"You'd better tell me—I'm too blimmin' busy and exhausted to watch the news." Then she softened. "I don't have much else to talk about. Those babies are my world now and I can't help fretting about them."

"And don't I know it." James said it so quietly, Saph wondered if she had heard right. Her pain must have shown for he looked apologetic. "You know I love those twins to bits, I truly do. I would give my life for them." James reached for her hand again and this time she didn't pull away. "The simple fact is I feel as though we're losing 'us'. We never seem to spend time together, just you and me. I realise it's probably selfish but I want you to pay attention to me for once."

Saph sighed. "I'm sorry James. I didn't realise the twins would take over our lives in this way." She squeezed his hand. "I agree, we do need some 'us' time and it's nice that we could have a night out on our own. It's simply that I'm exhausted. The babies need so much attention and when they're asleep, I'm too tired to socialise."

"I'm well aware it's tiring. Which is why I brought you out for a meal, to give you the opportunity to relax and so that neither of us have to worry about domestic duties …"

Saph sent him a grateful smile. "Very thoughtful of you."

"… or children. Can you remember what we used to talk about, pre-babies?"

Saph paused to think. "Our day, our jobs and what was happening at work. We used to dream about the house we were going to buy and we had the overseas trip to plan." She chuckled. "Do you remember when—?"

Her cell phone interrupted.

"Ignore it," James said but she was already checking the screen.

"I'll have to take this, it's Candace."

"Tell her to leave us in peace." James mouthed the words.

"Oh dear, we'll be home as soon as we can." Saph ended the call and snatched up her handbag. "Gemma and Chris will not stop crying and Candace is beside herself."

With an exasperated sigh, James threw his serviette on the table. "We'd better go then."

"Sorry Mum," Candace said when her mother burst through the

front door. But with barely a glance at her, Mum made a beeline for the nursery. A few moments later, she returned, snuggling Gemma, who was cooing and gurgling as though she hadn't been screaming her tiny lungs out just five minutes beforehand.

"Oh my poor baby," Mum said seemingly oblivious to all else, her words adding to Candace's already substantial feelings of inadequacy and failure. A whimpering came from the direction of the bedroom and Mum looked pointedly at Dad. "Can you go and see to Chris please?"

On his way past Dad glowered at Candace.

"I really am sorry, Dad," she murmured.

"Couldn't you have lasted just a bit longer?" he said.

She opened her mouth to defend herself but closed it again. What was the point? Maybe Mum would come to her defence—but she only had eyes for her younger daughter.

So much for her role as babysitter. She had failed spectacularly. Well, they were quite safe as she wouldn't offer again. What really hurt was her parents' attitude towards her; it seemed she wasn't required or even wanted here, just in the way. There was no place for her in what had once been her home. Her real home it seemed was in Hamilton. And she couldn't wait to return.

Chapter Ten

The afternoon had been trying, what with an hour-long wait at the doctor's, largely spent calming two fretful infants. By the time the lengthy routine appointment had finished, the traffic had built up and it was well after five when Saph at last made it home. She half-expected to find James on the couch reading the paper and drinking something cold. Or even better but less likely, organising the evening meal. However there was no sign of him.

It was starting to get dark. He should have been home half an hour ago. Surely he would have let her know if he was working late yet again? He'd been doing a lot of that over the past few weeks. And he had started going out for motorbike rides over the weekends too, leaving her to cope with the kids on her own. If he wasn't out, he was glued to his laptop. A recurring thought prickled. Surely not … no, she was not even going to entertain it. She shoved it back down again.

After Saph had gently placed a twin in each cot, she sat on the edge of Candace's old bed, crooning a lullaby. But it was not easy to be soothing, when being ripped up inside by paranoia. She tried not to let her anxiety show for even at that age the infants could still pick up on it—at least that's what she'd read somewhere. They fussed at first but it wasn't long before they settled down and she was able to creep from the room. Finally, she could cook dinner in peace.

At the usual meal time, she dished up two platefuls of food.

After ten minutes of waiting, she put one plate in the microwave and wearily sat at the table to eat on her own. James would have to reheat his dinner.

By eight o'clock there was still no sign of James. This was late even for him. She was too exhausted to stay up much longer. An early night for her. After checking on the babies, she headed for bed.

When she pulled her nightie out from under the pillow, she heard rather than saw the note as it rustled. Anticipation of what it was going to say filled her veins with ice. She gingerly unfolded the piece of paper—as if opening it slowly would make the contents any easier to bear.

Saph. I'm sorry. I need time out to think. James had signed it with his name alone and no endearments. With those few cold words, her life fell apart. He had left her. The crack in their marriage had become a ravine.

She collapsed onto the bed and sobbed. But grief eventually turned to anger. Time to think about what? Was having a wife and kids not enough for him? And how cowardly to write a note—even a text would have been preferable. A direct confrontation, although a daunting prospect, would have been best. He must have known he would be long gone by the time she read it.

Through her tears of rage, she noticed his wardrobe door was slightly ajar. She crept over to it and pulled it open, fearing the worst. But it wasn't empty—most of his gear was still there. It could be a good sign—perhaps he would only be gone for a day or two.

Preoccupied as she had been with the children, she had still noticed the symptoms of his discontentment with family life: supposedly working late and spending a lot of time on his own, either out or engrossed in his laptop. But he never openly talked about it.

He usually accompanied her to church but the drive there and back was often made in silence, interrupted only by the occasional squawks of the infants. Once there they would become 'happy couple' automatons and pretend everything was hunky dory. Inevitably during the service, one of the twins would start crying and Saph would have to go out to the mother's room, leaving James sitting on his own. At coffee time, he tended to gravitate towards the other men there and leave her to her own devices.

And then there was the motorbike. Just when finances were tight, what with two more mouths to feed and only one decent income, James had traded in his car to buy the machine. Without so much as asking her. Was it male post-natal depression? A mid-life crisis perhaps? Or was it to escape noisy family life and to gain some peace and quiet?

"But think how much petrol I'll save." He had tried to justify his purchase. "I'll only use it for the daily commute …"

That was a joke—he rode it nearly every weekend.

"… and so I won't get stuck on the motorway in rush hour traffic anymore."

She had fumed, her anger mixed with worry for his safety and fuelled by frustration over being left to cope on her own. They had rowed over it—they seemed to have been fighting a lot lately.

The motorbike! Snatching up a torch and the shed key, she raced outside. After unlocking the door, she shone the torch around the interior. Apart from a few spider webs and some tools, it was empty. But why was she surprised he had taken it? The precious bike was his only means of transport now.

Misery flooded her. The reason he had left so much behind was becoming clear; it wasn't necessarily because he was planning a brief time out, but because he could only take a backpack full on the bike. Would he return only to collect the rest of his gear? Was this the end? Would he ask her for a divorce?

Then the prickly thought she had been trying to avoid came

roaring up, louder than the motorbike. Was he having an affair, finding solace in another woman's arms? The idea was unbearable.

She had been so involved, so caught up in the new babies and permanently exhausted, she'd barely had time to think about her husband. Or herself for that matter. Oh, if only …

Back in the bedroom, she sat down and cried until she was dry.

"What am I going to do, Lord?" Her words sounded loud in the quiet of the unit. But there was no thundering response, not even a small still voice, just silence.

The old kind and caring James had long gone; had disappeared when the twins were just a few weeks old. The new and definitely not-improved James was no longer there physically—but ironically she longed to feel his comforting arms around her.

She wandered into the lounge with no aim in mind. On the book shelf as if to taunt her, was the photo of her and a beaming James holding the newborns. They had both looked so happy back then, before the twins had taken over their lives. James hadn't smiled like that since. At least not in her presence. The image twisted the knife in her current misery and doubled the pain—she knocked the picture face down, not caring if the glass shattered.

Her mobile rang. She fumbled in her haste to check the caller ID. It wasn't her husband but her daughter. She would have to answer it or Candace would worry. Still Saph hesitated. If she let on what had happened, even gave a mere hint of her dismay, her beloved eldest might very well interrupt her studies and come flying home. As tempting as that was, she couldn't allow it.

"Hi darling, how are you doing?" Was she being overly bright and artificial?

"I'm good, thanks," Candace said. At least she sounded cheerful. "How are you?"

"I'm not bad," Saph said in a non-committal way. Candace

started to talk about her life at university and didn't seem to notice the wooden responses.

"Sorry, Mum," she said at last, "I've been hogging the conversation. Are you all right? You sound a bit strange."

"I'm fine." Hopefully her reply was convincing. "Perhaps I'm coming down with a bit of a cold."

"Are those little tykes keeping you up at night? You're probably run down."

"Yes, that must be it. I'll take some extra vitamins."

"At least you've got Dad to help you. I hope he's pulling his weight."

"Sorry, Candace but I have to go. I think I can hear a baby crying." The beep as she disconnected was loud in the utter silence of the unit. Saph discovered she still had some tears left.

After she had hung up, Candace stared at the phone—as though it could give her some more information. Mum had not sounded right at all; nasal and slightly snuffly, and over cheerful as though she was trying to hide a sorrow. And most unusual for her, she had barely mentioned the children—in fact she had said very little. There was definitely something up.

She could pack a bag and head up to see Mum. But it would have to be by bus—a major hassle and there were none running so late at night. Anyway, whatever the problem was might be sorted in the hours it took to get there, and she would have wasted time and money on nothing. Besides, what help would she be? She had already proved herself to be a useless babysitter and in the way. No, best to stay put. Perhaps Mum was just under the weather.

Dad might know what was wrong with Mum. Candace sent him a text. He was normally useless at replying but she could only try. When she hadn't received an answer by ten pm, she gave up and went to bed. Surely no news was good news?

Through tear blurred eyes, Saph fired a message off to James. Not surprising, there was no immediate reply. After waiting half an hour, she tried again. Still no response.

For once the babies slept most of the night. In spite of her exhaustion, Saph didn't. Anticipating a text message made sleep almost impossible.

The next day seemed to drag by. To add to Saph's misery, the twins seemed especially fractious, perhaps picking up on her grief and stress. But in a way their misbehaviour was a blessing as it provided a distraction. There was no word from James that day. Or the next or the next.

She continued to exchange texts with Candace almost daily but it wasn't easy to sound upbeat when her heart was breaking. As long as her daughter didn't ring again …

When Sunday came round, Saph couldn't face church. Coping with two babies on her own was a daunting enough task, but the thought of trying to field the inevitable questions made her cringe. No doubt folk would ask her where James was. What could she tell them? Certainly not the truth—that she really had no idea.

On impulse she packed the car up, installed the babies and headed north. Blessedly the children were lulled to sleep on the smooth motorway. After that, concentrating on the twisting road provided a distraction for her. At the top of the Brynderwyn Hills, she pulled over to drink in the view of the sea and the Whangarei heads in the hazy distance. For the first time in what felt like eons her spirits lifted a little. It was tempting to get out for a stretch and to gulp in fresh air, but the twins were beginning to stir, so with some reluctance she merged her car into the northbound traffic again.

At last she pulled up outside her mother's café. The beach looked heavenly, and for a moment Saph sat in the car, breathing in the East Coast aroma and focusing on the ocean's gentle rhythm. At the sound of the French doors being opened, she turned to see her mother emerge.

"I'm just closing up." Mum's tone was gruff as she collected the sandwich board sign. Her glare became a puzzled squint. "Sapphire?" Gaping, she put her load down.

"Hi Mum." Saph climbed out of the car and stretched her stiff limbs.

"Sorry, I thought you were a late customer. What are you doing here? Is something wrong?"

All Saph's original intentions of playing it cool flew away as she almost fell into her mother's arms.

"Oh Mum, it's a total mess." The tears began to flow. Her mother said nothing, just put her arms around her, patted her back and allowed her to weep. Over her mother's shoulder, through blurry eyes she saw her father emerge from the café. He apparently summed up the situation in one glance for without a word, he picked up the abandoned sign and disappeared back inside. Presumably he figured it was women's business.

After some minutes of self-indulgent crying, Saph reluctantly let her mother go. "I really need to feed these babies," she said as a wail started up and was joined by another one, "and then they'll both need changing."

"I can help with the latter," Mum said. "Then you can tell me what's going on over a cup of tea."

It felt amazing to have another pair of hands to assist—for the first time in days. During the process, Mum asked no questions. Then once Chris and Gemma were contented, clean, and cradled on their respective grandparents' laps, Saph enjoyed leisurely sipping hot tea. There was something about being by the beach that was relaxing and she was already starting to unwind. Somehow her problems seemed not quite so enormous as she downloaded them onto her parents. It felt good to share the load. But she didn't mention her suspicions.

"So you have no idea where James is or when he will be back?" Mum asked.

"Not a clue. I haven't heard from him for days." She stared into her mug. "He could have left the country for all I know."

"Have you tried phoning him at work?"

"No, I'm not quite game enough." The number of times she had picked up the receiver—and then replaced it, scared of what she might find out … "He'll get in touch when he's ready, no doubt."

"I could throttle that boy." Dad was going on the offensive.

"I'm sorry for landing on you like this with no notice but would you mind if we stayed here for a couple of days please, Mum? Dad?"

"Of course you can," Dad said. "Stay as long as you like."

"It would be lovely to have you," Mum said, but with a doubtful look. "However we'll be busy so we can't offer you much in the way of babysitting."

"That's no problem—just so long as I can enjoy a change of scenery and some adult company."

In the evening, with her children in the tender care of their grandparents, Saph strolled barefoot along the sand, kicking up sprays of water in the surf and bending to collect the shells she fancied. It brought back childhood memories, of family outings to the beach before her parents had split. Oh, to be free of responsibilities, as she had been back then—how nice to be like that again.

But the carefree days had ended when Mum and Dad had parted. Then after many years, a miracle occurred and they had recommitted. If they could do it, perhaps there was hope for her own marriage. As she walked, she prayed a little. God would work this situation out. Somehow. She had almost forgotten her troubles by the time she returned to the café.

"Thank God you're back." Mum grimaced as she held a fractious child at arm's length. "This one's been squawking for the last fifteen minutes. He's been changed and I don't think he's hungry." She smiled at Saph. "He must simply be missing his mum."

By now she was so mellow, she calmly held her arms out to receive her noisy infant. It was gratifying when the wails died immediately. Whenever James had handed her an upset baby, she had tensed up, and the child, presumably sensing her stress, would continue to scream.

"That walk was just what I needed," she said as she cuddled her son, grateful for his comforting warmth. "I feel quite chilled out now." She smiled at her daughter snuggled in her grandfather's arms and gurgling up at him. He cooed back. "Apparently Gemma doesn't miss me at all. It seems she already knows how to charm the men, even at her tender age! She's got you wound around her little finger, Dad, good and tight."

After putting the children to bed, Saph closed the bedroom door and paused to gaze out the open hall window at the ocean. Her mobile trilled. Was it James? Every time her phone rang, she checked the ID with trepidation. No, it was Candace. It was enough to put a big dent in her mellow mood. What was she going to tell her daughter?

"Why can I hear gulls in the background?" Candace asked. "And is that the sound of waves?" Saph pulled the window shut.

"Sapphire," her mother called up the stairs. Her timing was dreadful.

"I'm on the phone, Mum." Saph tried to muffle the receiver. "It's Candace."

"Give her my love," Mum said.

"Is that Nana? Are you at her place?"

"Yes, just for a day or two."

"What are you doing there? Where's Dad?"

It was tempting to tell her daughter everything was fine. But she couldn't lie. "To be perfectly honest I don't know."

"What do you mean you don't know?" Candace's voice squeaked with alarm.

"Your dad's … gone away for a while. It's nothing to be worried about. He just needed some time out." Somehow she managed not to sound sarcastic.

"That's it, I'm coming home!"

"No! Don't you dare. You have to concentrate on your studies. You must have some major exams coming up soon. Besides which, there's no point as I'm not there."

"Well, when will you be back?"

"I'm not entirely sure. Anyway," Saph tried to sound more confident than she felt, "no doubt your dad will return soon."

Chapter Eleven

Her parents had split? Candace stared at the phone in disbelief. Of course Mum and Dad had had their arguments and neither was perfect, but they had constantly presented a united front, been a real team. Had it all been a mere façade?

How could Dad do this to Mum? And just when she needed him more than ever, with the two little ones. Was he planning to return? Or were the twins destined to be raised by a solo mum? Just like Candace had been, first by Kathy, and then by her real mother—until James had come onto the scene.

It was clearly no picnic trying to raise one child solo, let alone twins. Although Kathy had tried to hide it from her, Candace could tell she'd struggled, and she had seen the hardships of many of her schoolmates who were also being brought up by a single parent.

Time and again as a child, she had witnessed her friends' heartbreak over their parents splitting up, and thanked God it wasn't her—she wouldn't wish that on anybody and certainly not on her baby siblings.

Then again perhaps her father's departure wasn't such a bad thing after all—with him gone, maybe now she would be needed and wanted … no, that was selfish. Besides, she had her studies to consider—she couldn't just abandon them. It was frustrating being so far away and not being able to help out. The only thing she could do was to pray her father would stop being such an idiot and return.

Her original reason for phoning now seemed so pitiful compared to her mother's troubles. She had only wanted a bit of advice or just to be listened to. But she could hardly bother Mum with such minor issues when she had major worries of her own.

Would Mum have listened anyway? She had been so distracted since the birth of the twins. Those kids had a lot to answer for: her parents' split, her mother's absent mind and her own feelings of rejection. Candace sighed. No, it was unfair to blame the babies.

It was tempting to feel sorry for herself. Instead of a small mound of problems diminishing by being poured into a listening ear, they had been added to.

The trouble was Lance wouldn't give up, and Candace was tempted to give in. But she must stand strong and be true to herself; not break the resolution she had made at the start. Although he was quite a catch judging by the way other girls blatantly eyed him up, she knew he wasn't the one for her. Nevertheless, the Lance-quandary was beginning to distract her from her university work and she couldn't let it.

So if not Mum, who could she turn to now? Maybe Tiffany … but perhaps it wouldn't do to talk to her. It might be too tempting to spill the beans about her parents' problems. There was also the possibility Tiff would mention Greg. And Candace wasn't prepared to think about him. She put her cell phone aside and opened up a text book instead. Study should be a distraction from Lance, not the other way round.

After two relatively stress-free days, Saph reluctantly packed the car up again. Leaving the peaceful beach, family and the much appreciated help to head back to an empty house and the daily grind in the bustling noisy city was a depressing prospect. But although she had all the time in the world, she could only expect so much of her busy parents. She drove away with tear-blurred eyes, her farewell wave half-hearted.

In an effort to stave off the inevitable, she dawdled south, stopping at scenic lookouts along the way. At Orewa, she parked in the shade, wound the windows down and left the babies to sleep peacefully in the car. Then with her back against the bumper, she sat on the grassy bank, her bare feet on the warm sand.

Although her appetite had left at the same time as James, she forced herself to eat a meal of leftover café food, compliments of her mother. She ate slowly, trying to put off the departure. The sun's warmth made her sleepy and she was on the point of dozing off, when a voice startled her.

"Look at this, there are two babies asleep in this car, and the parent is nowhere to be seen."

"Should we ring the police?" a second voice asked.

In a superhero leap, Saph was up on the bank. "Don't you dare, I'm right here."

After giving her a filthy look, the two women backed off. That was just what she needed, to be branded a bad mother on top of everything else. The therapeutic effect of the beachside mini-break was rapidly eroding.

The babies started crying so on the grassy bank she fed and then changed them, half-wishing the women had stuck around to see her take care of her children.

Having no desire to drive in the dark, once the shadows started elongating, she reluctantly headed towards the motorway. The closer she drove to home, the more the good work and peace of the beach came undone. Had the trip been worth it? Or did it just highlight her misery? There was one tiny flicker of hope—James might have returned.

The sun had nearly set when she pulled up in the driveway. The moment the engine was turned off, the children woke up and started protesting. Her depression deepened when she caught sight of the locked-up shed.

"Hello?" she said as she opened the front door but any expectations were dashed when there was no reply.

Like an automaton she organised the children, all the time missing the extra pair of hands she'd had over the previous couple of days. The house smelt slightly musty from being closed up so she busied herself opening windows.

The bedroom curtains that she had drawn were now open. Perhaps James had returned home? But maybe it was only to pick up some more gear. She checked the contents of his wardrobe; nothing else appeared to be missing. At least, he hadn't moved all his stuff out while she had been away. Which could mean he was coming home one day soon—hope sparked again.

She wouldn't tell Candace she'd returned home but James hadn't. Her daughter might come racing back, anxious to help and disrupting her studies. It would be one more stress, something Saph did not need.

She turned the computer on and checked her emails. Nothing. Not even from James. A glance at the calendar showed it was pay day. With trepidation she scanned the online bank statement. God bless James—his wages were still going into their joint account. So at least he was continuing to provide for his family. That was one less worry. Her own on-call work pay wouldn't be enough for her to live on, let alone support the twins.

And unless that was holiday pay showing up in the account, it must mean he was still working. Which meant he had to be within commuting distance of his workplace, and hadn't left town.

Since he wasn't answering her texts, she could go to his office, but it would mean the confrontation, nerve-wracking enough, would be in front of his colleagues. No, better to meet him on neutral ground.

Most lunch times, he went to a certain café. Perhaps she could catch him there. It meant summoning up the nerve to confront him. But at least it would be an end to speculation.

"Thanks very much," Saph said as the man kindly held the heavy door open for her. He then helped her to manoeuvre the double pushchair into the crowded café. Once inside, ignoring the usual stares and smiles as people noticed the twins, she paused to look around. Her hunch was right: James was here, seated on the far side at a table that was dish-free, indicating he hadn't eaten yet. His dark fringe hung forward as he bent over his phone. It looked as though he was waiting for someone. Her insides began to twist.

So far he hadn't spotted her and it would be easy to simply turn around and leave, avoiding a showdown. But that would be cowardly. With heart pounding, she started to make her way over to him but … a woman was moving in his direction, a rather attractive one, carefully dressed and made up. A complete contrast to her frumpy self.

Saph froze as she watched the woman tap James on the shoulder. Raking his fringe out of his eyes, he lit up at her with his heart-warming grin. A knife of pain stabbed; it had been so long since Saph had seen him smile like that. Then to her horror he rose and gave the woman a hug. The blade twisted deeper.

She had to get out of there. With breath in short supply, Saph used the pushchair like a tank to punch through the crowd, tossing muttered apologies in her wake. Once outside she scurried along the pavement, ignoring the jostled babies' protests.

If any internal knots had been untangled at the beach, they were now firmly tied again, even tighter than before. Her worst fears were confirmed. Her husband was seeing another woman.

Once the fury and adrenalin had subsided, Saph wandered along the streets, oblivious of direction. It was simply putting off the inevitable but she couldn't face returning to the empty, depressing memory-laden unit just yet. What was she going to do now? It looked as though her marriage really was over.

With her head down, eyes blurred with tears, she bumped the pushchair into someone.

"Oops, sorry," she said, without looking up.

"Can't you watch where you're going?" a familiar and irritated-sounding voice said.

"Kimberly?"

"Sapphire! Haven't seen you in years. You've hardly changed."

Saph gazed at her old mate. "Neither have you." But even through her own misery, she was puzzled to see her friend's usually placid face wrinkled into a frown. "When did you get back from overseas?" Saph asked. "I can't remember the last time I saw you—"

"It must have been at your wedding."

That was the last thing Saph wanted to be reminded of. "I've become a mum," she said in an attempt to distract Kim in case she asked about James.

"So I see." Kim gave the babies only a cursory glance before averting her eyes—unlike most people who gushed over the twins. But then she had never been the maternal type. After all it had been Kim who had arranged for Saph's abortion to take place. And years later, according to Patti, Kim had barely reacted to the news the baby had survived.

Kim indicated a nearby bench. "Have you got time to catch up?"

"Definitely," Saph murmured. Especially since she didn't have to return home to prepare dinner for her lying, cheating husband. She parked the pram and sat down next to it.

"I really could do with someone to talk to," Kim said as she seated herself. She seemed dull and lifeless, not her usual upbeat self.

"Same here." Being a counsellor, her friend would be just the right person to offload to.

But Kim wasn't listening. "Saph, you have no idea what I'm going through. My partner's left me …"

"Oh yes I—"

Kim rushed on. "…after I miscarried our only baby. The idiot ran off with another woman and lumbered me with a mortgage." Venom infused her words.

Saph was rendered speechless. Somehow, her mountain of troubles had turned into a mere bump by comparison. After giving her friend a caring pat on the arm, she did her best to pay attention to what Kim was saying.

"It was his idea to have children—I really wasn't that keen. I quit my job when I found out I was pregnant and now I can't find another one. I'm broke and heartbroken and I don't know what to do."

With her own issues paling into insignificance, Saph let Kim talk on. Thankfully the babies kept quiet the whole time. In the light of her revelation, it was no wonder Kim hadn't wanted to look at them.

"Thanks for listening." Kim dried her eyes on the tissue donated by Saph. "I do feel a bit better now. Sorry for bailing you up like that and I hope I haven't bored you to tears. As a counsellor—when I had a job that is—I spent all day listening to other people's problems, but sometimes even we need a sympathetic ear."

"That's understandable."

"So what's happening for you?" Kim stared at her. "Did I hear you say you also needed someone to talk to?"

Avoiding the steady gaze, Saph shook her head. "No, it doesn't matter now." Not only did her problems seem minor by comparison, she at least had God on her side; Kim had nobody. Saph plastered on a smile. "I'm glad I could help. I'll remember you in prayer." She cast a sidelong glance at her atheistic friend to see how the comment went down. Instead of sneering, Kim solemnly nodded.

"I'd appreciate that."

"Do you want to come along to church?" Saph asked on impulse.

"I will seriously consider it."

Saph nearly fell off the bench and had to take a moment to regain her composure.

"This might sound corny but God cares about your problems. You could try telling Him all about it." Just like she hadn't—what a hypocrite she was. There had been that chat with Him at the beach but little else.

Rather than acting with derision and much to Saph's surprise, Kim appeared to be giving her words some thought. "Let's make sure we keep in touch," she said.

After they had checked and updated contact details, Kim stood up.

"I'd better go now," she said and lumbered off along the street. Saph lingered a while in the warmth and thanked God she still had a house, financial provision, and most importantly, her much loved and longed for children.

Until one of them started wailing, bringing her back down to earth. When she caught sight of the time, she nearly swore. It was approaching three and the Auckland school-run traffic was already building up. It was going to be a slow journey home.

Chapter Twelve

Listening to somebody else's huge problems had provided a distraction from Saph's own less weighty ones. But not for long. Now stuck in crawling traffic, there was time to think. Painful unwelcome images crept in: of James in the arms of another woman, of herself spending yet another evening alone in the double bed, sleep broken not only by the demands of the twins, but also by heartache.

At last after a frustratingly slow drive, they made it home. She had only just put the twins in their cots, when the landline phone trilled. Her greeting was listless—she lacked the energy to sound cheerful.

"Hi Saph, it's Patti here." One of her oldest friends from university days. Not that she had really been a friend back then—more like an over the top Christian pain-in-the-neck. When Patti had discovered what Saph was about to do with her unborn child, she had been horrified. Then she had stifled her dismay and showed her true Christian colours by selflessly offering to adopt the baby. And after the abortion, she hadn't been judgemental but more concerned for Saph's well being than her error. As for her reaction when Saph had at last revealed the truth regarding Candace, it could only be described as over the moon-ness—in great contrast to Kim's blasé attitude.

"I didn't see you at church on Sunday and I felt I should ring you, just to see how you are."

"Oh, I'm fine thanks." It was the automatic plastic answer. Saph paused as the dam started to crack, and then burst. "Actually that's a lie, I'm terrible, James has left me and the kids hardly ever stop grizzling." As if on cue, one of them let out a wail. There was a startled gasp on the other end before Patti spoke.

"I'm coming round. Put the jug on."

After placing a casserole dish on the kitchen bench—Saph hadn't given dinner a thought—Patti turned to give her a big comforting hug.

"Sit," Patti said in a no-nonsense voice, and once Saph had obeyed, proceeded to march around the kitchen as though she owned it. She made Saph a hot drink and wouldn't allow her to lift a finger. It felt wonderful to have someone look after her for once and to take responsibility.

Over a cup of coffee, Saph let her problems and her tears spill out. Unusual for her, Patti stayed quiet throughout, handed Saph the occasional tissue to mop up the flood and let her talk.

Patti spoke at last. "I suspected something was wrong but I didn't know what, or realise it was this bad. Are you sure he's being unfaithful to you?"

"I saw him with my own eyes. He was hugging the woman and smiling like he hasn't in a long time." It hurt to think about it, let alone say it out loud.

Patti looked thoughtful. "You go and rest for half an hour and I'll take care of the babies while the food heats in the oven. I'll call you when dinner's ready. And Saph? I reckon your children are simply picking up on your tension and that's why they're grizzling."

Saph gave her a grateful look. Now that she had unburdened herself, she could relax a little.

She awoke to the mouth-watering smell of the casserole and realised she felt hungry—for the first time in days. Patti had laid the table beautifully and she dished up for Saph before sitting down to her own plateful of food.

"But what about your family?" Saph asked after she had eaten a few mouthfuls.

"They'll be fine. Mike will look after the children." Patti grinned. "He knows how to operate the microwave to reheat the rest of this casserole. Or perhaps takeaways will be on the menu."

Saph managed a smile too. It was strange; her world was crashing down around her ears, but right now, she wasn't bothered.

"I bumped into your cousin Kim this afternoon," Saph said as she devoured the delicious food. Patti certainly knew how to cook. "She's going through an even tougher situation than me and I didn't want to bother her with my problems." At Patti's questioning look, she continued. "But I don't feel I should be the one to tell you what the trouble is. You might want to get in touch with her."

Saph was sorry when Patti had to go.

"Thank you so much Patti, for letting me offload," she said, while on the receiving end of another big hug. "It's so nice to be listened to—and pampered."

"I'm glad I could help. I'll definitely be praying for you."

"That's good because I can't even seem to manage that at the moment. The Lord seems miles away. Would you believe I suggested to Kim that she tell God all about her problems? I haven't even done that myself."

"I can't imagine James would be having an affair." Patti frowned and shook her head. He thinks the world of you. There's probably a perfectly logical explanation."

"You haven't seen what he's been like lately," Saph said.

"It would be wise to find out what's really going on, before you take any drastic action. Remember, I'm only a phone call away."

After Patti had left, Saph stared at her mobile as if it was dangerous. At last she reached for it. Might as well not beat about the bush—as Patti had advised, it was better to find out the truth.

Are you having an affair?

Before she lost her nerve, she sent the text on its way. Any semblance of peace was fast vaporising. With her heart in her mouth, she waited and tried to steel herself for his answer. If he denied it, would she believe him? When there was no reply, it went some way to confirming her suspicion. Once again she cried herself to sleep.

The next morning her nervous fingers shook so much, she nearly deleted James's text by accident.

Will ring you later.

He wasn't denying her accusation. So it was true? The pain was incredible. She could hardly see through the tears to write a reply.

Don't bother.

When her phone rang in the evening and James's number showed on the screen, she debated whether to answer it. He had ignored her last text, which was annoying but something of a relief too; it would be better to know for sure, one way or the other. Her stomach twisted. Was she about to have her suspicions confirmed? She pressed the button to receive the call.

"So is it true?" She didn't let him say a word. "Are you carrying on with someone else?"

"No." His answer was faint and unconvincing.

"But I saw you in the café yesterday. With a …" she choked, "… a woman. So who is she?" There was no immediate reply and nausea rose. Her thumb hovered over the disconnect key.

"In the café yesterday?" he said at last. "You mean Michelle?" So that was the other woman's name? It was like a slap in the face to hear him say it.

"She's just a … somebody I work with." His voice was quiet and strained.

"But you hugged her—I saw you. Do you normally hug your workmates, James?" With her stomach screwed in knots, she waited but he was silent.

"So it is what I think it is," she said dully.

"She's just a friend." He sounded defensive.

"It looked like more than that to me."

"There's nothing going on between us." He was a little too vehement. "She's only been in our office a month and doesn't know a lot of people yet. I got talking to her in the staff room one day, you know, just being friendly and … I found she was a good listener. And she seemed understanding."

Was that a dig at her?

"We've had lunch together on several occasions but all we do is talk."

"It still sounds like an affair."

"I swear to you, I have never so much as kissed her."

Saph snorted. "Not a physical one then but an emotional one. Almost as bad and just as dangerous. I suppose you told her all about our …er… situation?"

"Yes, I confided in her but it was therapeutic—like a counsellor."

"Couldn't you have talked to me?"

"Would you have listened?" James didn't give her time to reply to his kick. "Yesterday she invited me around to hers for dinner." More pain. "But it was the first time and she reassured me it was just to hang out together as mates. It seemed harmless enough and initially I agreed. Then just as I was about to go out, your text came through. Saph, it made me stop and reconsider. So I cancelled immediately."

"Why didn't you tell me this yesterday?" It had cost her a night's sleep.

"Perhaps I should have but I was too busy trying to sort things out in my mind. Honestly, I had no intention of taking it any further, even if she wanted something more."

Obviously interpreting her silence as doubt, James's tone was glacial. "So you don't believe me?"

"Would you blame me if I didn't?" Anger flooded her. "You take off, I don't hear from you for days, then I see you with your arms around an attractive woman. What am I supposed to think?"

"That you can trust me." James sounded irate and indignant. "Remember the vows I made to you on our wedding day? I am not having an affair! Believe you me, there were times when I was tempted, and who could blame me?" There was an irritating note of self-pity in his voice. "It felt as though you'd forgotten I existed, and when you did notice me, it was only because the children needed something."

Saph was too choked up to speak at first. When she didn't say anything, he continued. "So you don't trust me then?" His words were curt. "I told you, I just needed some time out."

"And you reckon I don't? I can't just abandon my children and ride off into the sunset."

"No, but you can neglect your husband."

"Oh, you poor thing." Saph couldn't help the sarcasm.

"Anyway you did go away. You weren't home when I came round last weekend, and some of your stuff was missing."

"Yes, I had some time out but I didn't leave the children behind when I went." It was a dig at him. "I took them to see their grandparents at the beach. It was wonderful having two extra pairs of hands to help." Another poke. Then his words sank in. "So that's what this is all about? You feel as though I've been neglecting you?"

"Have you only just figured it out?" He sounded exasperated. "It's what I was trying to tell you at the restaurant on our one and only night out. It was always the twins this, the babies that. There was no room for me." His voice softened. "Or for you for that matter. For us. I couldn't stand it anymore, the way in which our lives were revolving around the children. I had to get away and have some time and space for myself, and to process my thoughts. And before you say anything, we both need to do that, and not let the little tyrants rule us."

It was as though a light had been turned on—exposing the dim and dusty problem she had refused to acknowledge. Clarity made her fury dissipate. As galling as it was to admit it, it was true. She had been so engrossed in the demanding children—the answer to her desperate prayers regarding her barrenness—that her husband and marriage had all but disappeared off her radar. And she had almost lost herself too.

"Are you still there, Saph?"

"Yes, I'm just thinking. I hate to admit it but you're quite right." Shame and guilt made her mutter the words. "Sorry, James." It was hard to say.

"Saph, I'm sorry too." Finally he'd said the words she'd been waiting for, the anger had gone out of his tone and now he sounded humble—which loosened her internal knots. "I haven't lost you and the babies have I?" Dismay wobbled his voice. "There is still hope?"

"I'm sure we can come back from this," she said. "But how?"

There was a pause before he spoke. "While I've been on my own, I've been able to do lots of thinking. Obviously we need to pay more attention to each other and to set time aside just for us." He hesitated. "But I also reckon some outside help would be a good idea. Would you consider going to marriage counselling?"

How humiliating, needing a counsellor. Surely they could work through issues on their own? But this was bigger than both of them.

"I'll do anything to get our marriage back on track. And James …"

"Yes?"

"I miss you so much. And not just because I need someone to help out with the twins! Please come back soon. Our babies need their daddy. And so do I."

"I miss you too. And those little rascals," he said with mild exasperation, his tongue firmly in his cheek. "I am wholeheartedly committed to you and our marriage—to making it work."

"Me too."

It was as though a huge burden had been lifted off her shoulders. After the phone call ended, she danced around the lounge, thanking God. She poked her head into the warm darkness of the twins' bedroom and listened to their gentle breathing for a minute, enjoying the sound and the peace.

"Daddy's coming home," she whispered.

Chapter Thirteen

The new day brought doubts. Was James really going to come back to them? He hadn't said for sure he was returning or whether it would be today, tomorrow or sometime next week. Did Saph even want him back? After all he had nearly found solace in another woman's arms. He'd claimed he had resisted but was he telling the truth? It was going to take a lot of time to forgive him and even more to trust him again. Could she ever?

In the evening after putting the babies in their respective cots, she sat down on the couch and thumbed the TV remote in order to watch the news. But what had been happening in the world couldn't compete with what was playing over in her mind.

There was a faint rumbling outside. Could it be …? She dashed to the kitchen window just in time to see a motorbike roll to a stop on the driveway. After he had dismounted, James removed his helmet and stood gazing at the unit, his stance portraying uncertainty. His bag was on the pack rack; surely that meant he planned to stay. Even after all these years and his apparent betrayal, he was still attractive to her, and she went weak-kneed to the door and whipped it open.

"I want to come back—if you'll have me that is," James said. Although he looked unsure, he grinned at her in that way of his which would previously have melted her heart.

Out on the step however, she paused, torn. Her husband had returned and she was prepared to do whatever it took not to lose him again. But forgiveness wasn't going to be easy or instant. At last she moved over to him. Hesitant as though he feared rejection, he held out his hand to her, the stiff leather jacket creaking. With wooden arms she reached out to him and he tentatively pulled her close.

"All I can say is I'm sorry, truly and sincerely." He mumbled the words as though they were difficult. "I shouldn't have done that. Do you think you can forgive me?"

"That's going to take time. Perhaps if you'd told me what the problem was, instead of taking off …" *Into another woman's arms.* But she stopped short of saying it aloud.

"I did try." He was starting to sound defensive. She had to stop it in its tracks.

"I know. I apologise too." It wasn't just the face full of leather that muffled her words. "Sorry for neglecting you and sorry for making the babies the centre of my world. I should have put you first, before the children." James kissed the top of her bent head.

"Not me, but us," he said.

"They've only just settled down for the night so all is quiet. I'll make us some hot chocolate and we can have a good long chat." She pulled away to look up at him.

"With marshmallows?" His hopeful boyish look made her giggle and quickened the thaw.

Saph couldn't bring herself to discuss the other woman—at least not just yet. She took a sip of her drink and considered where to start.

"Did you not want children at all?" Even that was something of a touchy subject and took effort to say. "You should have said if you didn't."

James seemed to be searching for the right words. "It's not that I didn't want children," he said at length. "In fact when we first got married, I couldn't wait to become a dad. And I knew how much you longed for kids." He smiled at her. "But as time passed and there was no sign of a baby, I became used to it being only the three of us. Then it got to the point where I was looking forward to Candace leaving—not that I didn't want her around—I just thought it would be nice to have a peaceful house all to ourselves. By then I had basically given up hope of ever having more offspring. When you told me you were pregnant, it was quite a shock and I had to do some rethinking."

Saph looked at him. "I got the distinct impression you weren't over the moon about my news. But you didn't tell me why. I wish you'd said something at the start."

"You were so happy—I didn't want to rain on that." He shrugged. "Although it took a while, I eventually got used to the idea and even started looking forward to having a child I could call my own. After all I'll never know if Candace really is my daughter."

"And I wanted to have a baby with you," Saph said, "my husband, and not as the result of a drunken night. After missing out on Candace's babyhood, in fact the first nine years of her life, I wanted to know what it was like to raise a child from scratch as it were. Don't get me wrong, I love Candace dearly; but Kathy's fingerprints were all over her. Like you I wanted a child I could truly call my own, and put my stamp on."

"So other than being a bit disappointed that I wouldn't have you and the house all to myself, I was happy enough. But when I found out it was twins, I admit I was a little taken aback." James grimaced. "And then when they arrived … well, that was a whole different ball game. It was quite overwhelming. I didn't realise how much they would take over our lives and how obsessed you'd become."

Saph's face warmed. "To be honest I also was a little aghast at the idea of having two babies at once. But there wasn't much I could do about it and I figured between us, we'd cope somehow. And I was thrilled at the idea of having children at last." She shrugged. "We just got more than we bargained for."

"Yes, we sure did." His smile returned. "But now I wouldn't have it any other way. When I think how close I came to losing you and the children, it makes me cringe. I'll try and be more helpful with the twins. Just so long as I can have some space after I get home from work."

"Understood. I'm sorry for expecting you to take over as soon as you walk in the door. I know I'd hate it if you did that to me. But I would really appreciate your help too. Even though I used to be a solo mum to Candace, it was a rather different situation—she was older and a low-maintenance kid. When there are two demanding children, this single parent lark is no fun at all." She sipped her drink slowly, giving herself time to pluck up the courage to ask the question she had been avoiding. "What about this woman, your friend?"

He met her gaze. "It's all sorted. I told her today we shouldn't see each other any more, except in a professional capacity at work. In fact …" He held out his mobile to her. "I deleted her number."

The screen showed his contacts—there was no 'Michelle' listed. "Take the phone and have a look if you don't believe me, but as I said before, I've stayed faithful to you and I have every intention of doing so until 'death do us part'."

Strands of doubt still lingered, but she managed to push the phone away. "I believe you. But although I know I'm to blame too, there's still no excuse for that kind of behaviour."

"I realise that." James looked sheepish. "How can I prove myself to you?"

"You can't. I just have to learn to trust you again."

With cell phone in hand, Candace jigged around the room, before again reading the text her mother had sent. She hadn't imagined it.

Thank God! Your dad has returned! We're going to make it work.

It was an answer to prayer—and she had been praying hard for reconciliation. No need to catch that bus now. In fact it would be wiser to leave her parents alone—they could play happy families with their babies. There was only a minor sting of being left out.

Anyway she could ill afford the money for the bus fare or the time away from her studies. The end of the university year was looming and she needed to hit the books harder than ever.

But once the exams and assessments were over, then what? No point in returning to Auckland when there was no long term room for her at—she'd given up calling it home—the unit. That smarted a bit too. And she couldn't stay on in the hostel.

However a permanent flatting situation shouldn't be too hard to find at this time of year and she had a potential holiday job lined up. So it was looking as though Hamilton really would become home. It was where most of her friends were now anyway—Tiff was the only old mate still in Auckland. And of course, Greg. When she squeezed herself into the unit for a couple of days over Christmas, perhaps she could catch up with him then. Just as a friend. That's if he wanted to see her.

To avoid questions regarding their still unstable marriage, Saph did her best to play the part of the contented wife as she and James entered the church building. They were pushing the double stroller through the foyer when Patti made a beeline for them. Her face lit up as she looked from Saph to James and back again before she came alongside Saph.

"So I take it things have worked out?" Patti murmured, too low for James to hear. He wasn't listening anyway, having been distracted by a friend who had greeted him.

"We're getting there," Saph whispered, "thank the Lord. As you can see James is back and we're all living under the same roof, which is a good start. Things aren't completely hunky dory but we're communicating better and we're working towards clearing up some misunderstandings. We're going to get some … er …counselling." It was difficult to admit.

But Patti looked pleased. "Great idea. All couples need it at some stage or another. We've had some." That was both a surprise and a comfort to hear. "And were your fears confirmed?"

It took a second for Saph to click. Still being a bit raw, she wasn't ready to tell Patti about the emotional affair. "No, it wasn't quite what I thought." She broadened her smile to hide her pain. "Thank you for listening to me and praying for us."

Patti clearly didn't observe the underlying discomfort. "I love reconciliation." She gave Saph a big joyous hug. "You two are just right for each other and I'm so happy for you—"

"Good grief." Saph stopped her in mid gush and pointed. "Another miracle."

Patti twisted around to look at the entrance. "Kim's here!"

The woman stood in the foyer, looking awkward.

"Don't rush over to her, you might scare her off."

Patti paid no attention and full-sailed towards Kim.

"Nice to see you, Cuz!" Even from that distance Saph could hear Patti's enthusiastic greeting, before she engulfed Kim in a big bear hug.

"What's going on?" James asked, having finished his brief conversation.

"Kim's here. Could you keep an eye on the twins? I think I might need to go and do damage control." She followed Patti. But instead of heading towards the nearest exit, Kim waved as her cousin herded her into a row.

"Forgive us our sins as we forgive those who sin against us …" The congregation repeated the prayer every Sunday but this time, the line glowed neon and flashed. Did this mean she had to forgive James as God had forgiven her? Saph groaned quietly.

"How does the Lord forgive?" the pastor asked. Why of all the Sundays did he have to choose this particular one to do a sermon on forgiveness? He continued. "As though the individual has never sinned." The man must have some insider knowledge—indeed, he seemed to be looking straight at her as though he knew what was going on in her life and all the questions she had. "This is how we need to forgive too."

She glanced at James. Could she forgive him so completely?

The pastor went on. "It's not easy and you will need God's help to do it. But you won't regret it. And remember, love keeps no record of wrongs."

Which meant if she really loved James—which she did—she would have to scrub his past demeanours off her mental list. This was certainly going to require divine help.

It was a lot to think about. James had gone to get them both cups of coffee, so still musing, Saph pushed the stroller out into the foyer. But when she spotted Kim standing awkwardly on her own, she put her ponderings aside.

"Where's Patti?" she asked.

Kim pointed to the queue for hot drinks.

"What did you think of the service?" Saph asked, trying to be gentle. "I hope it wasn't too overwhelming."

"Apart from the sermon which was unrealistic ..." Her face darkened. "I doubt that I will ever forgive my ex for what he did. But overall I enjoyed it. I liked the singing and there's a nice atmosphere in this place." Kim grinned. "And even if I had hated it, I couldn't run away because Patti wouldn't let me out of the row. I actually do feel a bit better." Her smile became mischievous. "It was a choice of coming here or getting horribly drunk. And I couldn't afford the latter."

Chapter Fourteen

"Mrs Holden?" The gruff voice on the phone sounded familiar but Saph couldn't place it. "Is James there? It's imperative we get hold of him and he hasn't turned up at work yet." Impatience and irritation sounded in the man's tone. "We've tried phoning his mobile but it just keeps ringing until it goes through to voice mail."

The alarm bells began. Had James taken off again, for real this time? Into the arms of that woman? When he'd walked out the door this morning, he'd given no hint of any devious intentions—but that didn't necessarily mean anything. Her stomach twisted as mistrust resurfaced.

He had only been home a week but already she could see an improvement. The previously clogged lines of communication seemed to be opening up. It was going to take some time for the cracks to close, but she thought they'd been making progress. Until now. Perhaps the temptation had been too great and his 'friend' had finally worn him down.

"He left for work at the usual time," Saph said, trying to hide the note of panic. But when she glanced at the kitchen clock, an ounce of relief surfaced. "Oh, he's only half an hour late—probably still stuck in traffic. They said on the radio there'd been a couple of minor accidents on the motorway—that might have held him up."

"I suppose he was on his motorbike?"

She could still detect annoyance in the man's voice and it put her on the defensive.

"That is his usual mode of transport. With his helmet on there would be no way he could hear his phone."

"Well, if he contacts you, tell him to get in touch with the office. Immediately."

After the officious man had rung off with no good-bye, Saph tried James's mobile, her fingers fumbling with the tiny buttons in her agitation. No answer. He must still be in the jammed up traffic. Or was he with that woman? The thought intruded. She left a message and tried to go back to what she had been doing, but her earlier uneasiness had returned, stronger than before.

The phone rang again. Perhaps it was his workmate calling to say they had located him, or James reporting he had made it to work at last and not to worry.

"Hello, is that Mrs Holden?" This time a police officer identified himself. Any remnants of peace vanished completely to be replaced with ice.

"I'm sorry to have to tell you this." He sounded serious and official. "Your husband has been involved in an accident on the motorway."

The air in her lungs seemed to disappear. Saph had to sit down before she fainted. "He's not …?"

"No, he's not dead—"

"Thank God for that." She could breathe again. And, silly little thought, James hadn't been unfaithful.

"But it was quite severe and he's been taken to hospital, unconscious. No doubt you'll want to go and be with him?"

With her mind reeling, Saph couldn't answer.

"It's probably best if you don't go on your own. Is there anyone who could accompany and support you?"

No-one really. She would have to go it alone. After a frantic request for the details, she packed up a few of James's belongings and headed for the door. The twins! In her panic she had all but forgotten about them. What a great mother she was. For once they were both sleeping peacefully. What was she going to do with them? She couldn't take them with her to the hospital.

"Patti? I need your help. Urgently."

When Saph tried to rush to her husband's side and reach for his hand, the busy emergency staff kept her at a distance. They pointed her to a seat on the outskirts and wouldn't answer her desperate questions.

She sat helpless and agitated. It was all so unreal, as though she was a distant observer of a gruesome scene, and the man lying there was not James but a stranger. He looked so broken somehow; the big crimson lump on his forehead contrasted with his waxy complexion, as did the slash of red where his glasses had cut into the bridge of his nose.

His scuffed helmet sat with the rest of his belongings, the visor split in half, testament to how he had landed on the unyielding motorway. The remains of his precious leathers still lay under his crumpled body, from where they had been cut off him. But the expensive tatters would be the least of his worries when he woke up. If he woke up.

He couldn't die. It would be unbearable to lose him, and permanently this time. When he had left her, it had been difficult enough, but facing life without him would be unthinkable. Especially now, when they were just getting their faltering marriage back on track. Love for him welled up inside her, stronger than ever and she uttered more fervent prayers under her breath.

I need him, Lord. And his children need their daddy too.

But she must be brave and face up to the possibility he wouldn't make it. After a lengthy internal struggle she came to the point of giving him up to the Lord.

Trust Me. Two simple words—but so comforting.

"Sorry." The efficient looking radiologist interrupted her musings. "You'll need to vacate the room while we x-ray him." Saph moved out reluctantly, not willing to leave James even for a moment—it might be his last.

Although it was only a couple of minutes before she was allowed back in, it dragged like an hour. Again she had to sit at a distance, from where she watched his shallow breathing, his chest the only part of him moving. Then, as though a giant vacuum cleaner had been turned on, the room seemed to empty of staff until there was a solitary nurse left.

"Where's everyone gone?" Saph asked in a panic. "Why aren't they still working on my husband? They haven't given up on him have they?"

"They've done as much as they can." The nurse was brisk but somehow gentle too. "We just have to wait for him to wake up now. And unfortunately everyone else is needed for another emergency which has just come in."

For a moment irrational anger flared at the inconsiderate victim who had siphoned off the staff—surely her husband was more important?

After what felt like an age, James stirred.

"Where am I?" It was a hoarse murmur and barely audible. "What's happened to me?"

Saph moved over to him. "You're in hospital—you've been in an accident," she said, trying to sound calm and soothing.

James made an effort to look around for her but winced and gave up.

"Everything hurts."

"Thank God," she whispered. Surely feeling pain must a good sign—an indication he wasn't paralysed. "Poor darling," she said aloud.

He groaned in response.

"Am I allowed to touch him?" she asked. Under the watchful eye of the nurse, Saph was at last able to reach out and gently stroke his hand, hurting for him but whispering soft reassurances. At her caress, he seemed to relax a little.

A doctor entered the room. "Mrs Holden? A quiet word please," he said. It sounded ominous. With her heart pounding, she followed him out into the corridor. He must have noticed her stress for he gave her a reassuring smile. "Don't worry, in these circumstances it's comparatively good news. At this stage there is no major apparent brain trauma, just concussion. We will need to do a CT scan to check, but I don't expect any issues. After examining the x-rays, it appears his most significant injury is a broken collar bone."

Saph could have wept with relief. "Thank the Lord James was wearing his protective gear."

The doctor gave her a strange look before continuing. "We're debating whether to reset it under anaesthetic. If we don't operate, it might not knit together properly. It seems he's fractured two fingers and also cracked some ribs but really he's come off pretty lightly considering. Probably thanks to his protective clothing."

Or thanks to the angels looking after him. Saph didn't say it out loud.

"He was lucky his gloves stayed on. I've seen plenty of crunched up hands where the protective gear has come off. It's not pretty. His only other injuries are some grazes and heavy bruising. It's quite surprising his lung didn't collapse as it looks as though his shoulder took the full brunt of the fall. Although it will take some time, he should make a full recovery."

When she walked back into the room, James had his eyes closed and appeared to be asleep again.

"Do you want to take his belongings now?" the nurse asked. "He'll be moved to the HDU after his scan." Saph gathered up the helmet and patient property bag. She peeked inside to find his scuffed wallet, mobile and broken glasses. The cell phone looked miraculously intact apart from a cracked screen. She shouldn't really—but she just had to check. There might be some important messages to answer—that was one way of justifying it. Once she was out in the corridor again, she removed the phone and turned it on.

Surprisingly the battered mobile fired up without hesitation. There was no pin number—another indication of his trustworthiness. There didn't appear to be any new messages so with some trepidation, she checked through the old ones and could find nothing incriminating. She scrolled down the contacts list. No, 'Michelle' was not listed and neither was 'Shelly'—no unknown female names to be seen. Perhaps her husband really could be trusted. A mere twinge of guilt remained in amongst the relief.

"How is he?" Patti asked as soon as Saph walked through the door. The concern in Patti's eyes was so touching, and too shocked and too busy to cry before, the dam of tears broke and the tension and subsequent relief at the prognosis flooded out.

"Oh no, he's not … is he?" With a look of alarm, Patti threw her arms around Saph in her usual dramatic way.

"No, no, no." It was all Saph could splutter until the outburst had subsided. "Sorry Patti, I didn't mean to frighten you; it's a delayed reaction. James is going to be fine—well, eventually." She explained his injuries.

"Do they know how the accident happened?" Patti asked as she filled the electric jug.

Saph collapsed onto a chair, suddenly weary. "At this stage, James can't remember a thing beyond riding along the motorway," she said. "But according to police, witnesses reported a car cutting in front of him and he had nowhere to go. They reckon he wasn't riding at great speed or he would be a lot worse off. Apparently he was nearly collected by a truck, but he skidded out of the way just in time."

"The angels must have been protecting him," Patti said as she filled mugs.

"Yes, working overtime."

"If you need a hand with the babies while James is out of action, let me know."

"Thanks Patti, I might just take you up on that." Saph sighed. "It looks as though I'm going to be flying solo again for six weeks at least. And I don't feel right about asking Candace for help when she's knee deep in her studies."

It hadn't been easy telling James's parents. Although Saph downplayed the accident as much as possible, they naturally wanted to race up to be by their son's bedside.

However once they saw him sitting up in bed, smiling, it clearly put their minds at rest and they stayed at the hospital just for the afternoon. Only Saph knew James was putting on a brave face while gritting his teeth through the pain.

"Let us know if we can help in any way," Marion said as she followed her husband out the door.

Yes, please offer to babysit for a week at least.

"Thank you for the offer, but we should be fine." Saph forced a smile and prayed that it would be so.

Chapter Fifteen

Should she even tell her daughter about the accident? But if Candace found out through her grandparents, she might be upset Saph hadn't told her.

"Your dad has come off his motorbike." Saph tried to keep her tone light. "Don't worry, he's going to be fine."

"How bad is it?" Candace's anxiety was clear through the phone.

"He should be out of hospital soon." It was the wrong thing to say.

"That's it, I'm coming home." Candace sounded determined. "I'll try and get up after my tutorial tomorrow and stay for the weekend."

"There's really no need!" As difficult as it was for Saph to say, she had to be tough, for her daughter's sake.

The discouragement was met with silence. "I thought you might like some support and help with the twins," Candace said at last, artificially bright.

"But what about your end of year exams?"

"I'll bring some work with me and study while I'm there."

Saph's protestations were clearly too weak, and although she didn't say it out loud, the company and the extra helping hands would be a real boon.

"As long as you go back on Sunday evening." Now she was really being stern—not easy but necessary.

"I'll ask around," Candace said, in a dispirited tone. "Somebody is bound to be driving up to Auckland tomorrow."

If she couldn't find a lift she wouldn't bother going—Mum's less than enthusiastic response had been bruising. But upon making some half-hearted inquiries, Candace found a fellow student who was going to visit a relative in the same hospital. It seemed like too good an opportunity to miss.

Although Mum hugged her when they met in the foyer, it was brief and tense.

"Patti is looking after the twins," Mum said.

It would be like old times with just the three of them.

"So I can't stay too long."

Maybe not.

It was a struggle to hide her dismay when she first saw her father—he looked worse than she had expected. Clearly Mum had downplayed his injuries. He sat propped up in his hospital bed, the bump and scar still clearly visible on his pale face, and his well bandaged fingers protruding from the sling.

"You didn't tell me how bad it was, Mum." She murmured her accusation.

"I didn't want to worry you. Honestly it's not as serious as it appears. Believe me, he's improved a lot since the accident. He was unconscious when they brought him in."

"Hi Candace," James said. To her relief, he gave her his usual grin. But it became more of a grimace when he tried to push himself up in bed. Candace rushed to help him. "Did your mum tell you all my injuries?" He reeled off the list before she had a chance to answer. Although it sounded worrying, it was best to make light of it.

"It's amazing you're still here talking to us," she said.

He laughed even though it made him wince and clutch his chest.

"God's clearly not ready for me yet—He's throwing the tiddlers back into the sea. Obviously He still has something for me to do and …" he said in a stage whisper, "I haven't annoyed your mother enough."

Mum shook her head in exaggerated despair.

It was painful to see how the twins cowered away from Candace at first, as though she was a stranger. But she was really, since apart from the disastrous baby-sitting venture, she'd had little to do with them. Mum didn't seem to notice.

"So have any nice boys caught your attention?" Mum asked, teasing. The babies had at last settled down and the unit was peaceful.

For a moment Candace considered telling her about her issues with Lance. No, it was too trivial. Instead she rolled her eyes.

"They're hardly boys, Mum, they're men. Although they might act like children at times. Anyway I'm too busy studying to look." She didn't dare ask about Greg and risk being teased or worse still, find out he had moved on. A change of subject would be best.

"I'm glad to see Dad is on the mend."

"Yes," Mum said, her expression becoming solemn. "I doubt I could've borne it if he'd died. It made me realise how much I love him." They were both silent for a minute.

"Do you know when he's coming home?" Candace asked.

"Probably in a couple of days' time." Mum grimaced. "Although I miss him terribly, I'm not looking forward to having to cope with him and the babies."

"Do you want me to stay on then?"

"No!" Mum spoke a little too quickly and emphatically. "You can't. You've got to get back to your studies."

And although her mother didn't say it, she probably didn't want Candace getting in the way. She swallowed her pain.

"Anyway Patti's available to help out," Mum said. She's a dab hand with little ones."

Implying Candace wasn't. She really wasn't needed.

On Sunday afternoon, after one last visit to see Dad, Mum dropped Candace off at the bus stop.

"I have to get back to relieve Patti of the twins." With a brief 'thank you' and a farewell hug Mum was off, leaving Candace standing alone to wait. It was hard not to be hurt—it was like being pushed out of the nest all over again.

Two days later, James came home from hospital, still in pain and pasty-looking. Although Saph thanked God he was alive, after a week of waiting on him and the twins, her gratitude was muttered through gritted teeth. The broken bones prevented James from doing basic things for himself, and it was clearly frustrating for him. The children's fretting didn't help. Perhaps she should have taken up Candace's offer—she had been sorely tempted to. But no, her daughter must concentrate on her own life.

Anyway Patti, in spite of her bossiness, was turning out to be a real blessing. It was she who often provided the family with an evening meal, cared for the babies and rallied other church members to help out too.

"That was the insurance company." James groaned as he hung up, from physical pain or emotional—Saph wasn't quite sure. "Unsurprisingly the bike is to be written off." He looked grieved. "Alas poor bike, I did enjoy riding it."

"Yes, I'm sure it must have been fun," Saph said, "but to be honest, I'm not sorry to see that machine go."

"I didn't realise you felt that way." James appeared startled.

"That's because I didn't want to spoil your pleasure. I couldn't help but feel a little anxious whenever you were out on it and I did a whole lot of praying for your protection."

"I didn't think you'd even noticed my absence—you were too busy with the kids."

The sulky comment was like a slap and she reacted without thinking. "And I didn't know if I could trust you."

"Sorry," James muttered. "That was before." His apology soothed the pain. "It's nice to know you cared. Although the bike was a bit of a toy, I was a perfectly safe rider with all the protective gear. Almost over cautious."

"I know you were but it wasn't your driving I was worried about. It was the other motorists who are blind when it comes to motorbikes." She smiled. "We'll have to find you a nice safe car."

"Boring." Like a spoilt child, James pouted. "No fun at all."

"This is really nice." In the restaurant's waiting area, Saph shifted along the couch as close as she could to James. When he winced, she moved away a fraction. "Sorry, I have to remember you're still healing up." She patted his knee instead. "I'm glad the counsellor suggested a weekly date night."

After the accident it had taken great effort just to drag themselves through each day, unable to think of anything beyond the very basics of existence, let alone work on their relationship. But at last with James recovering, the previous week they had managed to attend their first counselling session.

"Don't expect to see instant results—it will take time," the counsellor had told them. "And a lot of hard work. But if you two are committed to your marriage and one another, then you will get there. Communication and trust are crucial. Be honest with each other."

Honesty … in all the craziness of the accident and its aftermath, Saph had all but forgotten a confession she needed to make. When, with teeth gritted against the pain James reached out to her, a twinge of guilt poked, her appetite dissipated and she nearly missed what James was saying.

"You look gorgeous." He nuzzled her shoulder, "and you smell so good."

"James, I have to tell you something." She pulled away again.

He recoiled a little. "Go on."

"I haven't been completely honest with you." She paused, nervous as to how he would react. "While you were in hospital, I checked your phone to see if there were any urgent texts—at least that's what I tried to tell myself. But I admit I looked through your inbox and contact list too."

"And did you find anything?"

She shook her head.

He shrugged. "Now maybe you'll believe me. I really can be trusted."

"So you're not upset?"

"No. It's quite understandable after what I did." He looked mildly embarrassed. "I truly am sorry and I really regret it. This brush with death has helped me to see things in a new light, to really appreciate you and all you do." With his apology and her minor confession lightening her, she floated.

"I do forgive you." At last she could say it with a measure of sincerity. One day it would be heartfelt. "Do you forgive me?"

"Of course." He smiled and nodded as the waiter approached and beckoned them to a table.

"That's wonderful to hear. All of a sudden I'm ravenous—I haven't even looked at the menu yet."

"It was a great idea of Candace's to get Tiff to babysit," Saph said, as they waited for their meals to arrive. "In exchange for looking after her son while she has a date night with Ryan."

"Yes, I left her with strict instructions to call us only if there was an extreme emergency. For example the babies have set fire to the house."

"At their age?" Saph frowned at her husband. But he just grinned.

"Or are in some sort of mortal danger. Otherwise I told her we don't want to know. Anyway that's enough of that subject—I'm not mentioning them again."

Saph smiled. "It was also a good idea of hers to bring young Johnny along to help entertain the—" James leaned over to press a finger against her lips, pre-empting what she was going to say.

"No more talk about them. You will not give them a second thought. I know it sounds heartless but I want to forget we are parents, just for a few hours anyway. I'm going to be completely selfish—I want you to focus on me and us."

Chapter Sixteen

"Welcome to the final Christian Fellowship meeting for the year. We—" The leader was interrupted by a tap on the door before it was tentatively pushed open. Perhaps Amanda had finally taken Candace up on her invitation—but it was Lance who entered the room.

"Do you mind if I join you?"

"We thought you'd left the hostel." The leader frowned a little.

"I have but I'd still like to come to the meeting," he said, looking directly at Candace. She blushed and pretended to examine a notice board. "If nobody objects?"

The others smiled and nodded. One girl beamed at him and shifted over to make room. But her smile was wasted, and her disappointment clear, when he headed straight for the empty chair next to Candace.

"How's the new flat?" she whispered.

"It's great. Come and visit sometime."

"Happy Christmas everybody," the leader said, concluding the meeting.

"Before you take off …" Candace squirmed a little as all eyes turned to her. "Does anyone know of accommodation going begging? I can't go back to Auckland as I've found a job down here." And there was no room in her former home—but she wasn't about to share that with the group.

"You could come and live with me," Lance said. Candace wasn't the only one to raise her eyebrows in surprise. He must have noticed the shocked looks for his face reddened.

"As a flatmate I mean, of course," he said in a rush. "And it would only be temporary. Both my flatmates are going home over the summer and I'm not, so I'll be rattling around in the house on my own."

Although it was a tempting offer, and he would probably be fun to flat with, living in a house with a man who was interested in her would be like playing with matches in a petrol station. She hesitated, not wanting to hurt his feelings.

Before she could reply, Vicky spoke up. "I need a flatmate. I've found myself a two bedroom unit but I can't afford it on my own. I was about to advertise."

Candace cast her a grateful look for the out. "Thanks, I really appreciate that." Although she didn't know the woman well, being the quietest and most reserved member of the group, Candace had heard nothing bad about her. She noticed Lance's puzzling frown and his grimace. When he subtly shook his head at her, she ignored him.

Once Vicki and the others had left, Candace stayed behind to help clean up. Lance joined her.

"Do you know what you're letting yourself in for?" he asked, stacking chairs. "Vicki was next door to me in the hostel and I can't imagine she'd be a barrel of laughs to flat with. From what I've heard, her sense of humour was removed at birth. You'll be bored stiff within five minutes—you'd have a lot more fun in my flat."

"Maybe I want sensible and quiet," Candace said going on the defensive. Was it just sour grapes on his part? Or was he genuinely concerned for her? She softened. "Thanks for your offer, Lance, but I think it would be best to flat with a woman. Besides, it's long term and the place is just around the corner from the university. It'll be so handy next year."

"If you last that long."

With her arms full of belongings, Candace stopped to examine a precisely lined-up page of house rules taped to the kitchen wall. She poked her tongue out at the offending list before lugging her gear to her new room. What had she let herself in for? Perhaps she should have listened to Lance. Once she had found places for her stuff, she joined Vicky in the super neat and clean lounge.

"I can't believe the university year is over already." Candace carefully sat in a chair, scared she might mess it up. "It's such a relief to have those exams behind me."

Vicky barely glanced up from the book she was reading.

"So, Lance has invited us both around for a small end-of-year social gathering. Are you interested?"

"Not for me," Vicky said.

"Come on, it'll be fun. It's just some people from church and from the group. I can't stay late as I have to get up early for the first day of my job tomorrow." She wasn't surprised at Vicky's response.

"It's not my thing. And should you be going when you have work in the morning?"

Biting back a retort, Candace retreated to her room. At least she could be herself in there. Perhaps Lance was right about her not lasting the summer with Vicky.

"Sorry, I'm late," Candace said when Lance opened the door. She had procrastinated, unwilling to go on her own.

"What, no Vicky?" he asked in mock surprise as he ushered her into the lounge.

"Where is everybody?" Candace asked, eyeing the room which

was devoid of people. Was this just a set-up to get her around there? The table however was laden with bowls of snacks.

Lance sighed. "You know how it is, people say they'll turn up and then don't. And they don't even have the common decency to let you know." He was clearly miffed. Then he smiled. "At least you're here, that's the main thing."

She squirmed and was thankful to hear a knock on the door. Lance hurried to open it and greetings were exchanged, before a couple followed him into the lounge. He introduced them to her as people from his church.

"And this is my—"

"Friend." Candace poked the word in, before he had a chance to say anything else.

"Please, help yourself to the food," Lance said. "There's plenty."

After half an hour of the four of them trying to make small talk over the nibbles and standing around looking ill at ease, the couple excused themselves with a mumbled apology.

"I'd better go too," Candace said, after they had left.

"No!" Lance said with a little too much vehemence. "I'm quite glad they've gone." Candace raised an eyebrow at him and he coloured up. "I mean it just felt awkward, surely you must have noticed?" He glanced at the time. "Oh well, it doesn't look as though anyone else is turning up and I've got a DVD here if you're interested. We can trough out on all this food while we watch."

It was still early and her dull new abode and antisocial flatmate held little appeal. After Lance had transferred some of the bowls of snacks onto the coffee table and put the movie on, he plonked down next to her on the lone couch

The film was so engrossing, Candace leaned forward. She started when she felt the hand on her back. Then Lance's arms were around her and he was turning her face to his. With all her senses on overload, she allowed it at first. But … he was moving in as if to kiss her. She pushed him away and leapt up. Unbidden, horrible memories of what that snake Doug had tried to do, poured in.

"No, Lance, I said I just wanted to be friends and I meant it." Indignation surged through her. "But even if we were an item, that still doesn't give you the right to pounce."

"Okay, I truly am sorry." Lance hung his head. "I got carried away. But it's so hard to resist you! I promise I won't try anything like that again."

The man was no Doug and at his apology, Candace's anger started to dissolve, especially when he looked up and gave her a hopeful smile.

"Remember how you told me you didn't want a relationship in the first year? Well, the year is over now."

He was right; it was what she'd said. While she hesitated, trying to dream up a response, he spoke again. "Go on a proper date with me, Candace, and I'll treat you like a princess."

No doubt he would but she had to be strong. "I'm sorry, Lance," she said and meant it. She didn't dare glance at him, in case he looked like a beaten puppy, and she did something she would regret purely out of pity. "You are a lovely guy. But I only see you as a friend. I'm sure God has somebody out there for you—but I don't think it's me. In fact I'm in love with someone else."

She slapped a hand over her mouth. Where had that come from? It wasn't what she'd intended to say. She snatched up her bag and sprinted. When she reached the front door, she glanced back. With an air of bewilderment, Lance stood motionless in the hallway.

Candace could not sleep. Too much to think about. Lance was one of the good guys and she could do a lot worse. But it would be unfair to lead him on when she wasn't genuinely attracted to him.

Nobly, she didn't want to get in the way of his happiness with someone else—and selfishly, for him to get in the way of hers.

And then there was what she'd blurted out tonight. She'd never said it out loud before. Was it just an excuse, a way of pouring cold water on Lance's passion? Or was she really in love with Greg?

She hadn't seen him for ages—perhaps it was merely a case of 'absence makes the heart grow fonder.' But right now, the feeling of missing him was overwhelming.

Even though it was past midnight she reached for her cell phone.

Are you around at Christmas time? Do you want to catch up? Unsurprisingly there was no reply.

While Candace fumbled her way around the unfamiliar keyboard and screen, she tried to hide yet another yawn from her new workmates.

"It's your first morning on the job and you're bored already?" her neighbour asked her.

"No, I ah, didn't sleep—" From the depths of her bag, her text alert sounded. She couldn't check it now; it would have to wait until the first break. Impatience and anticipation made it difficult to concentrate, and she had to retype several corrections.

At break time, the first thing she did was reach for her phone.

Sorry, not going to be around at Christmas.

Was that all Greg could say? He had given only the barest apology and no explanation, or expression of regret.

It was unusual for him to go away at that time of year. What on earth could he be up to? And where? But if she asked him what he was doing, it might sound as though she was checking up on him. Perhaps he simply wanted to avoid her. Best leave it. Last night, when she had been missing him so much, she had been eagerly anticipating returning to Auckland for Christmas. Now she wasn't fussed.

Chapter Seventeen

"Where are all the Christmas decorations, Mum?" Candace eyed her mother's half-hearted attempt to make the unit appear festive.

"I've been so busy, I haven't had the chance," Mum said.

"I'll give it a go." It wasn't as though she had anything better to do—her mother had been quick to refuse her offer of help with the babies.

Candace found the box of decorations in its usual place and lifted the lid.

"You have to make sure everything's up high out of reach of little fingers," Mum said, "now that the twins are starting to crawl."

On top of the pile were the ones that had been bought for their first Christmas together as a family—when it had been just the three of them. There was Mum's teddy bear and Dad's gold star. She carefully lifted her own glass angel from its tissue paper wrapping, and dangled it by the thread.

"You're not going to hang that up anywhere are you?" Mum said with evident alarm. "It would be so dangerous if it got broken."

Candace reluctantly nestled the angel back in the box. "It really belongs on a Christmas tree anyway. You're not having one this year?"

"Absolutely not. We don't want the twins swallowing something they shouldn't."

"So where should I put my presents then?"

"Hide them in your room—don't let the babies get hold of them."

The twins seemed to have brought about so many changes. Weren't children supposed to make Christmas? But this year, they were restricting it.

They had disturbed her sleep too, fussing during the night on the other side of the wall, the two cots crammed into the other bedroom. She failed to stifle a yawn and Mum noticed.

"The twins have been sleeping quite well in their room," she said dark circles under her eyes testament to her own tiredness. "Perhaps they feel disturbed having to share ours." It felt like a dig.

"Just as well I'm only staying two nights then." Her curtness was pain-induced but her mother didn't seem to pick up on it.

"I thought you would have been acclimatised to racket," she said, "after living in the hostel for all those months."

"But this is a different type of noise, one which I'm not used to."

"You wait until you have kids." Mum sent her a knowing smile.

"Who said I'm going to have any? Or get married?" Candace changed down to a mutter. This is almost enough to put me off."

Mum obviously heard her for she gave her a wistful look. "Please don't be. It will all be worthwhile in the end." Her weary face became mischievous. "Besides which I want grandchildren." She held up her hand in anticipation of Candace's indignation. "Although not just yet."

On Christmas morning, it was a relief to escape the crowded unit and sneak off to the church service on her own. In previous years they had attended as a family, but this time there was lunch to organise and infants to take care of. More disruption due to the children. It was a struggle not to resent them.

In the packed auditorium, Candace cast subtle glances around the crowd for Greg but he was nowhere to be seen.

"We pray for Greg," the pastor said. Her ears honed in on the mention of his name. "And his team as they make their way to

China on their missions trip." So Greg wasn't simply avoiding her. She bounced home, light with relief. Two cars were parked out in the cul-de-sac, indicating both sets of grandparents had arrived.

"Hello everybody." But there was no response and Candace's cheerful greeting fell flat. By the sound of it, her two grandmothers were in the bedroom fussing over the twins, and in between talking baby speak, having conversations with Mum about child-related topics.

It meant she wasn't going to get a look in. Meanwhile the men had drifted outside. Candace lingered in the sitting room, unsure of what to do and where she fitted in now—it seemed she didn't belong to either group. In previous years, she had been the centre of attention, being the only child on the scene.

Shortly after midday the seven adults squeezed around the table for Christmas lunch. The infants even managed to disrupt that— Mum had to settle them down to sleep before the family could eat. At last they were able to tuck into the food in peace and for the first time that day, things felt close to normal.

It didn't last long. Her parents looked too weary to truly enjoy the spread and her grandmothers wouldn't shut up about the babies. Only Gramps paid her any sort of attention. Oh for pre-baby Christmases.

Then there was the present opening, delayed until after the twins had woken up. Naturally most of the gifts were for them, but they were more interested in the packaging than the toys. The afternoon dragged as everyone dozed after eating too much.

"We'd better get going," Papa Bear said. Candace had her bags at the door before her grandparents had even started saying their farewells. Then she hovered impatiently as Mama Bear had to cuddle first one child and then the other. Papa Bear rolled his eyes and shook his head before sending Candace a sympathetic glance. She returned it gratefully. At least somebody understood. Finally, with a long drawn out sigh, Mama Bear relinquished the baby to his mother.

Bliss. No more fussing babies or fussing over babies. Candace settled into the spacious back seat, and tuned out Mama Bear's commentary on her youngest grandchildren.

This time she wasn't leaving home; she was going home.

PART TWO

Chapter Eighteen

Autumn 2009

"I'm so proud of you, Candace!" Saph's words were heartfelt. She stepped back to take a photo of the new graduate. Candace adjusted her gown and trencher before holding up her degree for the camera, her pride evident. All around them in the crowded foyer, there were flashes and clicks as fellow graduates posed for family snaps.

"And so am I," James said, also beaming. "You are and will be a brilliant teacher I'm sure."

"I don't know where those three years went," Saph said, examining the picture on the tiny screen. "It feels as though it was only last month we dropped you off at the hostel." The image blurred as tears of joy for her daughter mixed with sorrow for herself. This was so different to her own graduation day, when she had felt such a miserable failure. But she blinked the moisture away and lifted her head to smile at Candace—seeing her graduate was more than making up for it. "Don't move. I want to take another one."

Candace posed again, her proud smile as wide as her own.

"You could probably hear me applauding when you walked across the stage," Saph said, showing the photo to Candace, "I was clapping so loudly. I was tempted to holler and whistle—"

"I'm glad you didn't." Candace pulled a face. "It was terrifying enough negotiating the stairs in high heels, without you distracting me. I had to really concentrate so as not to trip and hurt myself—or my pride. To be honest, I can't wait to take these torturous shoes off. And this dress too—it's restricting my breathing."

Saph wrinkled her nose at her daughter. "It's a shame you find those sorts of clothes so uncomfortable—you look stunning in that outfit."

"If I ever graduate again, I'm wearing jeans and a t-shirt," Candace muttered. "And sneakers."

"I hope you're joking." But Candace shook her head.

"We have something for you." James removed an envelope from his jacket pocket and handed it to Candace. After unsealing the flap, she pulled out a card and opened it. Saph watched in horror as a slip of paper fell out and twisted away in the breeze. At great risk to her ankles, Candace scrambled for the elusive item amidst the assorted legs, and just managed to catch it before it sailed out the door. She glanced at it and then looked again.

"A cheque for one thousand dollars!" She blurted it out. "You can't afford this."

It had been a struggle scraping together the cash. But Candace didn't need to know that.

"Sorry." Candace looked apologetic. "I mean, thank you very much."

"You so deserve it," Saph said, receiving a grateful hug from her daughter. "You worked hard during the breaks and supported yourself all the way through your studies without asking us for a cent."

"Deposit it in your savings account," James said as he was hugged in turn. "Then you can earn interest on it."

"The money is to go towards your overseas travel," Saph said. "We know it's been your dream to go for so long."

"Are you sure you can spare it?" Candace frowned. "Don't forget I'm earning at the moment, at least until the end of the term. Plus, I should be able to get a job quite easily when I arrive in England."

"True, but you must have heaps of expenses. I bet not a lot of your wages make it into savings."

"I'll pay you back."

"You will do no such thing." James glared at her. "It's a gift."

"Thanks again." Candace draped her arms around her parents' shoulders. "You are the best Mum and Dad in the world."

"Would you still say that if we hadn't given you the cash?" James asked.

"Such cynicism, Dad. Do you really think I'm that shallow?"

He chuckled in reply.

"Although by giving you that money," Saph said, "I do feel as though I may be sending you to your doom."

Candace rolled her eyes. "Don't be so melodramatic, Mum. I'm a big girl now. God will go with me and I can look after myself."

"I'm sure you can." But it wasn't going to be easy to watch her daughter spread her wings even wider and fly further afield. "It's just difficult letting you go out into the big bad world on your own—so different from home." Unwilling to cop another scornful glare, Saph refrained from mentioning Candace's lack of worldly wisdom; she was bound to see some eye-opening stuff on her travels.

"But that's the appeal," Candace said. "I want to experience other cultures and ways of life. It'll be good for me—what you might call a stretching experience." She sighed. "Although part of me can't wait to go, another part of me doesn't want to. It means leaving Hamilton and all the friends I've made over the last three years." She smiled and waved at a man who stood nearby, also surrounded by his proud-looking family. "Pity I can't take all my mates with me," she said as the man returned the wave.

"Who's that?" Saph asked, trying to sound casual and not suspicious and parental.

"Lance. I met him in my first year at the Christian Fellowship group. We've hung out together over the years, been out to the movies and stuff now and then." She narrowed her eyes at Saph. "Don't go getting any funny ideas, we're just friends."

By the way in which the young man's gaze lingered on Candace, Saph wasn't convinced friendship was all he wanted.

"Your dad and I started out as," Saph made speech marks with her fingers, "just friends." James nodded and gave Candace an exaggerated wink.

"You told me that when Greg was on the scene," Candace said in a mock huff. "Many times. Now I hardly ever see or hear from him." She looked a little downcast.

"Speaking of Greg," Saph said, "I saw him at church last Sunday and he asked me to pass on his congratulations and to send his regards." And surely his love too, but she didn't say that out loud. She watched Candace's face light up again. Her daughter clearly still had feelings for her friend.

"We should be making a move to the restaurant for lunch," James said, nudging Saph and dislodging her romantic notions. "Afterwards we'll have to hurry off to rescue Mum and Dad from our dear sweet little children, before they drive the folks bonkers and they never speak to us again. Or offer to babysit. It's a pity you can't come out to Cambridge with us, Candace, but there's no room in the car."

Saph noticed the fleeting look of hurt cross her daughter's face, followed by a brave smile.

Even at her age, the rejection was still painful. This was supposed to be a happy day, when for once she was the focus of the family's attention. Her grandparents had been invited to the ceremony, but instead they'd jumped at the chance to babysit—it was clear where their priorities lay.

Now she wouldn't get the opportunity to show off to them and have them make a fuss over her for a change. Yet again, her young siblings were taking centre stage and she was left in the wings. Mum must have noticed for she sent her a sympathetic glance. Candace forced a smile to hide her sulk.

The twins hadn't just taken up her family's attention, but had taken over the home too. *Her* home—if it hadn't been for her, they wouldn't have the unit. Kathy had left it to her in trust until such time as she was old enough. Well, she was old enough now. She owned it and she had every right to kick the whole family out if she wanted.

And her parents giving her that money for the overseas trip— was that really out of generosity? Or were they trying to get rid of her? Although it was probably paranoia talking, it made her even more determined to go. In fact she couldn't wait. She knew when she wasn't wanted.

"Excuse me, I just have to go to the bathroom." She needed time to simmer down. Blessedly, there was no-one else in there. After a lot of deep breathing in front of the mirror, she gave her sour reflection a stern lecture.

"Grow up and get over yourself. They are only children and it's not their fault, they need lots of attention. In a couple of hours the focus will be back on them but in the meantime, I am determined to enjoy my lunch and lap up the admiration."

Back out in the foyer, at her mother's anxious look, she smiled sweetly to reassure her.

"Right, I'm ready to go now."

Chapter Nineteen

"This is all becoming very real." Candace gazed around the busy airport, trying to hide her nervousness beneath a calm veneer.

"Are you sure you've got everything?" Mum asked, equally strung-out and making no attempt to conceal it.

"Yes, for the hundredth time," Candace said with a roll of her eyes. "Stop fussing, Mum."

It was quite true her possessions were packed and ready to go—but was she emotionally prepared to fly into the sunset? The great OE had been a dream of hers well before the event of the twins; they had merely provided an extra incentive for action. However now that departure day was here at last, ironically all she wanted to do was cling to her family. But she couldn't let them see that.

Instead she stiffened her jaw to hide her fears and scanned the crowd again. There was still no sign of Greg. According to Mum, he had made a careful note of the departure time and declared he would be there to see her off. He'd better hurry up because she'd have to board soon. Perhaps he'd changed his mind. Maybe it was for the best—or she might have been doubly tempted to stay.

"So Vicky's going to meet you at Heathrow?" Mum asked, interrupting her search.

"Thank the Lord, yes. I'll be happy to see a familiar face and it'd be a nightmare trying to figure out the public transport system and find the flat on my own. She's been over there for a few months already so she knows her way around."

"It's such a blessing she has a room available."

"Even if it's not much bigger than a cupboard. But it's better than sleeping on a sofa or flatting with strangers."

It was nearly time to go. Candace crouched down in front of the double pushchair.

"Now Chris and Gemma, you two behave yourselves for your poor mum and dad." Two pairs of big round eyes gazed at Candace without comprehension. They still seemed unsure of her—but she only had herself to blame for that; her visits during her degree years had been occasional and reluctant day trips, even at Christmas. It was still painful though, to see that in their eyes she was like a stranger. Hoping they wouldn't take fright, she leaned in and kissed first one soft cheek and then the other before standing up again.

"So you're leaving Saturday afternoon," Dad stroked his chin thoughtfully, "and arrive in London on Sunday morning, their time. But it will be Sunday evening here? Sounds complicated."

"I think that's right. All I know is I'm going to be tired."

"As you bask in the English summer," he said, "spare a thought for us freezing to death in winter."

"You don't half exaggerate, Dad! Anyway, Vicky says it hasn't been that warm yet."

After giving her dad a hug, she turned to her mother, who enveloped her with the ferocity of a mama-bear.

"Please don't start, Mum," she said as she felt her mother's chest heave—her own thin veneer might crack and leak. And she was determined not to cry. She lifted her head to listen. "I'm afraid you're going to have let me go—that's my flight they're calling."

To her shock, her mother abruptly held her away at arm's length.

"Go into the world and have a wonderful time," Mum said with lowered eyes, her face expressionless. Without another word, she turned Candace around and gave her a light push in the direction of the security gate.

Slightly stunned at her mother's sudden change of attitude, and with her parents' farewells in her ears, Candace determinedly walked along the carpeted aisle. To her fate or to her future? She blinked her eyes against the tears and turned to smile and wave at her family. Two chubby little hands waved back at her.

It was so tempting to turn round and run back to the security of the familiar. But it was obvious there was no room for her here. Instead, she lifted her chin and squared her shoulders.

Where was Greg? She slowed her pace and again searched the crowd. No sign of him. He was rarely late and he was known for keeping his word. But not today it seemed. Best just to forget about him. Facing straight ahead, she resumed her marching. There was a big world out there that she couldn't wait to explore. Excitement replaced fear and sorrow. First stop, London. And after that, who knew where?

With a prayer for her daughter's safety, Saph watched as Candace disappeared into the dim hallway, like Alice down the rabbit hole. It was hard letting her go; akin to tearing a piece of her own self off and setting it out in front of wolves. Candace might be a grown woman, but she was still so child-like and vulnerable somehow.

It had been difficult enough sending her off to university—and that had only been a couple of hundred kilometres away. Now Candace was going to the other side of the world where anything could happen to her. There were such dreadful reports on the news these days: terrorist attacks, kidnapping—horrors—the plane could crash. She had already given her eldest daughter up once, when she had rejected her in the womb. Now she wanted to hang on to her and never let go.

But as much as she longed to run after her daughter and drag her back, she couldn't. This was Candace's choice, her life, her adventure. Somehow Saph managed to control herself and stay put.

James must have noticed her upset for he put a comforting arm around her. She leaned into his shoulder and wet his shirt with her tears.

"I hated pushing her away," she said between sobs. "But I had to, or she might never have gone."

"She's going to be all right," James said. "God will go with her." Although he spoke the truth, his words were of little comfort.

"Candace!" Saph and James turned at the sound of the familiar voice, tinged with despair. Greg came puffing up to them.

"You've just missed her!" Saph said.

"I know. I saw her just before she disappeared around the corner." He put his hands on his knees and panted. "Got stuck in traffic—my own fault—should have left earlier. And of course it was next to impossible to find a car park. Then I sprinted through the terminal, but it seems I'm still too late."

"The plane hasn't left yet, you can watch it taking off," James said.

"It's just not the same. Besides which, I had something to give her." He held up a pocket-sized teddy bear. "To remind her of me." He reddened. "And of course her other friends here at home."

Saph's heart went out to him. He was clearly still in love with her daughter.

Chapter Twenty

"Is there life beyond the jet lag?" Candace covered a yawn with her hand. "I thought it would be over by the third day."

"You'll be fine soon," Vicky said in her usual abrupt manner.

"Thanks once again for helping me out with a place to stay."

Vicky didn't acknowledge her gratitude. "When are you going to sign up at the job agency?" She was not being subtle.

"Probably early next week. I want to adjust to my new surroundings first. If I can stay awake, that is. I could hardly keep my eyelids up on the open top bus tour around London today—I probably missed some of the amazing sights."

But it was clear Vicky wasn't listening anymore.

"Don't worry." Candace stifled another yawn. "I can pay my way for some time yet."

Greg was standing in his usual place up the front at the morning service, with Candace next to him—wait, that couldn't be right!

Saph stared harder. The young woman had the same dark hair and petite figure—surely her daughter hadn't returned unknown to her? But when the girl turned to talk to Greg, the similarity diminished and Saph let out her held breath. She nudged James.

"Do you think Greg has found himself a girlfriend?"

He glanced at the couple. "She could just be a mate."

"I hope that's all she is. Although Candace wouldn't admit it, she'd be devastated if Greg had moved on."

"But she's on the other side of the world, so why would she care?" James said. "Besides, they were never really an item were they?"

"Only because Candace didn't want to settle down before she'd finished her degree and done the OE thing. Once she's got that out of her system …"

The band interrupted her and James was no longer listening.

Throughout the service, Saph kept a close eye on the pair's interactions. When Greg reached for his companion's hand, unreasonable indignation swelled. Candace had only been gone five minutes—and already Greg had moved on.

Afterwards, at coffee time, she tried to catch Greg's eye. But looking sheepish, he avoided her.

"Any sign of more permanent work?" Saph asked.

"The agency still only has relief teaching available," Candace said, her image pixelating on the computer screen. "But I've ended up working almost every weekday since I signed up. I must say it was a little disconcerting at first, trying to find my way around London and beyond, but now I've figured out the public transport system, it's reasonably straightforward."

"And surely you get to see a lot more of the country this way," Saph said, "rather than being stuck in one place with a static job."

"Speaking of getting out and about, I felt I should go and see Aunt Elizabeth … that is, Kathy's sister. So I visited her yesterday."

"What's Aunty Liz like?" Saph asked.

"Don't ever call her that!" Candace gave a mock gasp. "She's terribly English, complete with stiff upper lip. I got the feeling she saw me as a country bumpkin and wasn't particularly impressed to be the aunt of such a hick."

Saph chuckled. "That's funny—she's a born and bred Kiwi herself."

"She's certainly adapted to the British lifestyle," Candace said.

"Perhaps a bit too well. I don't think she's returned home once, not even for Kathy's or her parents' funerals. And now she has nothing to come back for." She shook her head sadly before continuing. "Aunt Elizabeth seemed to tolerate rather than welcome me. I gather she and Kathy weren't particularly close."

"Kathy told me they only exchanged birthday and Christmas cards and had no contact apart from that, not even a phone call. Does she live in a grand mansion?"

"The outside is fairly ordinary, but you should see inside her house, Mum—it's beautiful. Everything is so scarily perfect, it doesn't look lived in. I couldn't relax—I was almost afraid to breathe in case I disturbed something. We sat around and drank tea," Candace said, adopting a plummy accent, "out of fine china cups and attempted to make polite conversation. I was just waiting for the cucumber sandwiches to appear but no, she brought out supermarket biscuits. The whole meeting was rather uncomfortable and awkward."

Saph laughed and Candace joined in before she continued. "I don't know whether it was a wise idea but I finally plucked up the courage and told Aunt Elizabeth Kathy wasn't my real mother; that she'd adopted me at birth."

"How did she react?"

"She didn't say anything at first, just became even more stiff-lipped and stared down her nose at me for a while. Then she told me she'd just remembered she had urgent business to attend to. I was heartily glad to escape."

"Well, you've done your duty now. You don't ever have to go back there. Unless, of course, you want to."

"No thank you." Candace's response was vehement. "Any news from your side of the world?"

"Yes, actually." Saph paused. "And I don't know how you're going to take it. It looks as though young Greg has found himself a woman."

"Oh." Candace looked away from the camera and was quiet for a few seconds. Then she pressed her lips together in a strained smile. "Well, good on him," she said in an artificially upbeat way. "I'm happy for the man. I guess it wasn't unexpected."

The conversation didn't last much longer before Candace excused herself and made her good-byes. It was obvious she was more upset than she let on.

Since the walls of her tiny cupboard-bedroom were not totally soundproof, Candace muffled lonely tears with her pillow. The first few weeks of being in London had been an exciting distraction, but now the novelty had worn off and she missed all the familiarity of home, especially her friends. Her teaching assignments were too short for her to make any, although she had tried. So far she hadn't encountered any fellow Kiwis to connect with and the few Australians she had met, closed ranks and left her out. There were only two people she knew in this whole country: Aunt Elizabeth, who after just one meeting clearly wanted to have nothing more to do with her, and anti-social Vicky.

Mum's news this afternoon hadn't helped at all. It had taken great effort to hide her shock and devastation, to pretend not to care about Greg moving on. She did care—very much. How dare he? How could he look at anyone other than her? She raged silently at the dark empty air.

The loneliness was almost overwhelming. She missed her family, she missed her friends and right now—when she couldn't have him—she missed Greg most of all.

It was so tempting to jump on a plane and return home. But where was home now? She had given up the flat in Hamilton, and her family didn't have room for her in the tiny overcrowded unit; she would just end up being in the way there. In fact they were probably glad she was gone. And Greg clearly didn't miss her. There was really nothing to go back to. The self-pity brought fresh tears.

So returning to New Zealand was not an option. Besides, she could hardly give up already—she had only been here a month—not long enough to give it a real go. And there was still so much to see.

Of course she had God to help her. He was always there for her. Even if her own family rejected her, she was part of His. Which was a reminder—she hadn't been to church since she'd arrived. Going to a service might be a good way to meet people. She wasn't familiar with this area and she hadn't seen any churches on her short nervous ventures out, but Vicky attended a local church—perhaps she could tag along with her this Sunday.

From the outside, the church building looked majestic: all stone work and spires. Inside, it was equally impressive. But as Candace shuffled along behind Vicky between the pews, she shivered. The atmosphere was cold and gloomy, and not just physically but spiritually—it was as though God hadn't been invited to attend.

Organ music stirred the dead air and the choir, dressed in neat white robes, rose up as one to begin the service with a hymn. It was like walking through wet cement—the congregation droned the chorus without heart and seemed to be merely going through the motions. In the middle of the following song, Candace spotted a choir member hiding a yawn, looking as though she didn't really want to be there. Actually, nobody did—it seemed they had simply come along for their weekly religious inoculation.

The priest stood and spoke in a monotone, and the congregation responded by insincere rote. After a dreary half-hour, Candace was past ready to walk out. But she was blocked in on either side and Vicky clearly wasn't willing to go. Candace gritted her teeth and endured the long and unexciting sermon. At last the service dragged to a close. Prepared to write the whole experience off as a bad idea, Candace grabbed her handbag, intent upon making a rapid departure. However Vicky determinedly made her way to the adjacent hall where cups of tea were being served.

There was a strong chance she might get lost walking home on her own, so Candace trailed after her flatmate and joined the queue at the kitchen counter. The purpose of coming here after all, other than to connect with God, was to meet people. But nobody seemed keen to chat to a stranger; instead they clumped together in their own small cliques. So she hovered at Vicky's elbow and sipped the bitter brew. Her flatmate, apparently oblivious of her presence, engaged in a long-winded and earnest discussion with a fellow parishioner and didn't introduce her. With a vow never to return to this God-forsaken church, Candace drained her cup and wondered whether to have another. At least getting a refill would give her something to do while she waited for Vicky.

On her dawdle over to the tea urn, she glanced up to see a pair of fine male eyes gazing at her. Through coyly lowered lashes she examined the man, who stood alone also looking somewhat lost. He bore a slight but distinct resemblance to Greg, and a wave of nostalgia enveloped her. But this man was a shade taller, muscular rather than stocky, and better looking. She was filling her cup when he moved over to her.

"I don't believe I've seen you here before." He sounded Irish. "Are you new?" Candace nodded, not ready to reveal her accent just yet.

"Whereabouts are you from, then?"

"New Zealand."

His smile made him look even more attractive. "I've heard a lot about your country. It sounds amazing. Some people liken it to Ireland, another emerald isle as it were." He introduced himself as Neil and she lost track of time as they chatted.

"Are you ready to go?" Vicky had finally ended her conversation and arrived at her elbow. Candace reluctantly said good-bye to the charming man.

"Shall I see you next week then?" Neil asked.

"Yes, definitely." Vow forgotten, the formerly detested church now seemed like the best place to be.

Chapter Twenty-One

After putting the children to bed, Saph hastened to answer the phone before it disturbed them.

"Hello—"

"You'll never guess what, Mum!" Candace sounded super-excited. "I'm engaged!"

It took a couple of seconds for the news to sink in. Then, rendered speechless, Saph had to sit down.

"Last night Neil asked me to marry him and I simply had to tell you as soon as I could."

Instead of screaming negativity at her distant daughter as she wanted to, Saph gulped her feelings down.

"Who's Neil?" she asked, trying to hide her alarm beneath a calm voice.

"He's the most wonderful man: good looking, a real gentleman, and he treats me so well." Candace's wistful sigh was loud and exaggerated.

"So you like him, then?" Saph asked with mild sarcasm.

"Like him? I love him!"

"How long have you known this Neil? Why have we never heard his name mentioned before?"

"I only met him four weeks ago—but we clicked immediately. And I didn't want to say anything about a relationship before I was sure." Candace emitted a nervous giggle. "I never expected him to propose so soon, on only our second official date."

The alarm bells were jangling. A month, if that, was hardly long enough to get to know someone. "Is he a Christian?" Saph tied down her hysteria.

"He goes to church." Candace sounded slightly defensive. That didn't necessarily mean anything, but Saph kept her mouth shut and stuffed down the rising mothering instinct. "In fact that's where I met him. You should see the ring, Mum!" Candace stumbled over her words in her excitement. "I'm surprised you can't see it sparkling from there!"

A ring already? "So when do we get to meet this amazing Neil?" Saph asked through numb lips.

"One day." The vague answer added fuel to Saph's anxious fire. Then optimism sparked.

"Does this mean you're coming home soon?" She tried not to sound overly eager. "To introduce him to us?"

"No, not just yet." Candace's words dashed hopes. "There are still heaps of things I want to do over here, like seeing Europe, and the rest of the UK. Neil has offered to be my tour guide. He's from Ireland originally so he knows his way around."

Saph broke out in a mental cold sweat. A hot-blooded Irishman travelling with her vulnerable and innocent daughter? It was the stuff of nightmares. Perhaps it would be better for them to get married before they went. But then the wedding might be held over there and there was no way she and James could attend. And who knew when she would get to see her daughter again? In which case, it was best not to make the suggestion.

It was as though Candace had read Saph's uneasy thoughts. "Don't worry Mum," she said with a resigned sigh. "We won't be going on our own. Neil reckons he knows another couple who would be keen to come with us. Anyway, he's too much of a gentleman to try anything—if you know what I mean." Another coy giggle.

It was reassuring to hear, but still Saph wasn't completely comfortable. She had so many questions to ask but stuck to the safe ones.

"Have you started making wedding plans?"

"It's too soon for that! We haven't had a chance to discuss where or when. But I know Neil wants it to be some time in the near future. He reckons he can't wait for us to get married." More nervous laughter.

One question was particularly nerve-wracking. "Where are you planning to live?"

"Mum, it's still early days." Candace was being evasive. "We'll sort that out later. I know this is big news, but I'm over the moon and I want you to be happy for me."

"If you're happy then so am I." More like scared stiff. "Congratulations."

"I have to go now, Mum, this call is costing me a fortune."

"Wait, I've still got heaps to ask you. And don't you want to talk to your dad?" But Saph was speaking to the hum of a dead line.

"James, you might want to sit down before I tell you Candace's news."

He seemed less thrown by the announcement. "She's old enough to make up her own mind."

"But she hardly knows the man." Her protective maternal instincts were still at the fore. "He could be a homicidal maniac for all we know."

"There's not much we can do about it though, is there?" He was right, which made it all the more frustrating. "Other than pray for her."

"I could fly over there and sort her out." But it was an empty, irrational threat and James quelled it with a wordless raise of his eyebrows.

Early on Saturday morning, the Skype alert sounded. Saph answered it to find an excited Candace.

"Can you get Dad to come here please?" she asked. Saph beckoned James over to the computer screen.

"I want to introduce you, in a manner of speaking, to my fiancé." Candace seemed to savour the word. "He wants to ask you both something."

While Saph waited for James to pull up a chair, she watched the screen as Neil joined Candace. He really was a good-looking young man and she could certainly understand the attraction. However character was far more important than physical appearance.

To Saph's delight, James sounded protective of his eldest daughter as he proceeded to grill Neil about his job and home. The young man's answers were smooth and polished—perhaps a little too glib. He barely smiled once and although he said all the right things, Saph couldn't warm to him.

"Mr and Mrs Holden, I'd like to ask for your daughter's hand in marriage." Neil made his formal request with much solemnity.

"Great," James said. "What about the rest of her?"

"Pardon?" Judging by the young man's blank look, it was clear he didn't have the same sense of humour James did.

Saph nudged him none too gently in the ribs. "Be serious," she whispered.

"Yes," James said, sobering up. "You may marry my daughter. I appreciate you asking."

"What about you, Mrs Holden?" His eyes held a challenge as though he was daring her to defy him.

"If that's what Candace wants." She hid her uneasiness behind the noncommittal answer.

"Nice to meet you, even if it was only by Skype," James said.

"Likewise," Neil said.

"Hope to meet you in the flesh in the not too distant future." James rose and placed the chair back in its original position.

"I'll leave you to chat to your mother." Neil kissed Candace on the cheek, and with a farewell wave at the screen, was gone before Saph could respond.

Although Candace looked excited enough, there was no real sparkle in her eyes. Not like when Greg was around. Was this really the right man for her precious daughter, or could Candace be making the most horrendous mistake? Saph prayed for God's intervention if it was wrong in His sight.

Candace leaned toward the camera. "So what do you think?" she whispered.

"He seems like the perfect gentleman," Saph said. It was the only safe and sincere response she could come up with.

"Isn't he good-looking?" Candace said with a dreamy expression. "And he treats me so well."

Saph nodded and kept silent about her doubts.

After they had said their farewells, she switched off the monitor and turned to James.

"So what do you really think of him?" she asked.

"He seems a nice enough chap with good prospects. It was decent of him to ask me for Candace's hand in marriage, even if it was by Skype."

"He looks very serious. I don't think he smiled once. Not the type of man I'd have thought Candace would go for."

"He'll probably be good for her though. A solid and dependable sort."

"Sounds boring. And you can't judge on looks alone." Saph groaned. "Why does my darling daughter have to be so far away? And why did she have to fall for a foreigner? She'll probably end up living on the other side of the world and I'll hardly ever see her."

"At least if we go over there, we'll have free accommodation."

"Trust you to think of that."

"And there's always Skype, email and texts to help us stay in touch."

"It's just not the same. You can't hug a computer screen."

"Mrs Holden!" Saph turned at the sound of her name being called across the church.

"Hello, Greg." Slowed down by Gemma hanging on to her hand, and before she could dream up an excuse to keep on walking, he caught up with her.

"I haven't talked to you in ages."

There was a good reason for that; she had been deliberately avoiding him.

"Your daughter is looking very bonny." He smiled at Gemma, who was trying to hide behind Saph. "Where's the other twin?"

"Chris is with his dad, doing manly stuff."

"How's Candace?" Greg asked the question she had been dreading. "Is she still on the other side of the world?"

"Yes, she's living and teaching in the UK."

"I bet she's having a great time." There was wistfulness in his smile. "Do you hear from her often?"

"She usually texts or emails on a regular basis. But the other day she Skyped."

"Is she coming back anytime soon?" His eyes were alight with hope.

She would have to tell him the truth. "The reason she Skyped was because she had some big news to tell us. Greg, she's announced her engagement." Saph watched him closely for his reaction. "To an Irishman she met over there."

It was as if the light switched off inside him. He managed a smile, but it didn't reach his eyes.

"I hope she will be very happy with her fiancé." He muttered the words. "Give her my regards." But why should he care when he too was involved in a relationship?

"I see you've moved on as well—where's your girlfriend today?"

He gave her a puzzled look before he clicked. "Oh, do you mean Donna?" His attempt at a smile vanished completely. "We decided we weren't really suited. So we agreed to just be friends and she's gone back to her old church."

"I'm sorry to hear that, Greg." For two reasons: it meant he was available again, but now Candace wasn't. And she wanted to see him happy—with Candace.

After Greg had turned and sloped off, Saph continued to stare at him. Why did her daughter have to get engaged to a foreigner—a stranger—and in a country on the other side of the world? Couldn't she have stayed safely at home and married nice, kind, reliable Greg? He was the one for Candace—of that she was sure. And he would have made the perfect son-in-law.

Could she somehow stop her daughter from making what could be the biggest mistake of her entire life? Or was Candace about to learn a difficult lesson?

"Mum." Gemma was tugging on her hand, urging her to stop pondering and get going. The only thing doable was to pray. And hard.

"I haven't heard from Candace for three days now," Saph said, frowning as she once again checked her cell phone screen. "She used to make contact every other day, even if it was only a one-line text letting me know she was all right."

James looked up from his laptop. "I wouldn't worry about it. Apart from work, she's probably preoccupied with her new man. Plus, won't they be planning their tour around Europe?"

His words were mildly comforting. "True," Saph said. "And I

expect there'll be a lot for them to think about regarding the wedding and their future life together. Yes, that's what'll be keeping her busy and non-communicative. Hopefully she will contact us soon."

It seemed James was right. The following day there was a brief email from Candace, reassuring them she was happy. Apparently the new man, the tour, wedding plans and her job were all keeping her busy, as predicted. So she wouldn't be contacting them on a regular basis and they weren't to worry. But it wasn't enough to completely stop the anxious thoughts.

Chapter Twenty-Two

"Sorry Neil," Candace said. "I've already made plans for tonight."

"But we always spend Friday evenings together!" Neil's displeasure came through the phone loud and clear. "What on earth are you up to?" It was more of a staccato demand than a request.

"We haven't decided yet." It was the truth, although a meal at the local pub had been suggested.

"Who's 'we'?" There was sharp suspicion in his tone.

"Myself, Vicky and her friend, who's been staying with us. She wants to shout dinner as thanks for our hospitality."

"But I haven't seen you since Wednesday and that was only briefly. I've been looking forward to this date all week." Neil's whine was as sulky as a little boy's.

Immediately defensiveness sprang up. It wasn't her fault he had been anticipating it. True, a Friday night date had become the norm, but nothing definite had been arranged. Besides which, she had seen him nearly every day since they had officially become an item—surely he could live without her for one night?

Then guilt kicked in. Perhaps she should cancel or ask him to join them—but it would be purely out of obligation. And she had been hanging out for some girl time, where she could talk about shopping, fashion and such subjects that were unlikely to interest a male.

Anyway the other two might not appreciate his company. To be honest, neither would she. Not tonight.

"I'll see you tomorrow, Neil."

When no invitation was forthcoming, Neil abruptly said a curt good-bye and hung up.

The pub, one of the few Candace had set foot in, was typical 'olde English' with lots of dark wood, low ceilings and a fat fluffy ginger cat gracing the bar. Neil, who preferred fine dining, would not have approved of the casual atmosphere. Another good reason for not inviting him.

During the meal, even the usually serious Vicky smiled now and then at the light-hearted banter of her mate. They were such opposite personalities, how the two had ended up as friends was incomprehensible.

It was pleasant eating and chatting with the pair and for the first time since she had arrived in England, Candace unwound. Neil was always so serious and tense, something this evening was highlighting by contrast, and Candace hadn't noticed before. She couldn't joke around with Neil like this, not like she'd been able to with her mates back home … especially Greg. How comfortable and relaxed she had been in his presence … but it was Neil she was engaged to.

When Neil arrived on Saturday, dragging a dark cloud in with him, the figurative egg shells started crunching underfoot. How could she not have noticed the tension before? Or perhaps she had been in denial—subconsciously trying to ignore it. The alarm bells that had been faintly jangling were now positively clanging.

"Is something wrong?" she asked tentatively.

He kicked off. "Where did you go last night? What were you doing?"

"I told you I was going out with a couple of friends," she said, smiling in an attempt to pacify him. It didn't work; his face became more thunderous. "For a meal." *Not that it's any of your business.* His scowl stopped her from saying it out loud.

"Were there any men around?"

"We were at the local pub for dinner, so yes, there were men there." She kept her tone even and reined in her immediate defensiveness—the last thing she wanted was to aggravate him more. "But they were too busy playing darts and drinking beer to take any notice of me." The last bit wasn't strictly true—there had been some interested glances cast their way.

His eyes narrowed to slits. "How dare you go without me," he said through clenched teeth. "Don't you ever do that again."

His anger was frightening. She hadn't known him to be light-hearted, but this was the first time he had revealed a dark and possessive side.

"Neil, what's wrong? You know you're the man for me," she said in an attempt to placate him. He grasped her wrist and squeezed hard.

"And don't you forget it," he said with a hiss. Then he seemed to collect himself and relaxed his grip to become a hand hold. Although he smiled, it didn't show in his eyes. "Sorry, I can hardly bear to let you out of my sight," he whispered, and turning back into the gentleman she loved, tenderly took her in his arms. "You're just so precious to me." His words and touch were soothing. All her life, she had longed to be special to someone. And now she was.

But at what cost? She tried to squelch the wriggling doubt, to ignore the throbbing wrist reminder. Last night's pleasant out-ing had opened her eyes to the ever-present air of tension that surrounded him and enveloped her like a straitjacket. Without real-ising it, she had been constantly reining in her behaviour for fear of saying or doing the wrong thing in his presence and upsetting him. Was this what it was going to be like once they were married? Was it something she could live with? But she couldn't think about it while he was present.

At last he left and she could breathe again. Now she had time and space to untangle her scrambled thoughts. In all the excitement of the new romance and swift engagement, she'd barely had a moment or the inclination to think through the issues.

It might have been better to have never met Neil. She had ignored the internal Godly niggle which said Neil wasn't the man for her. Perhaps if she'd consulted God to start with, it would have saved a lot of heartache.

Dare she break up with Neil and call the whole thing off? There was no way he would go easily. But right now, she couldn't imagine being married to such a stress merchant.

Chapter Twenty-Three

Feeling as wooden as the church pew she and Neil were seated on, Candace barely dared to breathe. It had been a harrowing couple of months. Ever since that Friday night when Neil's dark and possessive side had begun to show, her happiness had been disrupted.

The revelation had goaded her into making a firm decision to break it off with Neil. But it had taken some time to pluck up the courage to take action. When she did, and before she'd had a chance to hand back the ring, he'd had a fit. He'd even threatened to kill himself, and she had been blackmailed back into the relationship.

But now the situation was simply unbearable; she couldn't go on like this. Neil's possessiveness lay like a dead weight upon her, crushing and suffocating. Stress had suppressed her appetite and she hadn't been eating properly. Her work was starting to suffer and she'd found herself trying to avoid him. There was one easy way out; she could jump on the next plane home. But no, that would be a cowardly thing to do, and admitting defeat.

Apart from the odd text, she had been avoiding contact with her parents for a couple of weeks now—in case they picked up on her anxiety and insist she return. Then again, they probably wouldn't have noticed anyway. They would be busy enough with the twins, without her problems as well.

The church service ended and they filed out for their customary cup of tea. While they stood and chatted, Candace noticed once again if she so much as glanced at another man, Neil would scowl.

"Dinner tomorrow night at my place," he said on the way home. It was a command, not an invitation. This could be the perfect opportunity to break the engagement off—she had to, or it would destroy her. Surely he was only bluffing about suicide. Still, she dreaded how he was going to react. But she would have to force herself to do it. Tomorrow night.

The table was beautifully laid out and meticulously neat, which was typical of Neil. Two slender candles with flames standing tall in the near stillness, provided the only brightness in the room. The mouth-watering smell of roast chicken filled the air.

"How lovely," Candace said as she eyed the table with a sinking heart. "You shouldn't have gone to so much trouble." Especially since she didn't plan to stay. This was really it; tonight she would return the ring and cut all ties with him, no matter what he threatened.

Lord, give me the strength to do this.

"Take a seat, please." Neil sounded menacing. He pulled a chair out for her and she obediently sat down. He poured her a small glass of wine in his precise fashion, twisting the bottle so as not to spill a drop on the pristine tablecloth.

"Neil, we really need to—"

"I'll be back in a moment. I just have to do something." She heard his footsteps along the hallway, followed by a strange metallic noise. It took a moment to figure out it was the sound of a key being turned in the lock and then removed. In spite of the warmth, it was as though ice shivered down her spine. She glanced around the room. Neil took his security seriously and although the curtains were drawn so she couldn't be sure, it was highly probable all the windows were locked. Was it to keep the criminals out? Or to keep her in? Best to try and appear calm.

She didn't get a chance to refuse the dinner as Neil had dished up two plates of roast chicken on his way back through the kitchen. Then he sat down and picked at his own meal, watching her, hawk-like, as she ate.

"Drink up." Another command. She obeyed but slowly, and in between mouthfuls of the delicious food. The wine seemed to go straight to her head and the room started to spin a little.

"You should have been a chef," she said, trying to sweet talk him. She gave him a placating smile, but there was no response.

"You'll be wanting dessert," he said, once again in a no-nonsense voice. She didn't. But since this was to be their last meal together, she had better humour him. And then she would have the serious chat.

There was something strong tasting in the chocolate sauce. It must be liqueur—and a powerful one at that, for everything was whirling past now. She put her spoon down but missed the table and it dropped off the edge—it seemed to fall a long, long way down.

Of late, Candace's texts had been sporadic and short at best. Last week they had dried up completely. So with no reply to her messages, Saph had emailed their important news. The weekend when Candace might have had time to respond, had come and gone. Still there was no word. Although Candace had warned her she didn't check her emails on a regular basis, the lack of a reply was surprising. Ignoring her daughter's previous advice, Saph's worry shifted into top gear. After she had tried and failed to get hold of her by Skype, she resorted to the expensive option of ringing Candace's mobile.

Lord, let her be all right. Eventually Candace's cheerful voice answered. "Please leave a message …"

"Oh Neil, I feel so sleepy." Candace dreamily pushed her plate away and made a vain attempt to retrieve the fallen cutlery. A strange warbling sound was coming from her handbag. Her phone. She should answer it … but now Neil had her bag. She tried to reach for it but her arm weighed a ton. Legs of solid heavy rubber wouldn't let her stand up and her eyes refused to stay open. "I need my …" Her mouth wouldn't work properly … there was something she was going to tell him … but what was it? Oh well, it couldn't have been important …

Chapter Twenty-Four

Although Candace sat up as slowly as possible, still the room seemed to whirl, making it necessary to sit motionless on the bed for a minute. A quick visual search for shoes and handbag proved fruitless. Bending to peer under the furniture produced nothing either; it simply made her dizzier. She had to sit back down before she toppled over. It seemed all she had were the crumpled clothes she was wearing. What had Neil done with her stuff? Or with *her*, for that matter? No, it was clear he hadn't touched her in the wrong way. Anyway he'd promised not to—they were to remain pure until their wedding night. What day was it? There were only hazy memories of the last few days. Or was it weeks?

Once the dizziness subsided a little, she pulled the engagement ring off her finger and laid it on the bedside table, the whole time listening for any signs of life in the house. All was quiet. Still woozy, she tiptoed out of the room. If only she could find her cell phone, she could ring for help. Perhaps it was in Neil's bedroom. She tried the door handle but unsurprisingly it was locked.

After a quick freshen up in the bathroom she made her way downstairs, clinging to the banister to stop from tumbling. She crept along the hallway, trying to be quiet in case Neil was lying in wait for her. But he didn't appear. He must have gone to work. A few sips of water in the kitchen helped to clear the fuzziness a little.

With the small amount of energy she had, she searched the ground floor for her phone, but there was no sign of any of her belongings. The study containing the computer and landline was locked, which ruled out the possibility of contacting help that way. To try and force her way in would take strength—which she didn't have.

It was tempting to crawl upstairs to bed, curl up in a despairing little ball and abandon hope. But she was tougher than that. And she refused to be defeated by the man.

There was nothing for it but to escape. With her stomach in knots and a fervent prayer in her heart, Candace went throughout the lower floor, trying the doors and impenetrable latticed windows. All locked. But what did she expect?

She was trapped. Once again she fought against energy-sapping despair. She needed some nourishment and a game plan. Back in the kitchen, some Hobnobs revived her somewhat and chased some more of the woolliness away.

There was still one window Candace hadn't checked. Previously dismissing it as being impossibly small to fit through, she was desperate enough to try now. Even if she couldn't get out, perhaps she could summon help. She padded into the downstairs bathroom. There was no sign of a lock on the window—clearly Neil hadn't considered it big enough to fit through. After twisting the latch, she held her breath and pushed. It opened to let in a gentle breeze. For a moment she stood, simply enjoying the fresh sweetness on her face. But there was no knowing when Neil would return, so with the small triumph energising her, she used the bath edge as a step and managed to squeeze through the narrow opening. Her landing on the grass below was far from dignified or graceful, but at least she was free.

After taking a few seconds to get her bearings, she stretched up on tiptoe to push the window closed—it wouldn't do to alert Neil prematurely to her escape. Then she stood hesitating, having not thought this far ahead. She glanced at her wrist but it was bare—he had removed her watch as well. Judging by the position of the sun, it must be about midday and time for Neil's lunch break. There was a good chance he could return any minute now to check up on her; she would have to form a plan, and fast. The shops were virtually next door; perhaps they would let her make a phone call there—if she could make it that far without getting caught.

The sound of crunching on the front path indicated someone was coming. With panic goading her into action, she scampered behind a bush to watch Neil approach the house. Once the front door had closed behind him she hurdled the gate, fear giving her wings. Ignoring the pain of the gravel digging into her bare feet, she sprinted along the street. It would only be a matter of time before he discovered she was gone.

Please be home. "Vicky!" Candace shouted. "Thank God you answered." The shop proprietor gave her a startled look, so she dropped her voice a notch. "Call a cab and come and get me please? I'm in desperate trouble. I managed to escape from Neil but I'm terrified he'll find me."

"What? Calm down, I can't understand you when you garble."

Frustrated and close to tears, Candace repeated herself, more clearly this time.

"Where have you been?" Vicky asked.

In a few staccato sentences, Candace explained the situation. "What day is it?" she asked.

"Wednesday."

"Seriously? I've been gone for almost two days?"

"Yes," Vicky said. "I was getting worried."

"So are you going to come and get me?"

"Can't you just catch a taxi?"

"I'm penniless. It looks as though Neil has taken my handbag which had my bank card in it, and I don't have any cash." Candace made an on-the-spot decision. "Can you bring all my stuff with you please? Most importantly, my passport and plane ticket. Oh, and my credit card—just as well I left it at home. I'll try and get a flight back to New Zealand as soon as I can. Once I have my card, I can reimburse you for the cab fare. And I'll give you some rent money too."

"It could take me a while to pack everything up."

"Just shove as much as you can into my suitcases. He even took my shoes so if you can leave a pair out of the packing, I'd be grateful."

"I'll do my best."

"God bless you, Vicky." It was heartfelt. "I'll explain all when I see you." She gave her flatmate a location and time for them to meet, and hung up.

After a glance towards the door to check for Neil, she turned to the man behind the counter. "Thank you so much for letting me use the phone. Do you mind if I hang out here for a while? I'm trying to avoid … someone." He nodded gravely and seemingly satisfied with her scant explanation, asked no questions.

While she waited, she moped in amongst the shelves of cans and exotic fare. She was torn; the only way to escape from Neil was to leave the country, but it was like admitting defeat and going home with her tail between her legs. And there was still so much of Europe and Britain she hadn't seen—Neil never had taken her on the tour they had planned—perhaps it had just been another false promise. But returning to New Zealand surely had to be the safest option.

When Candace spotted a grim-looking Neil peering through the shop window, she ducked behind a display stand, praying he hadn't seen her in the dim interior.

"It's him! The man I'm trying to avoid!"

The proprietor beckoned her behind the counter.

"Go through that doorway there," he whispered. She scurried

through the clattering beaded curtain and headed up a dark narrow staircase. When she went through the open door at the top, it was like entering a different country. In contrast to the musty gloominess below, the smell of spice and cooking filled the air and everywhere there was colour and movement. Once she had adjusted to the brightness, she found four pairs of dark eyes staring at her in surprise.

"Ah, hi," she said. "Sorry about the unexpected visit, your—er—the man in the shop said I could come in here because I'm trying to avoid somebody." How much did they understand? To her embarrassment, her stomach growled at the savoury aroma. Clearly the Hobnobs hadn't been enough.

The older lady, apparently the matriarch of the family, frowned and said something in her native language. Was she angry? Did she want her to leave? Candace hovered near the doorway, uncertain as to what to do. Should she risk going back down the stairs and encountering Neil? She was about to turn round when a teenage girl smiled at her, straight white teeth glowing against dark skin.

"My grandmother wants to know if you would like a cup of tea?" Her accent was British. "By the sounds of it, you need something to eat too."

Candace turned down the offer of a hot drink but accepted a small aromatic dish of something she didn't recognise; it was quite delicious. She was nibbling on a biscuit when the proprietor called up.

"It's safe, you can come back down now."

"Are you going to be all right?" the girl asked. "Is there anything we can do to help?"

"I'm going to be fine," Candace said, "thanks to you. God bless you all." Downstairs she cautiously emerged through the clacking plastic beads.

"I told him you'd come into the shop earlier," the proprietor said, "but I didn't see where you'd gone." He grinned. "Which is almost true, as I wasn't watching when you went up to the flat. I didn't tell him about the phone call."

After thanking him profusely, she paused at the shop entrance to check the coast was truly clear. Then she slipped out to mingle with the stream of pedestrians and make her way to the meeting point.

After wrenching open the taxi door, Candace threw herself in to land in a panting heap beside Vicky. It had been a mad dash from the small park where she had spent the last hour hiding, tensely eyeing up every passerby in case it was Neil. She risked a glance through the rear window to check for him, before hunkering down.

"Thanks heaps for managing to bring my gear," she said once she had regained her breath and they were on their way to Heathrow Airport.

"So what happened?" Vicky asked.

"I went to Neil's place for dinner." Candace frowned as she tried to recall. "Initially I thought it was the wine, or perhaps liqueur in the dessert which made me so sleepy, but now I'm sure Neil drugged me."

"How?" Vicky looked horrified.

"He must have put something in the food. When I woke up the first time, I found myself in the spare bed. I have a vague memory of trying to get out of the room—but he wouldn't let me and I was too woozy and weak to put up much of a fight. He's quite strong for his size and I was no match for him, especially since I was still not with it. So I went back to bed. Who knows?" She shrugged. "Perhaps that was all a dream. I kept drifting off to sleep again and only woke up properly this morning. I still don't feel quite right."

"Did he …" Vicky paused as though searching for the right words. "… do anything to you—if you know what I mean?"

"No, I'm quite sure of that. He's too much of a gentleman."

"You still think that even though he held you against your will in his house?" Vicky sounded incredulous.

"No, of course not. What I mean is when he proposed he told me he wanted us to stay pure and wait until we were married. I'm certain I was fully clothed the whole time. He must have only come into the bedroom to bring me food. I found trays on the bedside table but I don't remember eating much."

"He might have put something in that as well." With a look of concern, Vicky shook her head. "So what was his motive then?"

"I've been wondering that myself," Candace said. "Perhaps he wanted to own me."

"Don't you think you should call the police?"

"I just want to go home." It sounded pitiful but she didn't care. After clearing the sob from her throat, she continued. "Anyway he could simply deny any accusations and I doubt I could prove anything."

"So perhaps the rumour going around church is true after all," Vicky murmured.

"What rumour?"

"That Neil's a charmer who uses emotional blackmail on vulnerable women and that he *had* to leave Ireland. It was just a whisper and I dismissed it as gossip—but clearly I shouldn't have." Vicky shook her head. "I always had reservations about that man."

"Pity you didn't share them with me."

"Would you have listened?"

"Probably not." Candace sighed. "He seemed so wonderful at first, too good to be true. Which is exactly what he turned out to be."

"I almost forgot," Vicky said. "Your mother phoned for you yesterday. She sounded worried. I tried to allay her fears but I'm not sure she believed me. She wanted you to contact her as soon as you can. Apparently she has news."

"Oh dear, I can't ring her as I don't have my phone." It was a hint for Vicky to offer the use of her mobile, but she didn't pick up on it. "Perhaps I could try from the airport."

"Take this to cover my expenses." Candace removed a wad of cash from the ATM and handed it to her flatmate.

Vicky's eyes widened. "Surely that's way too much."

"I have kind of left you in the lurch, with rent and everything." Candace scribbled on a spare luggage label. "This is my address in Auckland if there's anything else to be sent on. Let me know if you need any more money. And if the job agency calls, can you tell them the situation?" Although Vicky nodded, she didn't look too pleased. "I promise I'll contact them once I get back to New Zealand," Candace said, in an attempt to smooth away the sour expression. "Thanks for everything, but don't feel you have to stay."

Vicky didn't need telling twice. After awkwardly receiving a hug, she took off. Candace hunkered down on a chair, fidgeting, on constant alert in case Neil showed up. It wouldn't take him long to figure out where she had gone. And since she was on standby, she might be stuck in the airport for days. How much more of this stress and constant looking over her shoulder could she take? All she could do was pray for a short wait and that she would be out of the country before Neil managed to track her down.

In answer to her prayer, her wait turned out to be a matter of mere hours. She was approaching the security gates when she heard her name yelled out and spun round. Neil was sprinting towards her. She started running, her carryall banging against her legs.

"That man is after me," she shouted at a nearby security guard. She nearly tripped trying to watch over her shoulder as he moved to stand in front of her pursuer. Neil tried to push past him, but the man was solid and unresisting.

"You're letting the woman I love get away," Neil shouted. "We're getting married this weekend." She nearly stopped in shock. Had that been his plan all along? The man truly was insane if he thought he could force her into marriage.

"By the way in which she's scarpering, it doesn't look as though you're the man *she* loves," the guard said, clearly unmoved. It was probably just as well she couldn't hear Neil's reply when she dashed into security.

Please hurry, please please hurry. Then she was through. She strolled along the aisle catching her breath, secure in the knowledge Neil couldn't get her now.

On board the plane, with the excitement over, she wilted into her seat. In all the chaos, she had forgotten to ring her mother. Oh well, she would see her soon enough.

Chapter Twenty-Five

Candace woke up with a jolt—the taxi had stopped. For a moment she sat peering through the windscreen at the building ahead, trying to figure out where she was or even which country she was in. It wasn't all just a dream, surely?

"Excuse me miss?" The announced cab fare at last registered through the sleep-fuzz, and she paid the driver.

"What's the time?" she asked. Judging by how dark it was, it must be late.

The cabbie checked the dashboard before opening his door. "Eight o'clock."

"Is that all? It feels much later. That's good—it means they won't have gone to bed yet."

Home. With a sudden burst of eagerness reviving her, she sprang from the car. While she waited impatiently for the driver to remove her luggage from the boot, she gazed at the unit, relishing the sight.

"Here you go, love." The cabby deposited her suitcases on the driveway. She snatched up the handles before picking her way between the so-familiar potholes. Loose stones rattled as the car backed out, her walking shadow elongated momentarily in the headlights. Then there was only the welcoming glow escaping from around the window blinds to see by.

When she reached the step she faltered. What sort of reception would she get? There would be no bed for her apart from the couch. But right now, when she could barely think an hour ahead, let alone plan for tomorrow, she didn't care. *Home.* It was all she could think about. She thumped on the door. It opened a crack.

"Surprise …" The word died on her lips. A stranger peeked cautiously through the gap, a puzzled frown on her face.

"Who are you?" Candace asked in shock. She collected herself. "Sorry, I don't mean to be rude, but where are Mum and Dad?"

"Who are you?" the woman echoed. "Who are Mum and Dad?"

Perhaps this was just a dream after all. More like a nightmare. "Mr and Mrs Holden. Do they still live here?"

The woman appeared to think for a moment. "Oh, you mean the previous tenants? No, they moved out just two weeks ago."

"What?" Exhaustion surged, absorbing her new found energy, and tears welled up. It was hard to think straight. Now what was she going to do? She was stuck out here, the taxi had gone, and even if she'd had a phone she knew of no numbers to ring. So much for being home.

"You must be the prodigal daughter," the stranger said. "Your parents told me they were having trouble finding you. They said there was a slim chance you might turn up here."

"Did they give you their new address?"

"I'm sure they did." The woman tapped her chin. "But wherever did I put it? I'm still not very organised yet." Compassion softened her expression. "You'd better come in while I hunt for it, you look as though you're about to collapse." She opened the door wide and held out her hand. "I'm Pam, by the way."

Candace barely had the energy to shake the woman's hand. Dragging her jet-lagged body into the house, she meekly followed Pam through the familiar kitchen and into the lounge. It was strange and somewhat disconcerting seeing her childhood home with completely different furniture and someone else's stamp on it.

"Have a seat and I'll make you a nice hot cuppa. Tea or coffee?"

"Herbal tea if you have it, please." Candace could hardly get the words out. She leaned back against the couch and closed her eyes.

It seemed only seconds later Pam was handing her a steaming mug.

"I've added some honey to give you a bit of energy. You look as though you need it. I'll try and find that address now." She began to rummage around in some papers on a desk sited where the small dining room table had once stood.

After a few sips of hot sweet liquid Candace revived a little, and the fuzziness cleared enough for the pain of rejection to register. Once again she had been left out of the family: abandoned by them this time.

"But they couldn't have sold this place to you." In her agitation she blurted it out. "It's not theirs to sell. Legally speaking it's mine!"

"Don't worry," Pam said, turning to face her. "They made that quite clear. They're just renting it to me." Fear crossed the woman's face. "You're not going to evict me are you?"

Candace wilted again and compassion kicked in. "No, you're quite safe."

Pam visibly relaxed. "That's why they were trying to find you—to ask for your permission to rent it out."

Was that the only reason her parents wanted to get hold of her—to sort out the flat? It wasn't because they cared. But she kept her rejection to herself. It wasn't Pam's fault and she wasn't about to take it out on her.

Pam continued. "It's not a proper official arrangement and they did warn me it might be short term, depending on how you felt about the situation. But I was desperate for accommodation and this place was a Godsend." She pointed towards some boxes in the corner of the lounge. "I haven't unpacked everything yet, just in case."

"Feel free to make yourself at home," Candace said, dispirited.

Pam gave her a relieved smile. "I think the address is in the kitchen."

While she was out of the room, Candace slumped further. Would her family even want to see her? But she had nowhere else to go.

"Here it is." Pam handed her a slip of paper. "They've left a phone number too. Do you want to ring them?"

"It's a bit late for that. I might wake the kids. Besides I want to surprise them." And give them a piece of her mind too—if she had the energy.

Candace glanced at the address, and had to check again before it registered. Once it did, adrenalin pumped and suddenly she was wide awake. She gulped down the tea, ignoring the heat. "Can I use your phone to call a taxi please?"

It wasn't ten o'clock yet, but Gramps's former villa was in darkness—they must have gone to bed already. Adrenalin rush over, Candace climbed the steps, not only weariness but trepidation making her drag her feet; she might not be particularly welcome, especially at this time of night. Using the last dregs of her energy, she pounded on the door before sinking down on her suitcase to wait. Were they ever going to answer? With nowhere else to go, she might have to sleep out here on the verandah. On the verge of exhausted tears, she at last heard footsteps and a light came on in the hallway. Then sudden brilliance flooded the porch, making her blink.

"Gramps?" she whispered. But of course this was no longer his house. It was her father's stern face that appeared when the door cracked open. He was being understandably cautious at this late hour.

"Who is it?" Mum asked in the background.

Dad's frown was replaced with astonishment. "You're not going to believe it!"

"Hi Mum and Dad, sorry to drag you out of bed."

"Candace!" Her mother tried to yank the door open before fumbling with the chain in her haste. Once she'd managed to disentangle it, she flew out and wrapped her arms around Candace.

"Are you safe and well?" Without waiting for an answer, her mother rushed on. "No need to apologise for getting us up. I'm so relieved to see you, we were terribly worried, we hadn't heard from you in weeks."

"Me too," Candace said, her words muffled by her mother's hug. "Relieved to see you, I mean."

At last Mum held her away from her and frowned.

"You look dreadful."

"Thanks, Mum."

"Sorry, I mean you look so pale and thin. You've lost weight— and you didn't have much to start with! Are you ill?"

"I'm just jetlagged and exhausted." Not to mention stressed, heart-broken and recovering from being drugged—but now was not the right time to tell her parents that.

Barely capable of standing, she had to let her mother help her into the house while Dad dealt with her luggage. Once in the dining room, Candace drooped onto a chair at the table and propped her head on her hand. Mum took a seat opposite, worry all over her face.

"I thought I'd lost you all over again," she said as Dad reappeared and joined them. "I was worried and not just for your safety. Since you didn't respond to my texts or email, I wasn't sure how to let you know we'd moved."

"We weren't too sure about what to do with the unit either," Dad said.

"Yes, Vicky told me you had some news. I'm sorry Mum and Dad, for losing touch with you. It's a long story that I don't have the energy to tell you right now. All I'll say is the wedding's off.

Now I just want to sleep. Do you have room for an extra?" she asked. "The couch will be fine."

"Okay—" Dad said.

Mum sent him a withering look. "There's plenty of space for you here. You can have Chris's bed."

Dad didn't look too happy. "I'll just move Chris back into Gemma's room then." It felt like a dig but Candace was too weary to care. She'd worry about it tomorrow, after she had caught up on some sleep. He arose and stalked off down the hallway. Shortly after, a childish voice made a sleepy complaint, but it didn't last long.

Mum also stood up. "I'll make the bed as fast as I can and we can talk in the morning."

Once again it seemed Candace was an inconvenience and in the way—but right now she just wanted to lie down and sleep for a very long time.

When Candace opened her eyes next, it was daylight and she was in an unfamiliar room. Had the plane trip home all just been a dream and she was still Neil's prisoner in England? She sat up in panic. No, her toy tiger and favourite childhood teddy bear smiled at her from on top of her old bookcase—she really was back in Auckland. It had been years since she'd stayed at Gramps's house and her mother's old room had apparently been redecorated in the meantime.

"Good morning Edward Bear and Tigger," she said. "Am I glad to see you!" She leaned back against the pillows and examined her surroundings, drawing comfort from all the familiar objects.

Then guilt kicked in. The soft toys were no longer hers—she had gifted them to the twins when they were two, and there was a fire engine pattern on the duvet. She was depriving her baby brother of his room. Once again she was in the way: the spare one of the family, the odd one out.

Energy gone, she flopped back onto the bed. Like heavy blankets, her failures piled on top of her. Her relationship had gone bang, she'd had to curtail her great OE, and she had been forced to return to her own country—to what? No job, little money and no real home. For a while she wallowed in luxurious self-pity and tortured herself with what might have been.

But as tempting as it was to stay put for the rest of her life, she must get up. She needed to set about finding a job in order to earn some money. Then she could move into a place she could call her own, and get out from under her family's feet.

Candace stumbled out into the dining room to find everyone seated at the table, eating a meal.

"Good morning, or rather good afternoon, sleepy head." Dad grinned at her.

"And who are these two young people?" She forced a smile and kissed each twin on the forehead. They giggled and squirmed and then regarded her with wide eyes. It was sad to think they were probably wondering who she was.

"Do you want some lunch?" Mum asked.

"Lunch? I thought it was breakfast time."

"You slept right through it," Dad said. "I wasn't joking when I said 'good afternoon'."

Mum made Candace a cup of tea and some toast which was all she felt capable of managing. After the twins had run off to play, Mum sat down at the table and gazed at her expectantly.

"We'd really like to hear the full story—but only if you're ready to tell us."

"Short version: Neil, the supposedly wonderful man I was planning to marry, turned out not to be so wonderful. A complete loss, in fact."

"I'm sorry to hear that," Mum said.

"He started getting all possessive which at first I found flattering;

that he couldn't bear to be without me. But when he kept wanting to know where I was and what I was up to, it became stifling, and then downright scary. I didn't want to tell you all this because I knew you would worry. Which is why I've hardly contacted you over the last few months."

"Is that why we didn't hear much from you," Mum said, frowning. "We didn't think you could be so busy that you couldn't send a short email, or at the very least a detailed text. When you didn't respond to my attempts to contact you, I got quite anxious."

As Candace filled in the details of her experience and her escape, Mum's horrified expression deepened and Dad's indignation increased.

"I simply couldn't warm to that man," Mum said, shaking her head.

"Why, that little …" Dad narrowed his eyes. "If I ever get my hands on him …"

Candace could have kissed him for being her champion.

"I searched for my handbag which had my mobile in it, but couldn't find it anywhere. I presume Neil confiscated it."

"So that's why you didn't answer when I rang."

"I couldn't phone for help either. Once I'd escaped, there was no opportunity to contact you as I went straight to Heathrow. I was going to ring you from there, but I was so stressed out I forgot. Blessedly I didn't have to wait too long for a standby flight. Neil turned up at the airport but by then I was about to go through security and he couldn't touch me after that."

"Thank the Lord for that." Mum breathed again.

"When I arrived back in Auckland, can you imagine my horror when I turned up at the unit only to find you didn't live there anymore?"

Mum grimaced. "I'm so sorry. We did try to let you know. Also we wanted to get your permission to rent out the unit."

"So I heard."

"Poor old Pam. We met her at church. She was stuck for a place to stay and her predicament was a catalyst for us to move. She can't afford to pay much, but what she can is rightfully yours. If you want her to vacate so you can move in, you have every right to do so."

Was this Mum's subtle hint Candace was in the way? If the unit had been vacant she would have wasted no time shifting back in.

"I couldn't be so mean," Candace said, trying to mask feelings of rejection. "It's just as well you left your forwarding address with her, or I don't know what I would have done—all my phone numbers were in my absent mobile. As a last resort I could have gone around to Tiff's mother's place—if she still lives there." Although it might have meant an encounter with Doug. Candace repressed a shudder. "Anyway Pam kindly made me a cup of tea and gave me your address. When I realised it was Gramps's old house, I was rapt. So how come you ended up here?"

"You know how Gramps had trouble selling this house," Mum said, "and rented it out? We moaned to him we were growing out of the unit, so when he had to evict his last troublesome tenants, he thought of us. We pay half the purchase price and the rest is my inheritance. It works well. I doubt we could afford to buy a house otherwise—certainly not one as nice as this."

"So is this just a visit? Or are you here to stay?" Dad asked.

"I'm not going back there again, at least not in a hurry." Candace grimaced. "But with all the craziness, I've had little chance to think about the future. Mind if I stick around here for a while? At least until I can find my feet." Mum smiled but Dad didn't react. "You can keep the rent from the flat as my board."

"But then you won't have an income," Mum said.

"I'll try to find a job as soon as I can and then I'll be out of your hair."

Was that a look of relief on Mum's face? And Dad's expression echoed it. Candace really needed to find a space of her own, somewhere to call home. And soon.

Chapter Twenty-Six

"Have you seen Greg lately?" Candace had been back a week before she was ready to ask about him—Mum had made no mention of the man since Neil had come onto the scene.

"Not for quite a while." Mum looked thoughtful. "We used to see him at church, but usually in the distance. Then he went off to become a youth pastor somewhere else and disappeared from our radar altogether."

"I didn't know he'd left." Hopefully Mum wouldn't notice the mild alarm in her voice. Greg's number had been in her vanished phone—and nowhere else. "Do you know if he still lives in the same place?"

"Sorry Candace, I wouldn't have a clue."

Panic bubbled—what say she'd lost touch with him completely?

"The last time I spoke to him was to tell him about your … er …" Her mother grimaced.

"My engagement. It's all right Mum, you can say the word; it doesn't particularly bother me anymore." It was true—now she was safe on the other side of the world that part of her life seemed like a half-forgotten nightmare.

"Greg certainly looked devastated when I told him your news. Apparently his own relationship didn't last long." Mum unwittingly answered the question Candace lacked the courage to ask.

"Hmm, interesting." She hid a smile.

"But that was months ago. Who knows? He might have found someone else in the meantime."

Candace's bubble of hope deflated. She managed not to react outwardly. "Even if he has …" she said, silently praying he hadn't but attempting to sound noble, "I'd still like to let him know I'm back and to have a catch up. But without my phone, my only option is to go round to his last known address. Hopefully he still lives there." Of course there was another agenda for visiting; to check if he was single and to subtly tell him she was—dare she say it—available.

"Thanks for letting me use your car, Mum," Candace said as she was handed the keys. "I only hope I can remember how to get to Greg's, it's been so long."

After one minor wrong turn, she pulled up across the road from the old villa: not quite as grand as her family's, but nonetheless stylish. It looked just the same as she remembered. Was this still Greg's home? What would it be like to live here? Now that was really jumping the gun.

Years earlier she had been astonished to find out Greg had his own place; and not a tiny flat either, but a proper three bedroom house.

"How can you afford property in Auckland?" She'd blurted it out before realising how rude it sounded.

He had reddened. "My parents helped me with the deposit," he muttered, "and I've had flatmates over the years who've contributed towards the mortgage." When she had discovered who his folks were, it all made sense.

While she waited for the stream of cars to clear, she watched a short stocky man exit the house—it was definitely Greg. Thank God, he hadn't shifted. Taking advantage of an opportune break in the traffic, she clambered out, and prepared to call a greeting. But the words died as she stared in disbelief. A woman had followed Greg out of the house. A curvaceous lady. Angie.

When Greg turned and smiled at his companion, she reflected it back with sunny warmth. Hopes began to fray. They looked so happy together—as though they were a couple. Something sparkled on Angie's left hand—a ring. Could they be engaged? Or maybe even married? From this distance it wasn't possible to see a wedding band. Oh no … they must be husband and wife … when the woman turned side on, there was a distinct bump. Angie was pregnant.

With dreams unravelling fast and before the pair could spot her, Candace slunk back into the car. In spite of the brave claims to her mother, she couldn't face a married Greg after all. He was lost to her for good. And to Angie, of all people.

But Candace had heard him vow he would never get together with that woman. So what had made him change his mind? Had Angie finally worn him down with her hounding? And perhaps news of Candace's engagement had been the last straw for Greg.

She could have kicked herself. Why hadn't she snatched him up when she had the chance all those years ago? Motives for visiting Greg surfaced and gelled—she *did* want him for herself. The tyres squealed as she pulled away.

When Saph arrived home from a walk with the twins, Candace's door was shut. She ushered the children into their room and although she instructed them to play quietly, the noise levels soon rose.

"Can't they just shut up?"

Candace had emerged, obviously in a foul mood. Although she tried to hide it, her eyes were red and her face flushed.

"Are you all right?" Saph asked. "You don't look very happy."

"I went to see Greg."

"So I take it he still lives in the same place then. Was he there?"

"Oh, he was home all right."

"How is he?" Saph asked. "Was he pleased to see you?"

"I don't know. I didn't talk to him." There was a dramatic pause. "Or his wife."

"Really?" Saph gaped at her. "He's married? That's astounding. I thought he only had eyes for you."

"So did I," Candace said, looking miserable. "But apparently not."

"I did warn you he could have moved on."

"Not helpful."

"And he must have thought you were married by now." Saph frowned. "It's strange I've heard nothing about his wedding on the church grapevine. Are you sure?"

"I saw him and …" —it seemed Candace could barely bring herself to say the name— "Angie together." She sneered. "And the ring on her finger."

"Angie? Wasn't she the one who was being bullied at school and was planning to end it all? If I remember correctly, Greg played the hero and talked her out of it."

"Yes, she owes him big time. But she was keen on him even before then, way back in youth group days. So much for his promise he wasn't interested in her. It gets worse." Candace sighed. "She's pregnant."

Saph mouthed a silent 'oh'. "I wonder why he didn't mention it during our last conversation." She counted on her fingers. "Which must have been about six months ago. You don't think he had to marry the woman because there was a baby on the way and he was too ashamed to tell me? No, that doesn't sound like Greg. Perhaps he married her on the rebound and she fell pregnant on their honeymoon."

"I'd rather not talk about it. Or think about it." With that Candace turned on her heel and stalked back to her room, slamming the door behind her.

With some trepidation Candace knocked and stood back to wait. It wasn't long before the front door opened. Thankfully it was Tiff's mother and not Doug who stared blankly at her.

"Hi, is Tiff around?"

"Oh, Candace isn't it?" Margaret smiled with recognition. "I haven't seen you in ages. You're in luck; I'm expecting Tiff and Johnny any minute now." She beckoned her in.

"I just returned from overseas last week and thought it was about time I paid her a visit." *And Tiff might know about Greg.* Candace followed Margaret into the kitchen. "When I tried her last known address, a stranger answered the door and wouldn't tell me where the family had gone. So I thought I would pop in on the off chance Tiff was here. I'm glad you haven't moved or I'd never be able to track her down. I've … er … lost my phone." Candace wasn't about to explain how. "Where's Doug these days?" It was a tentative question. The thought of encountering him had made her think twice about visiting Tiff's family home, and she could very well be opening up a painful can of worms for his mother. But Margaret smiled.

"Don't worry, you're quite safe. A criminal conviction turned out to be a good thing for my dear son—made him think about the consequences of his actions. He ended up turning his life around and moved to another part of the country where nobody knows his reputation. Now he's earning an honest wage and he's met a lovely woman whom he plans to marry next year."

"I'm happy for him," Candace said. The words came out with sincerity; she had truly forgiven him.

"Here are Tiff and Johnny now," Margaret said as a car came

up the driveway. Soon, Johnny ran into the kitchen, followed by a heavily pregnant Tiff. The boy pulled up when he saw Candace, and bravely hid behind his mum.

"Tiff! Wow, there's a lot of you to hug," Candace said as she embraced her friend. "Your mother never said anything about a baby on the way. When are you due?"

"Next week. But I'm more than ready to have her today. Now I know how a hippo feels." She gave a rueful smile. "I want to become a gazelle again."

"So you obviously know it's a girl."

"Yes." Tiff's smile wobbled, which was curious; but Candace didn't ask the reason. Instead she grinned and waved at the lad who was still acting shy.

"Young Johnny has grown."

"It must be a while since you last saw him. He'll be off to school next year."

During a good catch up over coffee, Candace explained her ordeal in the UK. Tiff looked suitably horrified before sadly telling of her miscarriage. That explained the wobbly smile.

"It was before the twelve-week mark, but still a big loss." Tiff patted her huge belly. "So we said a lot of prayers for this one."

"Obviously they've been answered. I'll have to dig out the knitting needles and get busy." Candace inhaled deeply, plucking up the courage to ask a burning question. "Have you seen Greg lately?" She held her breath while Tiff looked thoughtful.

"Not for ages. At one time he was coming to ours for dinner at least once a week. But when he found himself a girlfriend, he stopped turning up and we haven't seen him since."

With those words, the last ounce of hope vaporised. Tiff gave her a direct look before grimacing apologetically. "Oops, sorry. Didn't you know?"

"Sort of." It was a non-committal answer. Getting to her feet,

Candace plastered on a bright smile. "It's been lovely catching up with you, but I must go. Let me know when your baby arrives and I'll come and visit." She made a hasty exit before the tears began to flow.

Although she kept her head down, Mum must have spotted her tear-stained face.

"Candace, are you all right?"

She walked determinedly past her mother to her room, but before she could close the door, Mum followed her in. Candace sank down on the bed.

"I can see something's wrong." With a worried look, Mum also took a seat. Although she could feel her mother's gaze upon her, Candace couldn't meet it.

"Do you want to talk about it?"

"I've just been to see Tiff. She pretty much confirmed what I thought about … you know who." She couldn't bring herself to say Greg's name. Mum kept silent, but grimaced in sympathy.

"But it's not just him I'm upset about." With elbows on knees, Candace put her head in her hands. "Everything's going wrong. I can't find a job so I can't afford a flat … and I'm just getting in the way here."

"You're not in the way!" her mother said, aghast. "Whatever gave you that idea?"

"Ever since the twins arrived, I've felt as though I'm not part of this family anymore." She was letting it all out now. "As though I'm just a spare part, taking up space. I hate being a burden to you and Dad. The sooner I find a teaching position and move on, the better."

"Oh Candace, I'm so sorry," Mum said, dismay evident. "I've never thought of you as being surplus to requirements."

"I felt like an outsider." Candace couldn't hide her bitterness.

"You were so engrossed in the children—your perfect little family. There was no room for me."

"I had to apologise to your dad," Mum said, with head bowed, "for being obsessed with them. Now I apologise to you for the same reason, and for any time you thought you were being left out. You were mistaken, by the way—you're a real and vital part of this family." She reached across and grasped Candace's hand. "It hurt so much letting you go the first time you left home, for uni. It hurt even more when I had to farewell you at the airport."

"But it felt as though you were pushing me away, as though you couldn't wait to get rid of me." Candace wasn't quite done yet.

"That's only because I couldn't let you see how much I cared." Mum sighed. "What I really wanted was to cage you up and not let you out of my sight. But I had to set you free. You had your own life to lead, and your own adventures to have." She stared at her. "Have you honestly felt this way all these years? Why have you never said anything before now?"

"Because it seemed so immature somehow," Candace mumbled. "As though I was the spoilt only-child and jealous of two kids."

"They can never replace you. You're my precious firstborn. I nearly lost you once—I don't ever want to lose you again." She squeezed her hand harder. "This is your home now. You're most definitely not in the way and you never have been."

It was what Candace desperately wanted to hear.

Mum continued. "I felt so bad about not being able to let you know we'd shifted—I tried every way I could think of. Actually you were one of the reasons we moved. There wasn't enough space in the unit for guests and we hoped you and your … well, you would come and visit." She gave another resigned sigh. "I know I'll have to let you go one day, but … how can I convince you I want you to stay for as long as you need to?"

"I would love to, Mum." At last Candace looked up and smiled at her mother. "But doesn't Chris want his room back?"

"We'd only been in this house two weeks before you returned," Mum said. "He'd barely had time to get used to it. Although he might say otherwise, I doubt he even likes being on his own." She shook her head, apology and regret in her eyes. "I really wish you'd told me all this earlier."

"So do I, now."

"With regard to the lack of work, jobs are hard to come by these days—especially in teaching, now that the school year is winding down. Anyway you earn your keep working around the house, and you're a great help with Gemma and Chris."

"Now that they've got to know me," Candace said, "they actually seem to like me." Whenever she was around, the twins bugged her to play with them, and most nights it was their big sister rather than their parents they asked to read them bedtime stories.

"You're wonderful company and I love having you here. In fact, can you stay until you're thirty?"

Candace answered her mother's grin with her own, before giving a contented sigh—she really was home.

Chapter Twenty-Seven

"Hi, is this the Holden residence?" The friendly voice on the other end of the phone was only slightly familiar. "Can I speak to the young lady please?"

"Yes, this is Candace speaking."

"It's Pam, the tenant of your unit."

"Is something wrong?" Panic rose.

"No, no." Pam hastened to reassure her. "I just rang to tell you that a young man, claiming to be a friend of yours, turned up here a short while ago. He seemed desperate to catch up with you. When I said you didn't live here anymore, he asked me for your new address. I thought I should check with you before I give it to him."

"I appreciate that," Candace said, puzzled. None of her male friends knew she was back in the country. "Is he still there?"

"I suggested he wait while I phoned you, but he said he had to go."

"Did he tell you his name? Is it Lance? Or Greg, perhaps?" Would Greg be trying to find her if he was happily married? It was possible Tiff had told him she was back. Maybe he merely wanted to reconnect. Or—horrors—perhaps he wanted to tell her his news. Being happy for him was still proving difficult but at least the thought of Greg with Angie was now only mildly nauseating.

Pam interrupted her thoughts. "He didn't identify himself. He just said he would call back here later on."

Surely it had to be either Greg or Lance—unless it was an old university mate?

"I don't want him coming to my home address—at least not until I know who it is." Inquisitiveness wrestled with reluctance to see Greg—and won. "Could you pass a message on to the mystery man please? Tell him I'll meet him at ten tomorrow morning in the Amber café."

Being a fine morning, Candace walked the fifteen minutes to the café. In the doorway she paused, curiosity tinged with nervousness, to scan the crowd. There were no familiar faces or friendly waves to be seen. However she was slightly early.

After ordering, she picked up a magazine and found a table with a good vantage point of the entrance. The café was busy and the coffee took a while to arrive, so she flipped through the gossipy pages and tried to appear nonchalant. In spite of sipping slowly, by half-past-ten she was sucking dregs and knew far more than she wanted to about celebrities—still there was no sign of the man. Perhaps he hadn't received the message. Or maybe he had developed cold feet.

Disappointment mixed with frustration—she might never find out who it was. She was debating whether to order a refill or give up when a man entered the café and stood gazing around the room, clearly searching for someone. With the light behind him, his silhouette resembled Greg's. As she lifted her hand to wave, she got a clear view of the man. Recoiling down behind the open magazine, she did her best to look inconspicuous.

Neil! What was he doing here? Praying he hadn't seen her hesitant gesture, and from behind the cover she checked for any other exits. There were none to be seen. How was she going to escape when he remained standing near the doorway? Maybe he would give up and leave. She waited. But he stayed put.

There was nothing for it but to do a runner. With the pretence of dropping off the magazine on the stack in the far corner, she arose and edged around the room, attempting to maintain a safe distance. To no avail—Neil was moving towards her. She dodged between tables but anticipating her route, he blocked it before reaching out to grab her wrist. Patrons sipped on, seemingly oblivious. He squeezed—hard enough so that she had to stifle a cry.

"Don't make a scene," he hissed in her ear and twisted. She clamped her mouth shut against the pain. "How lovely to see you, Candace," he said aloud in an overly cheerful voice, the alcohol fumes on his breath faint but distinct. "Sorry I'm so late, this place is not easy to find." He led her out of the café. "It's been a while." Still with a firm grasp on her wrist, he marched her along the street. Being much stronger, he could snap her arm like a dry twig if she tried to struggle or run.

"Where are you taking me?" Candace spoke loudly in an attempt to get the attention of a passer-by. But the woman simply smiled at them. To her they probably looked like a young couple in love.

"First of all to my motel. Then back to England. I don't have long as I have to return to work next week."

Shock quelled a response. Surely he couldn't force her on to an aeroplane? Did he think he could somehow charm his way past her parents and make her pack a bag and grab her passport? The man clearly was insane.

After a short walk, they came to a park where he pushed her none too gently down on a bench and sat beside her.

"You have a lot of explaining to do, my dear."

The only thing she could do was pray. Which she did. Furiously.

"So?" Neil demanded. "How come you left me? I was devastated and my family was horrified to hear the wedding was off." When

Candace was speechless, he filled the silence. "Well, it's all right. We're back together again now which is what matters. Since I'm here, we can start making wedding arrangements. We could have a quick ceremony in your country for your family and then one back in Ireland for mine—"

"Candace!"

She looked up to see Greg smiling at her. With her grudge against him on hold, she thanked God at the sight of him. Neil moved his hand down to hers and gripped it tightly, disguising it to look like a loving grasp.

"I didn't realise you were back," Greg said with a warm smile. "This must be your fiancé." He stretched out a friendly hand to shake Neil's, but the man didn't respond.

"Ex-fiancé." Candace said it as clearly as she could, Greg's presence giving her courage. He looked startled before leaning down to give her a hug. The alcohol must have slowed Neil's thinking for he didn't react at first.

"Are you in trouble?" Greg whispered in her ear. "You're as white as a glacier."

"Call the police," she whispered back.

"Get your hands off my fiancé," Neil said in a low growl. Without letting go of Candace he stood up and aimed a woozy left-handed blow, but Greg ducked and the fist met air. Off balance, Neil loosened his grasp for a moment and Candace pulled her arm clear. Before Neil could prime his fist again, Greg gently but firmly tugged her to his nearby car, using his free hand to thumb a button on his phone.

"I need the police." He spoke urgently.

With alcohol-induced slowness, Neil stood wavering before stumping after them. Greg fumbled to unlock the car. "Jump in," he shouted before racing around to pile in the other side. He thumped the central-lock button and continued to tell the police what was going on.

"He's going to break something!" Candace shrieked and cowered when Neil began to pound the windows and panels.

"I'll drive you to the police station," Greg said, starting the car.

"Yes!" Candace screamed it. "Get us out of here before that maniac breaks in." To her horror Greg turned the ignition off again.

"The cops want us to stay put. They said they will come to us."

"But Neil might have wrecked the car and murdered us by then!"

Through the windscreen, which seemed in danger of cracking at any moment, she could see the frustrated fury in Neil's eyes as he continued to batter the vehicle.

"Oy!" A couple of men were running in their direction. For a moment Neil paused to look before returning to his assault. "What are you doing?" one man shouted. The pair, as burly as they were, had difficulty restraining the belligerent Neil. Greg hopped out and joined in to help. Some minutes later a siren indicated the police were approaching. With shaking legs, Candace made it out of the car and to the park bench where she remained, trembling, while she was questioned.

"They were assaulting me," Neil said to the officers, playing the pathos card. But it was his word against four witnesses and the police clearly didn't believe anything he said.

From the bench, Candace watched the officer push down on Neil's head to get him into the back seat of the police car. Although it was a relief to see him go, it was mixed with sadness; that Neil, the man whom she had once loved and thought had loved her, was now reduced to this. As the vehicle drove away, Neil turned to stare through the rear window and caught her eye. Her heart nearly broke. He looked truly pathetic.

"I'll walk—it's not far," Candace said when Greg offered her a lift home. The last thing she wanted was to be alone with him. But when she tried to get to her feet, her traitorous legs would barely hold her; she had to sit down again.

"You can hardly stand, let alone walk."

She acquiesced, but wouldn't allow Greg to help her to the car. After curtly giving him her address, the shock of the recent events and her antipathy towards him kept her silent during the short drive home. Her sore wrist, already starting to bruise, was massaged in secret to avoid Greg's sympathy.

By the time Greg pulled up outside the villa, she was feeling stronger. "Just drop me off at the kerb, thanks."

"Nice house," Greg said, eyeing it. "Somewhat bigger than the unit."

For a moment she let her guard down. "Yes, it was my grandfather's before he moved up north to be with Nana."

"Oh, dear old Gramps—you used to talk about him a lot but I never did meet him. Is he still going strong?"

"He's fine." The barrier went up again and she returned to being icily polite.

"So why didn't let me know you were back?" Greg sounded petulant.

Candace couldn't bring herself to answer. Praying he wouldn't repeat the question, she opened the car door. "If there's any damage to the panel work, I'll pay for it."

Greg shrugged. "Hey, what's a few more dings?"

"Thanks for coming to my rescue." *Just like last time, when the creepy Doug had tried to assault her.* But she wasn't going to remind him of that.

"Are you going to be all right?" Greg asked. "You still look pale."

"I'm fine," she muttered. Apart from the sore wrist and the trauma, it was mostly true.

"Perhaps I should walk you in. You look as though you could use a nice strong brew and we could have a catch up." His smile was warm. "You must have lots to tell me. I have some news of my own."

There was no guessing as to what that would be.

"I'm sure you need to get home to your family." She didn't hide her sarcasm. Without waiting for his reply, she scrambled out and marched up the path.

Her mother met her at the front door.

"I saw the car pull up. Was that Greg?" Mum asked. "Does this mean …?"

"Yes, it was him but no, it doesn't mean anything." Seated on the couch, she told her mother about the eventful morning, trying to downplay the danger so as not to worry her. But Mum still looked horrified.

"What are the police going to do?"

"I'm not pressing charges and neither is Greg." Candace grimaced. "Frankly I don't care what they do—all I want is for Neil to go away. He has to return home next week, so hopefully I'll never have to see him again. Perhaps I should have stayed on in London and reported him. It might have helped to save other women … but I simply couldn't face it."

"That's quite understandable. So how did Neil know our old address?"

"I've been thinking about that," Candace said. "He must've found it in my handbag."

"But there's no danger of him turning up here?"

"He doesn't know where I live now."

"Thank the Lord for that," Mum said, lifting her eyes to heaven. "What about Greg? Did he say anything about his wee family?"

Candace hid her pain. It was unlikely her mother was intentionally being insensitive, but still she'd managed to touch a raw nerve. "I didn't give him the chance."

"Was he wearing a wedding ring?" Now Mum was sprinkling salt on the already smarting wound.

"Sorry Mum, but I kind of had other things to think about. In all the excitement I didn't notice." She stood up and made to leave the room. "I don't want to talk about it anymore."

Chapter Twenty-Eight

Her bruised wrist healed a lot faster than her paranoia. With quick nervous glances Candace scanned the mall crowd for any familiar faces, as was her habit everywhere she went now. Neil should have long since left the country, but still she kept a lookout for him.

And for Greg. With Angie. Even after all this time, just the thought of them together still made Candace's stomach turn a little. As for seeing them in the flesh—it would surely be her worst nightmare. Angie was bound to look smug, being well aware of Candace's feelings for Greg. But she wouldn't give her the satisfaction by looking sour. She was determined to plaster on a smile and give them her blessing—although it would likely be through gritted teeth.

She headed to the notice board outside the supermarket to search for a job; anything to tide her over until she could launch her career. It seemed she had returned home just at the wrong time last year to find employment; the students had snaffled up the holiday jobs and the teaching positions had already been filled. And now, although she had signed up with a job agency, it was too early on in the school year for the requirement of relief teachers.

She was in dire need of an occupation, not to mention an income. The pitiful amount from the rental was going straight to her parents as board and her own savings were dwindling fast.

In amongst the many items for sale and desperate pleas for lost pets to be returned, there was only one job displayed: she considered it for a nanosecond. No, she had plenty of respect for care-givers, but it was definitely not her.

It was all rather disheartening, and the savoury smells wafting from the nearby food hall made her mouth water and stomach grumble. Breakfast seemed a long time ago. A bite to eat might help to cheer her up, although it meant spending what little cash she had left. After buying a cheap and filling cheese scone, she grabbed a newspaper abandoned on one of the tables. It turned out to be yesterday's news, but the Situations Vacant section was all she was after. The booths on the edge of the hall offered some privacy, so she parked herself in one and spread the paper out to scan the jobs listed while she nibbled.

Lunchtime was approaching, and the food hall was beginning to fill up. It was becoming difficult to concentrate due to the noise, especially the chatter coming from the newly arrived occupants in the next booth. She couldn't hear what they were saying but the woman's laugh was particularly grating. And familiar—there was only one person who sounded like that. Angie. Her companion was clearly a man judging by the deep tones. It had to be Greg, but the voice was too indistinct to tell. Was her worst nightmare about to come true?

She heard rather than saw them getting ready to leave. Holding the paper up in front of her face to avoid being recognised, Candace couldn't resist taking a surreptitious peek. Her stomach churned as Angie came into view. Since her back was to Candace, it was impossible to tell if there was still a baby bump. Then another nervous peek to see the man—she caught a glimpse of his face before he turned around.

It wasn't Greg. The relief was momentary. In horror she watched him take Angie's hand before they moved off. Candace sprang to her feet.

"Angie, how could you!" But her impulsive words were lost in the echoing Food Hall, and the couple didn't so much as glance in her direction. They wandered off through the crowd, hand in hand.

What should she do? Follow them and confront Angie? Still aghast and indecisive, Candace dithered until it was too late and they had disappeared from view.

How she longed to slap the woman's rounded face for cheating on such a lovely man as Greg. And so blatantly too, in public. Yes, she was still upset with him—but even so he didn't deserve this.

Out in the car park, after a cursory look for the miscreants, she climbed into the vehicle and sat for a while, fuming and trying to decide what to do. Should she or shouldn't she? Yes, she would. She turned the ignition key.

"Hi, Candace." The coward in her had hoped Greg wouldn't be home, but he smiled at her from the doorway. "This is a pleasant surprise." He moved towards her as if to give her a hug but she stepped backwards to evade him and nearly toppled off the porch. At her avoidance, his evident pleasure disappeared to be replaced with a puzzled frown. "What's wrong? You don't look happy."

"There's something I need to tell you and it's not pretty."

His expression went from confused to worried. "Come in and have a cuppa. You look as though you need one."

"No, I'd rather not." If she was alone with him in his house, she wouldn't be much better than his cheating wife.

"Okay, then," he said, clearly still mystified. "But shall we at least sit down on the steps?"

Ensuring there was as big a gap as possible between them, she sat. He waited in silence as she tried to figure out where to start.

"There's no easy way to say this." Now that the time had come, the words wouldn't. "I just saw Angie," she said at length, "down at the mall. I don't know how to tell you but she was with another man." She waited for his devastation, but instead his frown became deeper. "They seemed quite … er … intimate."

"Angie? With another man? How do you mean?"

"Your wife was with someone else," she said, close to shouting with frustration. "And he clearly was not just a friend."

"But … I don't have a wife."

It took a while for his words to register.

"You're not married?" she said at last. "But I thought … that is, I saw you and Angie together one day, coming out of this house. She was wearing a sparkling ring and appeared to be pregnant."

To her chagrin Greg burst out laughing. "Yes, Angie is married. But not to me. The man you saw at the mall would be her husband, Karl."

Candace stared at him, speechless. All this time she had been convinced Greg was wed to Angie—had been losing sleep over it and as unreasonable as it was, fuming at him …

"At least I hope it was Karl you saw or else Angie'll have some explaining to do." Greg chuckled. "It was me who introduced them to each other and they immediately hit it off—love at first sight, apparently. To be honest it was a relief to have Angie off my back and not hanging around me like a lovesick puppy. Their wedding was a couple of years ago now and I was the best man."

Right now the nearest wormhole was looking like a great place to crawl into.

"Oh, I'm such an idiot!" Candace put her head in her hands.

"No, you're not. You just added two and two and came up with the wrong number. They must have been visiting me that day you saw us together." His voice was gentle. "Perhaps if you'd waited for a few moments, you would have seen Karl park at the kerb to pick up Angie."

Out of the corner of her eye she noticed Greg shift closer and make as if to put his arm around her. She sprang to her feet.

"I'm so sorry, Greg," she shouted as she made a dash for the car.

"Candace!" Greg yelled after her. "You weren't to know." But she threw herself into the vehicle and drove off.

It was just as well there were no traffic officers around to charge her for erratic driving. In spite of several near misses which evoked much indignant tooting, Candace pulled up into the driveway miraculously unscathed. She sat for a while and gave into tears of self-pity. Nothing seemed to be going right. She had no job, little income and zero love life. And now Greg must think she was a complete idiot. He was probably on the phone this minute to Angie and Karl, having a great laugh at her expense.

Eventually she crawled out of the car and moped inside, planning to retreat to her bedroom and quite possibly never emerge again. In the hallway she narrowly missed bumping into her mother, exiting the twins' room.

Mum took one look at her face. "What's wrong?"

"Oh Mum, I'm such a twit."

"I very much doubt that. What's happened? Come and tell me over a cuppa."

They sat on the couch and Candace, unable to look her mother in the eye, related the afternoon's events. Mum hardly said a word the whole time, but merely nodded with no sign of a smirk.

"I hate to say it," Mum said after Candace had finished her tale of woe, "but I had serious doubts he was married." Her face lit up with hope. "He's always been so keen on you. Does this mean you two can finally get together?"

Candace snorted. "Mum, how can I ever face him again? Why would he want a complete idiot like me in his life anyway?"

"You're not an idiot! You simply jumped to conclusions and from what you said, it did look convincing. Probably anybody else would have thought the same thing." She gave Candace a comforting sideways hug.

"Do you really think so?" Candace squeezed back. "Thanks Mum for your reassurance. I feel a bit better now, having talked to you." She stood up and stretched. All the tears and tension were making her head ache. "Now I need some fresh air to clear away the cobwebs. I could take the twins down to the park to play on the swings if you like—give you some time out."

After the children had expended their energy on the playground equipment, Candace bought them all a snow freeze. It felt good to just sit on the sun-warmed park bench inhaling the sweet-smelling air, while licking cool creamy deliciousness. This was a reminder to count her blessings.

She had a place to live, a loving supportive family and although she might not have a job, there was a lot to keep her occupied. And now that she knew the truth about Greg … a microorganism of hope made itself felt—perhaps there was a chance for the two of them. If Greg could ever get over her stupidity, that was.

The twins sat still for once, intent on licking the overflow of ice-cream off the soggy cones and their little fists. She finished her own and made a vain attempt to clean their messy hands and faces with paper serviettes and tissues. Then they dawdled home, the children stopping to investigate the fallen russet-coloured leaves, snails and other things that delighted them but made Candace shudder. It was intriguing to observe what interested them, to see things through their eyes and to practice her teaching skills on them. At last they entered the house, healthily tired and sticky.

"Don't touch anything," Candace said as she led the children into the bathroom to wash their faces and hands. Mum appeared in the doorway, clearly dying to tell her something.

"Guess who came to visit?" She didn't wait for an answer. "Greg!"

Candace bent over to wipe a messy face, so as to hide a twinge of panic mixed with excitement. "What did he want? To laugh at me some more?"

"Not at all. He wanted to check you were all right—he was concerned with the way in which you took off." Mum's grin was mischievous as she stood aside to let the twins race each other out of the bathroom. "I gave him our landline number, so he might call later."

"What on earth did you do that for?" Hopefully her outward annoyance hid her internal pleasure.

"It's my phone number and I can do with it what I like." Grin still in place, Mum folded her arms and lifted her chin. "Besides which I want to keep in touch with him, even if you don't. He's such a lovely young man. I've got his mobile number too."

"You talk to him then," Candace muttered as she dried her hands.

"Don't you want to be friends with him anymore?"

Without answering, Candace escaped to her room. Of course she still wanted to be friends with Greg—and more than that. But did he?

Chapter Twenty-Nine

When the phone rang, Mum hurried to answer it.

A minute later there was a knock on Candace's door and Mum peered in.

"Greg's coming around for a cuppa shortly," she said. "Somehow I doubt he's turning up just to see me. I hope you'll come out and join us."

"I'll think about it." Candace tried to sound blasé while her heart skipped with nervousness, or maybe it was excitement. This would be the first chance she'd had to chat with him since her return, and beyond all the misunderstandings. She yanked the band out of her hair to let it flow freely, brushed it smooth and applied a quick dab of lipstick. When she entered the kitchen, deliberately casual, she noticed her mother try unsuccessfully to hide a smile.

"You look very nice," she said.

To hide her blush, Candace busied herself filling the electric jug. "I'll make the hot drinks. I remember just how he likes his coffee."

"I'm sure you do," Mum said, almost under her breath.

Greg duly turned up with hair neatly combed, fresh-shaven, and smelling of something masculine. Candace blushed more when she felt his gaze upon her.

After the trio had made idle chit-chat at the table, Mum drained her cup and rather unsubtly excused herself.

"The children must have finished their afternoon naps by now," she said with an innocent smile. "I'll just go and check up on them."

"So why didn't you let me know you were back?" Greg asked once Mum had left the room on her imaginary errand. He sounded hurt.

"Don't you think I tried? I couldn't text you originally because my so-called wonderful fiancé kindly confiscated my cell phone." She couldn't help the sarcasm. "It had all my friends' numbers in it, including yours."

The light dawned on Greg's face. "That explains why you haven't returned my texts then—ever since the incident with that man, I've been trying to contact you to find out if you were all right. When I didn't get any replies, I thought about coming to visit, but wondered if perhaps you were snubbing me for some reason."

"I admit I was, but only because I thought you were married! The week after my return, since I couldn't contact you by phone, I tried to pay you a visit."

"Was that when you saw Angie at my house?"

"Yes. I spotted the ring on her finger and jumped to conclusions. The wrong ones, as it turned out. After that I avoided you because I couldn't bear the thought of seeing you with your …"—she made quote marks with her fingers—"…wife."

"So that's why you were so short with me when I rescued you." Greg looked thoughtful.

"Then I saw Angie at the mall. I didn't tell you I challenged her, did I? Blessedly she didn't hear me or I would have made a fool of myself in public … instead of just in private with you. After that, I was so embarrassed I couldn't face you. I thought you'd all be having a good laugh at my expense."

"I wouldn't laugh at you, you should know that," he said with indignation. "So why didn't you want to see Angie and me together?" He feigned innocence, but there was mischief in his smile.

She examined the tablecloth so he wouldn't see her blush.

"Do I really have to answer that?"

"If you don't, I'll make up an answer. And you might not like it." Greg chuckled and Candace looked up.

"Partly because you said you'd never go there with her," she said.

"True, and I don't go back on my word. So perhaps you should have believed me."

"At the risk of sounding egotistical, I thought perhaps when you found out I was engaged, you'd been so devastated, you'd succumbed to her charms. When I saw you together, it seemed obvious you two were an item. You both looked blissfully happy." It was Candace's turn to smile and stir. "Such a lovely couple."

Greg pulled a face. "She's a good friend—if a rather needy one. But she's not my type. Not like someone else I know." He grinned at her and she reddened again. "So what's the other part of the reason?"

"I was jealous." She mumbled it to the table. "I couldn't bear to lose the man I thought was once my … bestest friend."

Greg chuckled at first before becoming serious. "So why did you get engaged to that … monster?"

"It's a bit embarrassing but to be honest, I'm not quite sure. I think it was because I was in a foreign country where I hardly knew anyone, and I was homesick and lonely. Then Mum told me you had a girlfriend."

Greg seemed to be trying to recall who she meant. "Oh, her. We were barely an item."

"But I didn't know that. So I was at my most vulnerable when along comes this 'prince charming' who proceeds to sweep me off my feet. At the time I sure needed a dose of ego boost, and like a drug pusher, he provided me with that in buckets." She lifted her eyes to meet his. "Also, he reminded me a little of a certain friend I had back home, but only physically. This particular person is so much nicer and easier to talk to. And he listens."

"Sounds like a great chap," Greg said straight faced but with a twinkle in his eye. "You must introduce me to him one day."

"And he doesn't try to manipulate me. Or kidnap me."

He gaped. "That man tried to kidnap you?"

Downplaying it, she gave him sparse details about the incident and how she had managed to escape and return home.

"He's clearly dangerous." Greg's frown deepened. "And deranged. Thank the Lord I found you that day he turned up. Otherwise you might be locked in a house in England by now, married to a psychopath." There was a bitter note in his voice, unusual for him.

"Yes, you've come to my rescue twice now. If it happens a third time, I might have to become your slave. At least I think that's what happens in some cultures."

With a grin at her he didn't commit to an answer. "So what about that guy I saw you with in your first year at university?"

Although he sounded nonchalant, Candace was sure he was holding his breath. She had to think for a moment. "Oh, you mean Lance? That was so long ago. Lovely guy but just a friend, that's all. He wanted to be more, but I dissuaded him."

Greg let out what sounded like a sigh of relief. "It's been ages since we hung out together. How about we go and grab takeaways and eat them at the beach tonight?"

After she had agreed, and he left, Candace called to her mother. "You can come out now, the coast is clear."

"Look at you, you're all flushed and your eyes are sparkling," Mum said as she entered the dining room, suspiciously fast. "I take it you've sorted everything out now?"

"Yes," Candace said as she floated around the room. "We're friends again."

"The temperature is so mild, it's hard to believe it's autumn." Candace flapped her hands to shoo away the opportunistic gulls swooping over the pile of takeaways. "Such a shame daylight saving will be ending soon. No more long evenings."

"Better make the most of it then. I haven't had junk food since …" Greg paused to savour a fat chip in its thick coating of tomato sauce. "I can't remember how long."

"Me neither," Candace said as she helped herself to a chunk of battered fish. "Probably the last lot I ate were in the UK. But they were so greasy I could have wrung them out and used the oil to lubricate a car. The next day I was one big pimple."

"I can't believe that," Greg said with a laugh. "You wouldn't know how to have zits! Do you even have pores?" He leaned in, pretending to examine her face. Candace let him, noticing the sparkle in his eyes. Was he going to kiss her? But instead he looked down to select a piece of fish.

"Tomorrow I'll be back on the healthy stuff." He sighed. "But I am half the man I used to be. Well, three-quarters perhaps?" It was good to see he had managed to maintain his physique over the years, ever since he had helped Angie to slim down by joining her in healthy eating and exercise.

They ate as much of the mound of fish and chips as they could before tossing the remnants out for the noisy gulls to fight over. Then Candace removed her shoes in order to feel the cool silky sand beneath her feet.

"What a wonderful evening," she said, as they strolled along the beach watching the sea turn into pale green satin. She wasn't just referring to the weather and the view. When was the last time she had felt so happy and relaxed in the company of a man? It all seemed so natural, two close friends spending quality time together.

Now and then, Greg looked as though he might reach out to take her hand. But then he would hesitate before putting his firmly back into his pocket. It was disappointing—she wanted him to.

Once it was too dark to see the beach, they crossed the road to a café and indulged in hot chocolates.

"It feels as though we've never been apart," Greg said slowly. Was he going to ask her something? She held her breath as he paused, appearing to pluck up courage.

"Shall we do this again?" he asked.

"Yes, please. And soon."

"They're not dates, we're just friends," Candace said as she rushed around trying to get herself organised.

Her mother raised an eyebrow. "What, every Friday night? You don't meet up with any of your other friends that often."

Candace didn't reply. Annoyingly, Mum was right. Hanging out with Greg was the highlight of Candace's week but she wasn't about to give Mum the satisfaction of knowing that.

"If they're not dates then why are you going to so much trouble over your appearance?" Mum looked smug.

Candace stopped in mid rush and peered down at herself. "I'm not exactly wearing my best dress."

"But you're neat and tidy and your hair is styled."

By way of an answer Candace huffed off to her room. It had been months now and in truth she was getting impatient for their relationship to move on to the next stage. But she wasn't about to initiate it.

As they sipped their hot chocolates in the café, Greg began to tap a nervous rhythm on the table. Then he danced his hand over to hers and took hold of it.

"We've been hanging out together as friends for a while now," he said. Candace gave him an encouraging smile. "But I would like to be something more." Butterflies started dancing in her stomach. "Now that we're both single and you've tried out your wings … that question I asked you all those years ago, I want to ask you again. Candace, will you go out with me? On a real date, I mean."

She didn't need time to think about it but nodded hard while squeezing his hand, enjoying the strength and solidness of it. He had dependable hands, just like the man himself.

"You obviously had a nice time," Mum said with a mischievous smile as Candace wafted into the house.

"We're going out next Friday. On a real date. To a proper restaurant."

Mum's smile broadened. "I thought you told me you were just …?"

But Candace didn't stick around to hear her mother's smug triumph. She had outfits to plan.

Chapter Thirty

This dress hadn't seen the light of day since graduation—when Mum had given her glowing compliments. Now Candace wriggled and tugged. She must have gained weight since then as the bodice felt even more restrictive and uncomfortable—she could hardly breathe. Her hairdo, secured with a multitude of clips, was so tight it was making her head ache. She pulled a face at her reflection. Yes, she wanted to look nice for Greg, but this was so not her.

He would be here soon. She reluctantly strapped on her high-heels and immediately wanted to kick them off again. Why was it seemingly impossible to be comfortable and look good at the same time? It was making her irritable—if this was what a 'proper date' was all about, her enthusiasm was waning. It was bringing back bad memories too; when Neil had taken her to fancy restaurants he had insisted she dress up. She was teetering on the brink of undoing all her hard work and throwing on jeans and a t-shirt, when there was a knock on the front door. Too late.

"Greg's here, Candace," Mum said.

Candace took as deep a breath as her bodice would allow and entered the lounge. Greg gaped when he saw her. Obviously Mum was right.

"Candace, you look …" He was clearly lost for words. Her face warmed—his reaction almost made up for the discomfort. Until she pulled on a coat to ward off the cold and felt even more restricted.

Greg, apparently just as uncomfortable in his formal attire, held the car door open for her and she carefully stepped in. Judging by the small talk made during the journey, he was equally as tense as she was. Her exit from the car was awkward, and she prayed she wouldn't fall off the heels and make a complete idiot of herself.

The restaurant Greg had chosen was impressively fancy. How could he afford it? She nearly blurted out the question. While they waited to be served, conversation was overly polite, punctuated by a lot of silence where usually there would have been laughter.

At last the food arrived. Although the ridiculously small portions were delicious, she was too busy minding her table manners and trying to be lady-like to truly enjoy the meal.

Greg seemed to grow more tense and distracted by the minute, while she sat hating every moment. What were they doing here? This so wasn't them. It made her long for their relaxed and casual unofficial dates.

After they had finished their main meal, she opened her mouth to suggest they skip dessert and escape, when she noticed him fishing around in his jacket pocket. No, he wasn't—was he? He put a small round box clad in midnight blue velvet on the table and reached for her hands.

"Candace, will you—"

"No!" she shouted and pulled away. Greg sat frozen, eyes wide. The other diners turned to gawp at her outburst, but she didn't care. She had to get out of the place. After shoving her chair back so hard it nearly tipped over, she snatched up her coat and purse, and scarpered as fast as the high heels would allow.

Outside she tottered over to a nearby taxi stand and plunged into a waiting cab. As it moved off, she glanced out the rear window. Greg stood motionless in the doorway, staring after her.

Her burst into the house brought her parents out to the hallway. Ignoring their startled expressions and questions, she made straight for her room. Once she had clawed the clips from her hair, she wrenched the hateful dress off and crumpled it into a corner. After throwing on pyjamas, she crawled under the covers and pulled a pillow over her head. A muffled noise reached her ears. From the depths of her handbag, her phone was ringing. She hauled it out and, without bothering to check the screen, silenced it.

All she wanted was for them to be a real couple at long last, to simply be boyfriend and girlfriend for a time, without the added pressure of planning a wedding. So why did Greg have to go and spoil everything by proposing on their first proper date? Was there any hope for their relationship now or had she mucked everything up? Wondering and worrying kept her awake until the early hours.

After what felt like one minute of sleep, Candace woke up to find it was light. Had it all been a dream? Or perhaps a horrible nightmare. She reached for her phone and reality hit. Five missed calls and as many texts from Greg. She read through them all: his hurt and embarrassment were clear. Horrified at her own rude behaviour, she replied.

Greg, I'm so sorry. I owe you an explanation.

It would be quite understandable if he didn't respond. But she didn't have to wait long.

You certainly do.

Do you want to come round tonight? That is if you still want to talk to me.

There was no reply. Well, if he didn't turn up, she deserved it.

Candace couldn't bring herself to look Greg in the eye. "I know it's getting dark, but how about we go for a wander?" That way she wouldn't have to face him while they talked and there would be no chance of her parents eavesdropping.

They walked in silence at first until Greg spoke.

"I felt like such an prat last night." There was more than a hint of accusation in his tone. "I'm sure everyone in the restaurant was looking at me. That is after they'd finished watching you make a spectacle of yourself." She could hear unusual anger in his voice. His words were not making her feel better and she squirmed.

"I know, I really am sorry." Shame made her mutter. "You're not the idiot—that was me. I panicked and I just had to get out of there. If it's any comfort, it makes me cringe to remember what I did."

"But why did you run away, Candace? We've known each other for so long and so well. Surely we're ready to move on to the next step?"

"I totally overreacted." Candace hesitated. "It's the whole proper date-thing … it felt so formal and uncomfortable, not us at all. And then a proposal on our first official date—it was all way too soon. It brought back horrible memories … of Neil. He proposed after only a few weeks."

Even in the dim light, she could see Greg look stricken. He gulped. "Oh Candace, I had no idea."

"How would you? I didn't tell you that part. Then he turned into a possessive, controlling monster."

Under a street light Greg stopped and, taking her by the shoulders, turned her to face him. "Candace, I would never do that. I only proposed so soon—or at least tried to—because I was sure you're the one for me, God's intended."

"You're the sweetest guy I know, Greg." She smiled up at him. "I can't imagine marrying anyone else." When he opened his mouth as if to interrupt, she held up a hand. "But I'm simply not ready yet—it took your proposal to make me realise that. I've ended up with as much baggage as an international airport. I need more time than I thought to heal up from that traumatic relationship, and to find my feet."

"Yes, I know." Greg looked mournful. "I'm sorry Candace, it was thoughtless of me."

She laid a hand on his arm. "Not at all. I appreciate the gesture and I'm incredibly flattered. It's not an outright 'no', it's just a 'not right now'. Also, to be boringly practical, I must concentrate on finding work rather than a wedding venue."

"Do you want me to give you some space?"

"Yes. No." She shrugged and sighed. "I don't know."

"Best to start heading back," he said before lapsing into silence again.

"Do you want to come in?" she asked him at the front door, more out of politeness than an honest desire for his company.

"No, I'd better go home. I'll leave you in peace to think. Good bye, Candace." Without a hug or a peck, he turned and stalked down the steps.

"I just need time to process everything," she said to his receding back. "I'll contact you when I'm ready. Please don't give up on me." But he had gone.

For a week Candace moped and prayed, unsure of what to do with herself. She wrote cathartic screeds in her journal and arranged to see a counsellor. As a way of keeping busy and distracted, she upped her job hunt and frantically sent off CVs for the following year's teaching positions. To Greg's credit and her disappointment, he left her alone; not a beep of the cell phone out of him.

On Monday morning the phone rang. She was wanted for a day's work at a nearby school. They asked her to return the following day and then for the rest of the week to replace a teacher who had to take off in a hurry. More days of work were a blessing, and not only for her finances—employment provided a distraction and a much needed confidence boost. Relief teaching had been sporadic for most of the year but now just when she needed a diversion, it was blessedly ramping up.

By the end of the week she was exhausted, but it was a good sort of weariness; not from depression but rather from seeing a job well done. There was also the satisfaction of being wanted back on the following Monday—and for the rest of the term.

On Saturday, after a sound night's sleep, she realised she was missing Greg terribly and ready to associate with him again. She fired off a text.

Do you want to do nice casual takeaways in the food hall tonight?

It would be a great way to relax and they would have plenty to talk about. To her dismay and after constantly checking her phone, it was hours before his reply came through. By which time it was too late.

Sorry, busy.

She read the message with shock and disappointment. Was he genuinely occupied—or merely fobbing her off?

Another time maybe? Her text was hopeful. But there was no answer.

The weekend dragged past and it was something of a relief to have a job to go to on Monday—it would take her mind off her problems. In the evening a text came through. When she saw it was from Greg, she opened it with some trepidation.

Sorry, I was at a youth camp over the weekend and the kids were keeping me busy. What about a beach walk on Friday night before it gets too dark?

So he hadn't gone off her … unless this was going to be a fare-well speech.

Work made the week go fast. At least until Friday afternoon which seemed to last an entire year. When Greg came to pick her up, it was awkward at first. The drive to the beach was largely made in silence and on their stroll, he kept his hands firmly in his pock-ets. Not a good sign. At last they found a spot to spread a beach towel out and sit down. They talked about nothing much until the light started to fade, Candace waiting nervously for the dreaded indication he was intent on splitting up. But it didn't happen. On the walk back to the car, she held out a trembling hand. At first he didn't seem aware of it.

"Are you sure?" he asked once he'd finally noticed.

"Yes, I'm positive. If you are. Unless you brought me here to dump me?" It was a tentative question.

"What gave you that idea?" He looked aghast. "It didn't even occur to me! Is that why you've been on edge all night?"

"Well, after our last meeting, I thought you might have had enough."

"And I was under the impression you wanted to take things slowly. Which is why I didn't make any moves this evening." He turned to face her and took her hands. "After God, you're the best thing that's ever happened to me."

"You too." Relief made her mischievous. "But if you ever arrange another fancy date like that, I'll never talk to you again."

"Pity—you looked stunning in that dress!" He pulled a rueful face.

"Thank you. But it's so uncomfortable. You try walking in high-heels and wearing an outfit like that."

Greg chuckled. "I might lose my pastoral position if I did! Right, so no more posh dates then." He pretended to write a memo before taking her hands again and giving her a shy smile. "Anyway, you'd look beautiful in anything, even an old sack." Candace glowed at the compliment.

Chapter Thirty-One

Candace tried not to pull a face.

"This was my daughter's car," the seller said, indicating the small and decidedly untrendy vehicle. "Now she's moved on to something a little more upmarket. It may be basic, without all the bells and whistles, but it's really reliable, economical and tidy."

"That's all my daughter requires," Dad said.

"That's all I can afford," Candace said in a mutter not loud enough for the seller to hear. "But I really do need transport to get to work." She was fed up with having to rely on buses and her parents. Judging by the enthusiastic way Dad had stumped up some money and Mum had searched for suitable vehicles, they were tired of it too.

After a quick test drive, with the paperwork and finances sorted, Dad headed homewards. But Candace made her solo maiden voyage to Greg's place to show him her new acquisition. It was a non-date night, but hopefully he would be home …

Not again. Who was the woman with Greg this time? It certainly wasn't Angie. Paranoia and angst kicked in as Candace watched him give the slim attractive female a hug, followed by an apologetic grin as he disentangled his fingers from her long hair.

Was there much point in bothering to get out of the car? But it wasn't worth suffering like the last time when she had jumped to conclusions. It was best to confront him now and get it over and done with.

He's trustworthy, there's probably a perfectly simple explanation. It didn't loosen the internal knots.

"Come inside," Greg was saying. With his hand on his companion's back, he nudged her along the path. It was the mystery woman who turned at Candace's approach and gave her an uncertain smile.

"I'm not interrupting anything, am I?" Curtness soured Candace's tone. Greg spun round and his initial surprise was swiftly replaced with obvious delight.

"Candace! I wasn't expecting to see you."

She instantly regretted her suspicions, but he must have caught a glimpse of her acidic expression before she rearranged it; his pleasure faded.

"Candace, meet Penelope—"

"I've heard so much about you," Penelope said, her face lighting up.

"Pen is your younger sister?" Candace returned the warmth. "The one you talk about a lot?"

"Yes, she's visiting from England. You didn't think—"

"No, of course not," she said with a dismissive wave. She wasn't about to tell him her paranoid thoughts.

"Pen only turned up a couple of minutes ago when Mum and Dad dropped her off on their way into town. I was going to text you to come round and meet her. Now I don't need to."

Candace gave him a sheepish grin, but still his expression remained solemn.

"I have an introduction of my own to make." She indicated her purchase. "Do you two want to jump in and we'll go to a café? Or would you rather not be seen dead in such an untrendy car?"

Pen turned out to be as cheerful and as humorous as her brother, and the three spent a pleasant hour together. Perhaps it was just Candace's imagination but Greg seemed a little off with her.

"Mum and Dad will be coming by to pick me up soon," Pen said, draining her hot chocolate.

Back at Greg's place, his parents stopped in briefly. After his family had left, he confronted Candace.

"I could tell you didn't trust me."

"I'm sorry." She couldn't meet his eyes. "It's part of the baggage I was telling you about."

He took her hands in his. "I'll tell you something which you must remember." His face was earnest. "I have no intention or desire to look at another woman."

By Friday afternoon, Candace was almost ready to quit after being stuck in a stuffy classroom with noisy unsettled children. All that kept her going was the anticipation of escaping to the beach with Greg. When at last she headed to her car, the overcast sky steadily darkened. During the drive home the clouds finally gave way, leaking sheets of rain. It looked as though it had set in for the evening and by the time she'd dashed into the house, her spirits were as damp as she was. She sent Greg a petulant text regarding the weather. His invitation to come round to his house for a meal cheered her a little.

"I have a wee surprise for you," Greg said as soon as she came through the door. "Close your eyes." He took her hand to lead her and she felt a breeze on her face. "Okay, open them now."

On the lounge floor, a rug had been spread and set with paper plates and plastic cutlery. A picnic hamper full of food sat to one side. The French doors were wide open.

"To create that indoor-outdoor flow. Sorry I can't give you sand and sea, but there's plenty of moisture out there. I can make gull noises if you want." He proceeded to squawk.

"No, it's all right," Candace said, covering her ears. "Thank you Greg, this is so thoughtful of you."

After they had eaten, Greg put a DVD on and they snuggled up on the couch to watch the movie.

All was dark. A strange noise had woken Candace—or had she dreamt it? Where was she?

She was warm and comfortable, but certainly not in her own bed. There was that weird sound again. It was a snore. And it was coming from Greg.

Alarm surged—but she restrained herself from springing to her feet. She must have fallen asleep cuddled up to him on the couch. He was clearly out to it; although he stirred slightly, he didn't wake. She really should go … but she didn't want to disturb Greg. Besides which, she was delightfully cosy and too tired to move …

Saph tiptoed along the hallway. Strange, Candace's door was open. Even in the dimness of the early morning, she could see the bed was empty. It was most unlike her daughter to stay out so late. Several different scenarios played—and none of them pretty. Horrors, perhaps her daughter had been involved in an accident and was lying injured or maybe even—. No, she wouldn't allow herself to go there.

Or there was another possibility, almost as unpleasant; Candace usually spent Friday evenings with Greg. She was well past the age of having to check in with parents, but still …

"Oh girl, what have you done?" Saph whispered into the cool night air. Surely her precious daughter hadn't stayed over at her boyfriend's place? No, she had more sense and morals than to do that. Didn't she?

Perhaps she should text Candace. But then it would look as though she was checking up on her. Better to give her daughter the benefit of the doubt. Saph returned to bed, but not to sleep as she strained to hear the sound of Candace's vehicle returning.

The dawn was glowing through the curtains when Candace opened her eyes again. This time she was lying on the couch, covered with a blanket. Her human pillow was gone, but had thoughtfully replaced himself with a cushion.

"Hello, sleeping beauty!" Greg smiled at her from the doorway. "You dozed off in my arms last night—it was … rather nice. I managed to reach the remote to turn the TV off but I couldn't bear to disturb you, you looked so peaceful."

She blinked away the sleep. "Your snoring woke me up in the middle of the night—"

"I don't snore—do I? I've never had anyone to tell me that." He raised his eyebrows at her.

"But I didn't want to bother you."

"Do you want some breakfast?"

Candace caught sight of the time and sat up, wide awake. "Oh dear, I'd better go or I'll have some explaining to do."

"It was lovely to snuggle like that," Greg said with a wistful look.

"Yes, it was." Candace grinned, the memory of his warm arms around her still fresh and buoying her up. "But we'd better not do that again."

"Not unless we're married," Greg murmured with a faraway look.

"See you later," Candace said. With a swift departing hug, she scooted.

After turning the door key and handle as noiselessly as she could manage, Candace crept into the house and along the hallway.

"And what exactly have you been up to?"

Dad was in the kitchen and he sounded unimpressed. Clearly it was a waste of time trying to be quiet. "Were you going to sneak in and pretend you'd been here all night?"

Candace slumped. "It was all perfectly innocent, Dad. We started watching a movie but we were both so tired—it's been a long hard week—and we fell asleep on the couch." Defensiveness made her rude. "Anyway, what business is it of yours? I am an adult."

Dad looked a little taken aback and put his hands up. "Backing off now. But no matter what age you are, it doesn't stop us from worrying about you. You could have been involved in an accident for all we knew."

Immediately her defensiveness dissipated.

"Sorry Dad, I know you're just looking out for me."

Mum appeared and gave her a questioning look. Candace repeated the story.

"I'm glad to hear you were safe and sound," Mum said with a relieved smile. "And weren't getting up to anything you shouldn't." She must have noticed Candace's frown. "Don't worry, I know you're not that sort of girl and I believe Greg is trustworthy. I was sure there must be an innocent explanation."

Later in the morning the phone rang, and Mum answered it. It wasn't long before she tapped on Candace's door.

"I'm afraid we have a situation," she said when she entered. "Mrs B from church—she lives along the road from Greg—spotted your car parked in his driveway yesterday evening. And early this morning … it was obvious it was there all night. You know what a gossip she is." Mum shook her head. "This is not a good look for a pastor."

Candace gulped. "I hadn't thought of that."

Greg's annoyance was evident on the phone. "Would you believe someone has reported my supposed philandering to the senior pastor?"

"That's terrible," Candace said. "We had a call this morning from a certain busy-body, so I knew we'd been spotted. But I didn't think she would dob us in."

"No, don't tell me, I have a fair idea of who it is." Greg sounded miffed. "This morning the senior pastor called me to ask what was going on. I explained what had happened and how we hadn't done anything wrong."

"It was all quite innocent," Candace said, with rising indignation.

"I could tell he believed me, but as he pointed out it didn't look good—people always think the worst, and I could be setting a bad example for the youth. But as I said only if somebody tells them. And I promised I wouldn't let it happen again. He said he wouldn't say a word to anyone else—but warned me that rumours have a bad habit of spreading."

"Especially if Mrs B is involved."

"He reassured me he'd had a word to her too, about gossiping, and reminded her she needs to hear the full story before making such an accusation. I semi-seriously offered to resign, but he refused my offer."

"Thank the Lord for that," Candace said with sincerity. "Besides, what else would you do? Greg, this is your calling. I'm so sorry, I should have left the first time I woke up."

"And I should have sent you home last night—but I just couldn't."

"Right, no more movie nights at your place. At least not when we're in danger of falling asleep. Maybe we should only be together in public."

"There are a couple of other options …" Greg sounded mysterious. "See you Friday night?"

Chapter Thirty-Two

"Aren't we stopping for takeaways?" Candace asked in dismay. Greg didn't slow down, and she gazed longingly at their regular haunt as they sailed past.

"No, I've organised something else."

The week had dragged by. As usual she'd been looking forward to their Friday night date, and mildly intrigued by his mysterious comment, but the last few days of work had been so busy and distracting. Now she was too tired and hungry to care.

At the beach Greg removed the picnic hamper from the car boot. When he saw Candace's questioning look, he merely gave her an enigmatic smile and raised an eyebrow. Hefting the basket in one hand, he reached for hers and led her along the shore.

The tide was going out and the lowering sun gilded the few clouds, reflecting on the calm water. What could have been a romantic stroll was spoiled by her grump and Greg's silent tenseness. After they had walked for what felt like miles, her mood darkened further.

"I'm so hungry," she said. As if on cue, her stomach growled to confirm it. "Can't we eat now?"

"Soon." Greg appeared distracted. His downward gaze suggested he was searching for something. She sulked and stumped along in silence.

"Stop," he said as they neared an old fallen tree trunk, worn smooth by the wind and the waves. "This is just the right spot."

He deposited the basket on the beach and opened it to remove a blanket. After he had spread the rug out on the log-seat, with a sweeping bow he gestured for Candace to sit there. Then he bent down and rummaged around in the sand.

"Perfect," she heard him mutter as he picked something up and slipped it into his pocket.

"What are you doing?" Candace asked, his puzzling behaviour distracting from her rumbling stomach.

Without answering, Greg planted one knee on the damp sand and took her left hand in his. He fumbled in his pocket and pulled out the object. It was the lip of a shell that had been worn down to form a ring.

"Is it still too soon to ask you?" He slipped it onto her finger. "Candace, will you marry me?"

In an instant, her grump and hunger was forgotten.

"Yes, please!" Her response was so loud, Greg winced and several loitering gulls took to the air. They were about to settle again when Greg yelled too.

"We're getting married!" He punched the gull-laden air before hauling her to her feet and doing a jig with her in his arms. Then he grinned. "Soon you'll be able to stay over and no busy-body can dob us in."

To hide her blush, Candace pretended to admire the ring. It was too big and she had to hold her hand up to prevent it from falling off. "How do we get this resized?"

Once again there was no answer. Instead Greg opened up the picnic hamper and pulled out what appeared to be a bottle of wine and two elegant glasses.

"Is that what I think it is? Champagne?"

With a silent smile, Greg sent the stopper flying high into the air before it arced down to land in the lower branches of a tree.

"Remind me to retrieve that later. Right now I have more important things to attend to." With foam flowing out of the bottle and down over his hand, Greg poured bubbles and handed her a glass. She hesitated to take it. "Don't worry," he said, "it's just sparkling grape juice. I still have to drive us home." Then he reached into the basket again and removed a small round box, clad in midnight blue velvet; one which Candace had seen before …

"So what was the other option?" With all the excitement Candace's appetite had dissipated and now she toyed with the little food she had on her plate.

"A chaperone," Greg said and grinned. He didn't seem very hungry either.

With an answering smile, Candace held her left hand out in front of her, the sunset dancing on the diamonds.

"It's a gorgeous ring."

"Sorry, it's not exactly extravagant."

"To me it's just right because it's from you. Besides, you know how much I hate pretension." She flipped it around her finger. "It might pay to get it resized. I don't want to lose it."

"No problem, but not today. Now, where were we?"

"Oh," Candace said, startled. "My feet are getting wet!"

"The tide is coming in. We'd better get going." Greg snatched at the picnic basket which was in danger of starting a seaward voyage, and hoisted it onto the log. "I was going to get that plastic stopper." He peered through the twilight at the tree branch. "It's almost too dark now to see where it went. You stay here and I'll go and retrieve it."

"Is it worth worrying about? We don't want to be caught out by the tide."

"But what about the environment?" Greg asked. "Don't worry, I won't be long."

She lifted her feet up onto the log to keep them dry and watched him pull on the low branch. There was a loud crack, a splash and then silence. Hauling up her trouser legs as she went, Candace ran through the small waves. It seemed to take an age to get to Greg where he lay motionless on his back in the shallow water.

"Are you all right?" When there was no response, panic began to stir. Frantic glances each way along the beach for help showed it was deserted. Ignoring the inches of water she knelt down and leaned over to check his breathing. She found herself in his embrace.

"You little …" She pulled away. "I was really worried about you."

"Ouch, that fall was not nice. I've been winded." He sat up and coughed. "It was worth it though." She could see him smiling in the fading light.

"Was that all just a stunt?" She couldn't really be angry with him.

"I certainly didn't do it on purpose." He rubbed his back and winced before gingerly standing up. "Now that I'm thoroughly soaked, we'd better get out of this water before we get swept out to sea."

"True. If we don't get moving, this incredibly memorable engagement might turn out to be an incredibly short one."

"Have you still got the ring?" Greg asked. Candace waggled her ring-clad finger at him, the diamonds catching the last dying rays of the daylight.

Using a corner of the blanket, Greg dried himself off as best he could. Then huddling together, Candace wrapped the dry part around their shoulders to ward off the chilly evening air. Still they shivered. By the light of her cell phone they found what little sand there was left to walk on and made slow progress back along the beach to the car park. When Greg pulled off his soaked shirt, under the street light Candace could just make out the redness on his back where he had landed.

"Are you sure you're all right?"

"I'll be fine," he said, his voice muffled by the sweatshirt he was pulling over his head. "Here, put this on." He removed a jacket from the backseat and she took it gratefully.

They spoke little in the car on the way home, as Candace alternated between worrying about Greg and thrilling over her engagement. His teeth chattered audibly in spite of the heater blasting out warmth.

"I must look a right mess," Greg said in between shivers as they pulled up outside the old villa. "How can I ask your dad that all-important question looking like this?" He peered in the mirror. "I'll nip home and come back later."

"No, I won't be able to keep the secret for that long."

He looked down at his trousers. "I really need to get out of these wet jeans."

"Dad might be able to loan you some."

"I can just imagine that—'can I borrow a pair of your trousers? And by the way, I'd like to marry your daughter'." He gave her a peck on the cheek. "I'll be back in half an hour."

There was no way she would be able to hide her shining face or sparkling ring from her parents. Blessedly they were in the lounge so after calling out a brief greeting, Candace headed straight to her room. Anyway, it wasn't as though she would need to avoid them for long, just until Greg returned and they could make their announcement.

She changed out of her damp gear and sat fidgeting, unable to settle as the half hour dragged by. And then another.

There was no reply to the text she sent Greg. Perhaps he was in transit. Another hour slowly went past before she tried texting him again. Still nothing.

Her parents called good night to her through the closed door. Should she tell them not to go to bed yet? But it was getting too late for Greg to visit now. Maybe he had fallen asleep—how disappointing. She slid the ring off her finger and carefully placed it in the box. The announcement would have to wait until morning.

Wedding excitement and worry about Greg made sleep elusive. By the time Candace crept out of the house, the sun was only just above the horizon and her family were nowhere to be seen. When she pulled into Greg's driveway, she spotted his vehicle in the garage. At least he had made it home.

There was no response to her repeated knocks on the door. Perhaps he was still snoring. With mild resentment at his ability to sleep when she couldn't, she walked around to the back. His bedroom curtains were open and his neatly made bed looked as though it hadn't been slept in. It was quite possible he had crashed out on the couch. Or he might be in the bathroom. She pounded on the back door, but still there were no signs of life. After completing her circuit of the house, fretting and pondering as she went, she checked the garage—it was strange that the door was open when it was so early. In the dimness and through the fogged-up windows of the car, she could just make out a figure slumped over the steering wheel.

"Greg!" She yanked the door open and reached for his wrist with one hand and her mobile with the other. To her relief, his pulse was strong. She jumped when he stirred.

"Huh?" Greg lifted his head and squinted at her. "Candace? What are you doing here?" He struggled to sit up. "Ooh, it hurts to breathe."

"That does it." Candace primed her phone. "I'm calling an ambulance."

"No, I'm all right." Greg held up a hand. "I'm just stiff and sore from sleeping in the car and from my little mishap last night."

"Well, at least let me take you to a medical centre."

"Okay, but I need to change into some dry trousers."

"You mean you slept in those wet clothes all night—you could have pneumonia!"

"The last thing I remember is parking in the garage."

"So you didn't hear my texts?"

With much groaning, Greg hauled himself out of the car. He pulled his phone from his damp pocket and gave it a rueful examination. "It looks as though it went for a bit of a swim too. It could be terminal."

"As long as it's the only thing that is. I'll put it in the hot water cupboard."

Inside he went off to change while Candace waited impatiently in the lounge. She was about to knock on the bedroom door to check if he was still upright when he emerged, looking tidy but hunched in pain.

"We need to get you some medical attention right now," Candace said, not giving him room to argue.

The doctor diagnosed bruised but not cracked ribs, ruled out anything worse and prescribed at least one day of bed rest.

"When we get back to your place," Candace said, as they made their way to the car, "you should go straight to bed."

"As tempting as that is, first we have to pay a visit to your parents." Greg managed a pale smile. "I have a serious question to ask them."

Chapter Thirty-Three

"I wonder what happened to Candace last night?" Saph gazed out the kitchen window as she washed a cup and placed it on the rack to dry. "She was awfully quick to go to bed and I haven't seen her this morning."

"It's none of our business," James said, wielding a tea towel.

"Yes, I know." Saph sighed. "But I can't help being a mother—my maternal instinct tells me something's up." Suds splashed the pane as she pointed a soapy finger. "Here's Candace now. With Greg." She watched her daughter help him from the car. "He does not look well." She hurried to open the door. "What's wrong?"

"Hello Mrs Holden," Greg said. "Don't worry, it's nothing. I'll tell you about it soon." He managed a tired but jubilant smile and paused to draw a painful breath before facing James. "Mr Holden, can we have a chat please?"

After the men had retired to the lounge and closed the door, Saph raised her eyebrows at Candace. But her daughter's only response was a smug grin.

After what felt like a month, and with the suspense threatening to do her in, James and Greg emerged again. Saph hovered and waited for an announcement.

"Greg is going to take Candace off our hands," James said in his usual dry fashion, "in marriage."

"If that's all right by you?" Greg asked Saph.

"Most definitely!" It would have been undignified to do a dance of joy, so she restrained herself. "Congratulations—I'm so happy for you both."

"Humph, it seems you can't wait to get rid of me," Candace said, folding her arms in mock indignation.

Saph gave her daughter a delighted embrace. "Of course I don't want you to go, but I'm just so glad you're marrying Greg." *The right man this time.* She stopped short of saying it out loud. Greg's slight physical resemblance to Neil was hopefully the only similarity.

Then suspicion flickered. A proposal so soon after a night spent together seemed mildly dubious. Surely they weren't in a rush to get married?

"So have you set a date yet?" she asked, subtly digging.

Candace opened her mouth to speak but Greg beat her to it. "The sooner the better, as far as I'm concerned." He raised hopeful eyebrows at Candace. His words did nothing to ease Saph's concern. But his grin was mischievous. "So in future Mrs B won't be able to accuse us of getting up to anything we shouldn't."

"Steady on, Mum," Candace held up a hand. "Greg only proposed last night. It might not be for a year or so. There's no hurry." With that Saph's fears were allayed.

"I know." She tried to rein it in. "I'm just so excited for you." Turning to her future son-in-law, she hugged him as gently as possible, aware of his discomfort. "Welcome to the family, Greg."

"I hope you know what you're letting yourself in for." James looked pleased too, although he didn't show it as much as she did. "We'll have to warn you all about Candace's idiosyncrasies." With that his daughter turned on her heel and marched out of the room.

"Did I say something wrong?" he asked, grimacing. But his face lightened when Candace emerged seconds later and held out her left hand. A simple but charming ring adorned her finger.

"I've been dying to show this to you. The big announcement

was all supposed to happen last night, but it didn't quite work out the way we'd planned."

"So that's why you went straight to your bedroom," Saph said. "I thought perhaps you were really upset."

While Candace was telling them the story of the proposal and the drama that followed, the twins bounced into the kitchen.

"Greg's going to be your brother-in-law!" Candace told them.

"What's that mean?" Gemma asked, screwing up her face in puzzlement.

"It means I'm going to marry Greg and go and live with him."

"Can I have my room back?" Chris asked, ever the practical one.

"Now if it's all right by you," Greg said, visibly drooping after all the excitement, "I just want to go home and wallow in luxurious misery on my sick bed."

After Candace had left to drive Greg home and the twins had returned to their play, Saph noticed James's sober expression.

"How on earth can we afford to pay for a wedding?" he asked.

"Oh, is that what you're worried about? I hadn't thought that far ahead. Trust you to be so practical."

"We might have to save for a decade," James said. "Or perhaps we could put a ladder up to her window as a hint for her to elope. Offspring are expensive, don't you think? Even at Candace's age."

"We'll manage somehow. Perhaps I could increase my hours of work. And I'm sure Candace will be able to contribute."

"Maybe we could sell something."

"Like what?"

"How much do you get for a kidney?"

Saph rolled her eyes before grinning. "Wow, I've just had a thought. One of my favourite rock stars is going be my daughter's father-in-law!"

"I can't wait for you to see where Greg's parents live, James," Saph said. "It's practically a mansion." Her enthusiasm was only mildly dampened by the discomfort of being squashed between two booster seats full of dozing infants. Although Candace was smaller, she had used the excuse of travel sickness to claim the front seat.

James grunted a reply as he concentrated on negotiating yet another bend in the Waitakere Ranges. "It was nice of the Stones to invite us for lunch," he said, once they were on a less complicated stretch of road.

"It's just around this next corner," Candace said. When James pulled up in front of the gate, she hopped out of the car to speak into the intercom. The gate slid back with only a faint squeak and James steered the car through into a tunnel of trees.

"There is a house at the end of this driveway, isn't there?" He peered out the windscreen. "All I can see is bush."

"Wait till you—" Saph said, just at the moment they emerged from the tree-tunnel.

"Wow!" James said. "That is impressive."

The house, which appeared to be in danger of sliding down the hillside into the surf, looked grand against the awesome backdrop of the shining sea. They pulled up in front of the garage and just as on a previous occasion, the two dogs, now both grey around the muzzle, barked and came bounding.

At their alarm call, Greg and his father emerged from the house. Once the dogs had obeyed the command to 'sit', the family climbed out of the car. Saph stammered a greeting, suddenly awkward with embarrassment of how gushy she had been last time she had met the great rock star, and still in awe of him. But his cheerful reply put her at ease.

"This is my husband James," Saph said, her tongue now untied. The two men shook hands. "And these are our other two children, Chris and Gemma." Jerry bent down and with much solemnity, shook each miniature fist. When the two dogs sniffed the twins, Chris stood his ground but Gemma squealed and hid behind her mother.

"Roxy, Rambo, heel you two," Jerry yelled and the dogs obeyed. "Leave those kids alone. They're here to eat lunch, not to be eaten for lunch." Hero or not, Saph frowned at his terrifying comment, which Gemma thankfully seemed too distracted to hear. After instructing the dogs to 'stay', Jerry ducked into the house.

Greg led them into the kitchen where his mother was organising the meal. After the round of introductions, they followed Flo out onto the deck where the table was set for lunch, and Jerry was heating up the barbeque.

"Since it's such a lovely day, I thought we could eat out here."

James breathed in the sea air. "That is one spectacular view." There was barely a breeze and the ocean was gently rolling.

"Yes," Flo said. "The scenery changes daily—it's something I'll never get tired of."

"It's lovely to have something nice and positive to celebrate." Saph passed a food platter along the table. "We're so happy to have Greg joining our family."

"We feel the same way about Candace," Flo said. "It's a pity Penelope isn't here to celebrate with us. I Skyped her last night with your news. She hopes to come out for the wedding but she will need a fair bit of notice to get a decent deal on flights." She smiled at Greg and Candace. "So any ideas when your big day will be?"

"We haven't had time to set a firm date yet," Candace said, looking at Greg.

"Tomorrow would suit me." He grinned back at her. "Yesterday would have been even better."

"It takes time to plan a wedding." Candace's glare at her fiancé didn't hide her coy blush.

"Especially if you want the full pav," Saph said.

"What do you mean by that?" Greg looked puzzled.

"A big flash do with a dress that's as white and fluffy as a pavlova. What with the flowers, the photographer, the venues for the ceremony and the reception, there's a lot to organise."

James's shout rudely interrupted the planning.

"Chris, come away from the glass railings."

"Don't worry, they're childproof," Flo said, "being extremely tough and shatterproof. You'd have to be the incredible hulk to break them."

"Yes, but are they small-dirty-hands proof? I don't want to be held responsible for greasy marks on the clean glass."

After they had eaten, Jerry and Flo fetched the guitars.

"You're in for a treat," Saph murmured to James. The two children sat in quiet awe of the music, although Gemma put her hands over her ears when the volume increased.

"Do you think you could play at our wedding?" Candace asked as the instruments were being placed back in the cases.

"I'd be delighted to." Jerry chuckled. "But on one condition—I don't get recognised."

"We'll have to dream up a disguise for you," Greg said.

"James," Saph said, "is that your mobile ringing?"

He retrieved his phone from the dining table, glanced at the screen, and answered. "Hi Mum."

Alarmingly, the smile slid off his face. With one finger in his free ear, he moved away from the chattering group. After a minute, he beckoned Saph over.

"It's Dad," he whispered. "He's been rushed to Waikato hospital. It's not looking good, I'm afraid. We'll have to go."

Chapter Thirty-Four

It was a quiet and tense drive back through the ranges. Saph was kept busy praying under her breath while James and Candace were obviously lost in thought.

"We'll nip home and everyone can grab some fresh clothes and toothbrushes," James said once they were back in the city. "We may need to stay the night in Cambridge. Candace, do you want to come with us?"

"I want to see Papa Bear too." Candace's words were clear but quiet and her face was a little pale.

"Are we going to see Papa Bear?" Saph felt Chris's excited wriggle through his booster seat, and Gemma copy him. "I want a piggy back."

"I'm afraid he won't be able to play with you," Saph said, "because he's very sick in hospital. So you'll have to be quiet around him."

Leaving the twins in the waiting area with Candace, Saph followed James into the hospital room. His mother was sitting in the chair next to her husband's bed, anxiously clutching his limp hand. She looked up at them, exhaustion and worry clear in her red-rimmed eyes.

"Oh, James." It was almost a wail. She arose to give him a tight hug and seemed reluctant to let go. Saph was next on the receiving end.

"How is he?" James asked, eyeing his father and all the gadgets attached to his prone body. "What happened? Why has he got that huge red lump on his forehead?"

"He was in the laundry on the step ladder trying to repair the shelf and he asked me to get the jar of screws." Marion grimaced at the memory. "So I was off searching for them when I heard a groan followed by a bang. I ran back in and found him lying on the floor in a heap. The doctors think he probably had a massive heart attack and cracked his head on something as he fell." Her voice became a whisper. "I don't think he's going to make it."

At James's stricken expression, Saph's heart sank. She needed to inject some optimism.

"My dad was in the same situation years ago," she whispered to James and Marion. "But now look at him. There is hope for Len too."

James nodded and gave her a wan smile, but his mother shook her head.

Saph and Candace took it in turns to sit with the children. But after an hour of milling around and not being allowed to touch anything, the twins had apparently had enough.

"I'm hungry." Chris's whine was loud enough to be heard at the bedside.

"This is boring." Gemma chimed in.

Marion handed Saph a house key. "You take the kids and go back to our place. Stay the night if you want."

"I'd prefer to be here with you and James," Saph said. "Anyway if I take our car, how will you get back to Cambridge?"

"Although I so wanted to go with Len in the ambulance, I drove here. It was a complete nightmare, but I didn't know how I was going to get home otherwise …" Marion's voice faded.

Saph went out into the waiting area. "Candace, do you want to take the twins back to your grandparents' place?"

"I just want to see Papa Bear one more time." One last time, her words implied. She spent a couple of minutes with her grand-father, holding his limp hand and murmuring to him. Although Saph couldn't hear what she said, it could have been a prayer. Then Candace gently kissed him on the cheek and patted his arm. He barely responded to her touch. "Goodbye, Papa Bear." She sounded so sad and wistful Saph was touched by the finality of her words. Did Candace somehow know she wasn't going to see him again?

"Say good-bye to Papa Bear," Candace said to the children before wiping away a tear.

Chris and Gemma stood in the doorway.

"Bye Papa Bear," Gemma said. Her sad little wave nearly broke Saph's heart and when Chris followed his sister's lead, she had to gulp back a sob. Their solemn faces indicated they too must have picked up on Candace's instinct.

"We'll let you know if his condition changes," Saph whispered, "hopefully for the better—but prepare yourself for the worst."

With one last look of regret at her grandfather, Candace led the twins away.

Saph was all but asleep when she heard her father-in-law stir and groan. Through bleary eyes she looked up in time to see the man reach for his son's hand. Marion slept on obliviously, slumped in a chair.

"What is it, Dad?" James leaned in.

"Son." Saph struggled to understand the faint words. "I think I'm dying."

"Dad, you're going to be fine." James sounded artificially bright and quite insincere.

"I don't want to die. I'm scared, James." Clearly Len didn't believe the unconvincing attempt at reassurance. He was suddenly lucid. "I don't know where I'm going …"

"Do you want me to pray for you, Dad?" Len gave a weak but

distinct nod. Saph held her breath; her in-laws had never before shown the slightest interest in faith.

As James prayed, the sick man nodded affirmation and feebly squeezed his son's hand. A sense of peace filled the room and Saph found herself smiling as she watched her father-in-law heave a sigh and relax. Then his eyes opened wide and he pointed to a corner of the room.

"I can see Him!" he said in a clear voice, startling his wife awake.

"Who, Dad?"

"What have you done, James?" His mother's alarm sounded loud in the quiet room.

"He's over there!"

Saph looked in the direction Len was pointing but could see nothing. A sudden loud and prolonged beep from the machine ripped the peace to shreds, and she turned back to see his eyes flutter closed. Then he lay still, with a slight smile on his lips. When the medical staff burst into the room filling it with urgent noise, any remnants of tranquillity fled.

After Saph had planted a farewell kiss on the cooling cheek of her father-in-law, she left the room to allow James and his mother to say their final good-byes. Out in the waiting area she reached for her mobile to call Candace with the sad news—but it was so late at night, and it would be better to tell her in person. She put her phone away again.

When mother and son at last joined Saph, it seemed grief had aged Marion twenty years in as many minutes. In contrast, although James had clearly been crying, he wore a serene smile.

"This time yesterday …" the new widow said as they supported her along the corridor, "I had a husband and no idea …" She shook her head in despair. "There was no warning, nothing." Marion looked up at her son. "James, how can you be so calm about this?"

"I'm convinced Dad is in a better place now." The doors slid open and they walked out into depressing drizzle, glowing orange under the car park lights.

She snorted. "As you well know, he wasn't the least bit religious and he was certainly no saint. Don't get me wrong, Len wasn't a bad man—he never broke the law and he was always ready to help others—but he didn't believe in God or anything. Remember what he used to say? When your time's up, that's it. Oblivion."

"Didn't you see or feel anything in the hospital room just now?" James's tone was gentle. "That was the presence of God."

His mother's only answer was another derisive snort. When they reached the car, she opened her handbag and pulled out the keys.

"You'll have to drive, James," she said, handing them to him. "I don't feel up to it."

Once they were all in, his mother turned to him.

"This so reminds me of your dad, James—I can smell his after-shave." James patted the hand she laid on his arm. "I don't know whether I can face going home—it's going to be so empty without him."

"We'll be there with you," Saph said.

Marion twisted around to look behind her. "His old jacket is still in here."

Saph removed the garment from the back seat next to her and handed it over to the grieving woman. "We can help you through this."

"Why did he have to leave me?" Marion cuddled the jacket. "I still needed him. I thought we had years left together."

Her words were so full of pathos, Saph shed another quiet tear.

At the sound of tyres crunching gravel on the driveway, Candace was instantly alert. For the others to come home in the early hours and without warning most likely meant bad news. After hauling on her dressing gown, she stuffed the pockets with tissues and went out onto the porch. Mum was the first up the steps.

"I'm sorry …" she said, holding out her arms.

"He's gone, isn't he?"

At Mum's silent nod of affirmation, Candace reached for a tissue before moving into the hug.

"I know you've grown close to your grandfather," Mum said, giving her back a comforting rub, "since you found out the truth. We're all going to miss him."

Candace pulled back to wipe her face. "What hurts most is the thought of Papa Bear dying unsaved."

Through her tears, she was surprised to see Mum smile.

"But your dad and Papa Bear prayed together," she said in a low voice. She swiftly explained the astounding news.

"Hallelujah," Candace whispered.

Over her mother's shoulder, she could see Mama Bear standing frozen on the lawn, staring at the house, Dad's arm around her.

"Mum, we have to go inside now," Dad said, gently coaxing her. "It's cold out here."

When her grandmother came up onto the porch, Candace gave her a hug, which was received wordlessly.

"Mum, you must be exhausted—don't you want to go and get some sleep?" Dad asked his silent white-faced mother once they were inside. At the vehement shake of her head, he sat her down at the dining room table and Candace made hot drinks for everybody. The four of them sipped and quietly reminisced, although Mama Bear said little.

"Why is everybody crying?" a small voice said.

"Chris! What are you doing up?" Dad pulled the boy onto his lap. "Sorry, son, did we wake you? We're all a bit sad because, well … shall I tell him?" He mouthed the words at Mum and she nodded. "Papa Bear has gone to heaven."

Candace noticed her grandmother scowl at his words.

"So when's he coming back?" At the lad's words, James had to use his handkerchief. Once he had recovered, he continued.

"He's not coming home, Chris. He's gone to live with God now."

"I had a feeling this might happen," Saph murmured to Candace with a restraining hand on her arm. "Give them a little bit of space." From a short distance, they watched James and his mother hesitate at the entrance of the funeral parlour.

"I know it's difficult, Mum," he was saying. "But we have to go in." Linking his arm through hers, he coaxed her forward.

"What's wrong?" Candace asked in a low voice.

"This is where Darryll's funeral was held," Saph whispered. "It brings back unhappy memories even for me—and I barely knew him. I can only imagine what it must be like for James and his mum." She shook her head. "It was such a sad funeral and your grandmother was beside herself. In fact she was so bereft, James and his dad had to help her out of the church. But whereas there was no hope for Darryll, at least we know your grandfather is in heaven."

"This is the part I hate," Saph whispered as the first clod of earth thudded onto the coffin. "It always seems so final."

Candace nodded. "Blessedly it's only his mortal—"

With a cry rending the solemn atmosphere, the widow rushed towards the open grave. Several horrified onlookers reached out to her, but she pulled up at the grassy edge where James grabbed her before enfolding her in his arms. He began murmuring soothing words to calm her down.

After the small crowd had dispersed, Marion towed James across the cemetery. "I want to go and see Darryll."

Once they reached his headstone, she hugged the cold granite and sobbed while James stood with clenched jaw. Saph nudged Candace away to allow mother and son time to grieve in private.

"Now I've lost two men in my life," Marion said, her tone dismal, as they made their way back to the car. "James, you're the only one left." She clung harder to him.

"It's good that Candace can stay on and keep your mother company," Saph said as she drove the car back towards Auckland. "She seems to be taking it really hard."

"Yes, I'm glad Mum won't be on her own," James said. "I hated leaving her but I need to get back to work and we can only expect Tiff to look after the twins for so long."

"In spite of the humorous things people said about your dad at the funeral, they all looked devastated."

"That's probably because he was comparatively young and it was so unexpected. It just goes to show you have to be prepared because you never know when your time is up. At least we have hope—both for him and for ourselves."

"It seemed we were the only ones there who did. I noticed there was not a single hymn or any mention of God at all during the service. At least not until you spoke."

James nodded. "I had to tell them he was in a better place. But even though I know he's at peace, I'm still going to miss him heaps." Saph glanced at him. By the set of his jaw, he was clearly holding back tears.

Chapter Thirty-Five

There was so much to organise—Candace sagged on the park bench. During her stay in Cambridge to help Mama Bear grieve and sort out issues, she and Greg had agreed to put the wedding plans on hold. They had even made the tentative offer of postponing it indefinitely. "Absolutely not," Mum had said. "The family all need something positive to look forward to in the near future." When Candace had phoned Greg to tell him the good news, her fiancé's sigh of relief was louder than hers. But it meant the flood gates had suddenly opened, releasing a cresting wave of preparation chores to crash down on her.

The sun was low on the horizon, the temperature was dropping, and she shivered where she sat. They should have left ages ago, but the children were having such a ball and Candace was reluctant to interrupt their fun. Or perhaps it was just an excuse to think of all things wedding.

She and Greg still hadn't set a firm date, but figured March or April was probably best, before winter set in. Which didn't leave them much time. There was the venue to organise; it would be lovely to get married in a garden setting, or perhaps the church where her parents had tied the knot. Then there was the reception to sort out. The Pavilion would be perfect—but it was probably booked up months in advance, especially for that time of year. And just the thought of what it would cost was frightening. Although wasn't it the bride's parents' responsibility to pay for the reception?

Mum and Dad were hardly flush at the moment. No, she wouldn't put that burden upon them.

She still had to find a dress. And outfits for her attendants. Tiff had jumped at the chance to be her matron of honour and young Gemma was to be a flower girl. Then there were the flowers … the list seemed eternal and headache inducing … she just wanted to get married!

A sudden cool breeze brought her sharply back from planet wedding to earth. She glanced at her watch and leapt to her feet.

"We have to go home now, kids," she yelled across the park. "Mum and Dad will be back soon."

The children ran towards her, still playing tag, their high-pitched giggles and yells filling the air. At the pedestrian crossing, she stopped to wait for them.

"Are they twins?" A passer-by smiled at the boisterous pair as they scampered circles around Candace. "I suppose they're excited about Christmas."

Candace groaned at the reminder—she had barely given it a thought, although Santa and the church nativity play had been mentioned more than once. Christmas preparation was yet another thing to squeeze onto her already full plate.

"The little girl looks just like her mother," the woman said, looking from Gemma to Candace.

"I'll tell our mum that when we get home." Candace grinned at the woman's obvious puzzlement. "They're my brother and sister. Don't worry, I get this all the time." She held out her hands for them to grasp. "Come on, you two."

"Wasn't that a lovely movie?" Saph said wistfully. "So romantic. Just the sort of film I enjoy on our date night. And just the right amount of violence for you."

James turned to flash her a grin. "You know me so—"

"Look out!" Saph shouted as two small shadows darted in front of the car.

Time changed to slow motion. She closed her eyes at the screech of the brakes, followed by a nauseating dull metallic thud, which seemed to echo on and on. She didn't want to look. But she had to. Opening her lids only half-way—as if that would help minimise the damage—she scanned the whole tragic scene. Intermittently bathed in the ghastly yellow of the pedestrian crossing light, a marble statue with hands on mouth, stood on the traffic island. On the pavement opposite was a small girl, face so pale it glowed in the dusk. At her feet in the gutter lay something resembling a crumpled rag.

"Mummy? Daddy?" the girl said. *Gemma.* Which meant the rag must be Chris. They had knocked down their own son.

As though she was swimming through jelly, Saph struggled out of the car and crawled and clawed her way through the sticky-fluid air to the rumpled body of her son.

"Don't move him!" James screamed at her.

"What's wrong with Chris, Mummy?" Gemma asked. Saph couldn't answer, couldn't speak. In her peripheral vision, she saw the statue unfreeze to become Candace, and James reach for his phone and Gemma.

"She's okay," he said. "Thank God!"

Saph ignored them, instead collapsing down beside Chris where he lay motionless on his side. She stretched out a tentative hand to stroke the boy's waxy fingers and silky face, and watched in horror as the blood poured from his mouth and pooled under his ear in an alarming fashion. His eyelids fluttered and then closed again, his faint breath bubbling the red puddle.

With Gemma clinging to his arm, James moved to crouch down on the other side of the boy. He spoke urgently into the phone held in his shaking hand, his white face reflecting the blinking car hazard lights. A distraught Candace knelt down beside Saph.

"Oh Mum, I'm so sorry! I tried to grab their hands but they were playing tag and just ran straight past me onto the road."

Saph could only shake her head, unable to form words. Candace began to rub her back, obviously meant to be comforting, but it was just irritating. Saph shrugged her daughter's hand away—too bad if Candace felt rejected—and continued to stroke her son's face. He was all she could care about right now.

They couldn't lose him, they just couldn't. Surely she hadn't waited so long for this boy, prayed for children so hard, only to have him taken away?

No, Lord, please no.

She glanced around her. Where was the ambulance? It seemed to take an entire month to arrive. A police car pulled up close behind it. The others backed off, but Saph stayed where she was.

"I'm afraid you'll have to move away so we can do our job." The ambulance officer spoke kindly but firmly.

"But I can't." She was unwilling to let go of her son's hand even for a second, afraid that if she did, he would let go of life. The man gently moved her aside.

She hovered as close as she could. While the medics assessed her son, the police officers questioned James.

"I knocked down my own boy." His voice was almost a wail. "I wasn't speeding, I promise."

"We can see by the tyre marks you weren't going too fast when you put on the brakes. But sir, you should have noticed you were approaching a pedestrian crossing." In answer, James wept.

After they had finished with him, it was Candace's turn.

"I looked away just at the moment it happened. I was so distracted by … I'm supposed to be getting married next year …" Her words fizzled out.

Then the officers approached Saph. As she gave her dull and monosyllabic answers, she kept her eyes on Chris the whole time—she couldn't bear to look away from him, not even for a moment.

When the medics loaded the tiny body onto the stretcher, the tears finally began to flow. She followed him into the back of the ambulance, still doing her best not to let him out of her sight.

"Where's Gemma?" Candace's panicky voice barely penetrated Saph's brain fog. Where was her precious daughter? Saph did a visual search through the vehicle doorway for her.

"I popped her in the back of the car," she heard James say. He climbed in beside Saph and put his arm around her. She barely noticed. "Are you going to be okay?"

"What do you think?" Grief and shock was making her rude and abrupt, but she wasn't about to apologise. He clenched his jaw.

"First Dad and now Chris," she heard him mutter.

"He is *not* going to die," Saph said through gritted teeth. "He just can't."

"We'll follow in the car," James said in a flat voice as he exited. Before the ambulance doors were closed, she watched James hesitating to get into his vehicle—as though he was summoning up the courage to get behind the wheel again. *Serves you right.* She shouldn't be thinking that—shouldn't be blaming him for the accident. But if she didn't, she might have to admit culpability. And right now, she couldn't face it.

Finally they were off. As they sped along the motorway, Saph continued to pray silently.

"Are you all right there, Mrs ..." The ambulance officer checked his notes. "Holden?"

"He is going to live." She couldn't stop a sob from escaping. "Isn't he? I pray to God he will."

The man smiled. "Me too." It was a comfort to know there was someone else praying as he cared for her son, and a fraction of the tension left her.

"We're nearly at the hospital now." He sounded kind. But he hadn't answered her question.

"As difficult as it is, it's better for you and for your son if you wait out there." With a kind smile, the nurse shooed her out of the room. So while the medical staff worked on Chris for what felt like all eternity, Saph fidgeted in the near-empty waiting area, alternately worrying and fuming. Where were the others? Not that she really wanted them there. She was still too upset with them—and with herself, if she were honest. At last they appeared, James looking pale.

"Any developments?" he asked, avoiding Saph's eye.

"No news yet," she said in a monotone. He took a seat on the other side of the room—which was just as well because right now she didn't want him anywhere near her—and sat with his head down.

Candace slumped in the chair next to her. "I had to drive," she whispered. There was a wobble in her voice and her face was a blank white. "Dad was too traumatised. He might get done for dangerous driving—because of what he … did."

Good job. But Saph resisted the urge to say it.

For a while nobody said a word. Saph couldn't trust herself not to utter something she would regret.

"This is all my fault," Candace said, her dismal words loud in the quietness.

"No, it's mine," James said, without looking up. "I should've been concentrating."

"I'm sorry for running out on the road, Mummy." Gemma burst into tears.

"Will you all shut up about who's to blame?" Saph couldn't help her viciousness. "I'm the one who distracted James. But it's done now and can't be undone. Let's just pray Chris will be all right."

At her outburst the others sat in stunned silence, broken only by Gemma's sobs.

Saph held out her arms to her youngest daughter. "I'm sorry, baby. I'm just worried and it's making me grumpy."

By midnight Gemma was asleep, lying full length on the bench seat while Candace and James dozed in their respective chairs. Saph alone was wide awake and resenting her family's ability to sleep through all the trauma and stress, when a man entered the room.

"Hi, I'm the doctor looking after the young lad," he said, wearily rubbing his stubbly chin. At the sound of his voice, Candace and James woke up. "You must be the Holden family."

The doctor's grim expression was enough to send Saph's heart plummeting.

He must have noticed her dismay for he managed a reassuring smile. "Sorry, it's been a long busy night," he said. "We've done all the necessary tests and now your son is going to be transferred to the children's ward."

"How is he?" James sounded hesitant, asking what Saph was too scared to.

"He's only suffered a mild concussion and some cuts and bruises. There were no fractures. He's very lucky—it could have been catastrophic."

"But what about all that blood?" Saph asked, not allowing the relief to sink in just yet.

"He bit his tongue—they always bleed a lot and look much worse than the true extent of the wound. Also he split his ear—another profuse bleeder. Apart from a couple of minor scars, your son is going to be fine."

"Thank the Lord!" James murmured.

"Amen," Saph added.

The doctor gave them a puzzled look and then a tired smile. "It will take a little while before he makes a full recovery. To be on the safe side we'll keep him here overnight. So you might as well all go and get some sleep. You should be able to take him home tomorrow."

"Can I see him?" Saph asked.

"He's still out to it, so just a peek and come back in the morning." His smile broadened. "Then you can remind him there're only a few more sleeps until Christmas—that should get him buzzing."

Chapter Thirty-Six

Although it was mildly surprising Greg still hadn't replied to her earlier text, Candace wasn't greatly bothered. The hours spent in the waiting room had been a good opportunity to think—and not just about the accident. An idea had seeded, but it was only now after the doctor's reassurance of Chris's recovery that she dared allow it to sprout and grow into a plan.

It had to be put on hold however, as she concentrated on driving the family home from the hospital. Dad, still too upset to get behind the wheel, insisted on wedging himself in the back between the booster seats: one sadly empty, the other containing a dozing Gemma. Meanwhile Mum sat gazing out the passenger window, pale-faced and withdrawn.

And once they had safely made it home in the early hours, it was impractical to take action. After mumbling good night to her parents, Candace headed straight for her room, fell into bed and was asleep almost immediately.

In spite of her exhaustion, Saph couldn't sleep. And judging by the restless movement on the other side of the bed, James too was suffering. The whole accident scenario played over and over like a horror movie on repeat; there was no way that sickening thud could be forgotten. In between replays, she was plagued by a series of 'if onlys'—if only she hadn't distracted James, if only the twins hadn't been so busy playing …

But she wasn't about to let on she was still awake, as that might have meant conversing—and she wasn't ready for that. Not yet and not for a while. Anyway it was apparent James didn't want to talk, either.

What felt like mere minutes later, Candace awoke to find the sunrise giving the curtains a golden lining. She dozed for a few moments more, until the memories of the previous evening came flooding back. *The accident—but Chris is going to be all right.* There was something else, too … like a dose of caffeine, it woke her up fully. Now was the time for action. Without even a glance at the bedside clock she reached for her phone and stabbed a button.

"Hello?" A sleep-filled voice answered at last.

"Greg, we need to talk. As soon as possible. It can't wait. I'm coming round to your place. I'll bring breakfast."

After making a hasty stop at a bakery to buy some food, Candace arrived to find Greg unshaven and dressed in clothes that appeared to have been slept in. He greeted her, looking puzzled and more than a little anxious.

"Is Chris going to be all right?" he asked. At her nod he continued. "Sorry, I was out last night and I've only just read your text." He gazed wistfully at the kitchen. "Can you tell me all about it while I make coffee? I'm still half-asleep."

While he brewed up, Candace leaned against the door frame and gave him a potted version of the events of the previous evening. He made an empathic face as she hesitantly skimmed over the details of the ghastly accident—the memory and guilt still raw.

"Don't worry, Chris is going to be fine."

"What about you?" His look of concern made her fall in love with him all over again. He led the way to the lounge, where on the couch they balanced plates on their laps.

"There's nothing wrong with me, at least not physically," Candace said between swift bites. "I do feel a lot of guilt and I can't unsee that awful scene." She squeezed her eyes closed against the image. "I'm sure I'll remember it for the rest of my life. But I know it wasn't entirely my fault and I have apologised for my part in it."

"So please put me out of my misery." Greg's question was tentative. "Have you come to tell me we have to put the wedding off?"

"What happened last night has made me realise life is simply too short." She told him her idea and watched the initial surprise be replaced by a spreading smile that chased away the worried look. They were interrupted by her phone ringing. With an exasperated glance at the ID, she answered.

"Sorry, I'm not interested in any relief teaching—not until next year."

After she had hung up, she noticed Greg's startled expression. "There're only a couple of weeks left of term anyway," she said with a shrug. "So, are you on board with this?"

He nodded hard and beamed as she took his hand and hauled him up from the seat. "We have to get going," she said.

To her dismay, his smile disappeared and he clutched his stomach with a groan.

"What's wrong?"

He grimaced. "Indigestion—from eating too fast."

Once daylight arrived, Saph waited for James to get up, but he stayed lying with his back to her.

"I can't face work today," he mumbled, the first words he had spoken that morning. "I'll call in sick." She left him wallowing and went to check on Gemma. Normally she would be up and playing by this time of morning but she was still in bed, apparently exhausted from the late night and the trauma. Saph left her sleeping peacefully and picked at a sparse breakfast alone while James stayed out of sight. She was putting her dishes in the sink when he appeared in the doorway and announced he was going out for a walk to clear his head.

It seemed Candace too had left the house, and early, which was puzzling after such a late night. Whatever it was, it must have been something she considered urgent. But Saph dismissed it—with the others out of the house, she now had time and space to think.

They all had reasons to feel guilty. James had taken his eyes off the road for a second because she had distracted him. Candace hadn't been paying attention, little Gemma had been carried away with the game, and Chris hadn't listened to his big sister. It was going to take a while to process things and forgive everybody—including herself.

Saph drifted towards the twins' room to stand in the doorway. It hurt so much to see just one small body tucked between the sheets, while the other bed stood vacant. Sitting in front of the empty pillow was Chris's favourite teddy bear. Saph picked it up and held it to her, drawing comfort from the soft fur. His toy trucks were scattered on the floor of his side of the room. He was so different to his sister; Gemma was amazingly neat for one so young, and Chris's mess was never allowed onto her patch.

Was it really only yesterday Saph had, with barely stifled exasperation, told Chris for the umpteenth time to pick them up? He obviously hadn't listened. But she couldn't be angry with him now; in fact, how could she ever tell him off again?

Still clutching the teddy, she tiptoed over to the sleeping girl and touched her soft face. The child stirred but didn't wake. Thank God Gemma hadn't been hurt. She could so easily have been—perhaps even killed. It was almost unbearable to think about. She was absolutely precious. As was Chris; two little miracles sent from God.

Of course the twins were no angels; at times they were downright brats and tested patience to the limits. But how devastated would she have been if anything more serious had happened to either of them?

This must be how You think of us, Lord. Even when we're ratbags, You still love us and can't bear to be without Your children.

She whispered her gratitude to God; for His love, for Chris coming home today and the fact that he was going to be all right. Her prayer was interrupted by the click of the front door closing. Moments later James appeared in the bedroom doorway.

"Would it better if I just moved out?" His muttered question was despairing.

She stared at him, words failing her.

"I'll go and pack then." He retreated into the hallway and she sprinted after him.

"Why on earth would you leave?"

"Because I've mucked up majorly." James stared at the carpet. "I've let you all down. How can you bear to look at me after what I've done?"

Resentment made it difficult but she forced herself to put her arms around his waist. Although he received her hesitantly at first, she could feel the tension begin to ooze out of him.

"We've all messed up here," she said as they clung to one another. "You and I have to stick together through this; we need each other now more than ever." She took a deep breath in preparation for what she had to say. "I forgive you." It took considerable effort, the sincerity lagging a long way behind the words. "I'm sorry for being so distant and snappy. Do you forgive me?"

His only answer was a sob.

It was difficult to ignore the white-knuckled fists James clenched in his lap, and his sharp intake of breath as they approached the pedestrian crossing. On edge herself, Saph snail-paced the car through it and managed not to react to his tension. When she parked the car at the hospital, his audible sigh of relief mixed with hers.

On the cautious return journey to Saph's relief, James insisted on sitting in the back, using the excuse of wanting to comfort his son. Once they had made it safely home, he carried Chris into the house as though he was handling fine china. Then he hovered while Saph tucked Chris into bed.

With an affectionate pat on the boy's cheek, James left Saph to linger by the bedside. She gently stroked Chris's hair, making sure to avoid his sore ear. It nearly broke her heart to see her usually lively son so still and quiet, with every breath seeming to hurt. But once the pain relief kicked in, he soon dozed off.

She continued her caressing. It was going to take a long time to truly forgive the family, including herself. But blaming anyone wasn't going to help; the past could not be changed. Instead they would have to make the most of the future, hope that Chris had learnt his lesson and thank God he was not going to have any life-long disability.

This Christmas was going to have to be extra special, to celebrate the second chance God had given them with this child.

It was the best present ever.

Chapter Thirty-Seven

When Saph recognised the voice on the other end of the line, she let out a quiet groan. It proved to be well founded.

"You'll never believe what I've just seen!" Mrs 'Busybody' paused, perhaps to lick her lips as she savoured a juicy piece of gossip. "As Candace's mother I thought you should be the first to know …"

Before she spread it far and wide. But while Saph was busy dreaming up an excuse to get off the phone, the woman started in.

"I don't how to tell you this," she said, her smirk audible. "As I was driving past a motel this morning, I spotted your Candace emerging from one of the units. With a man! And you'll never believe who."

The woman was all but crowing—indeed, it was a tasty titbit. This was going to be fun …

"I presume it was Greg?" Saph asked.

"Yes, it was. The pastor of all people." Mrs B sounded shocked. "Do you mean to say it doesn't bother you?"

Here was another piece of gossip for the woman; Sapphire Holden doesn't have a problem with her daughter sneaking around with the pastor—what a great headline that would make in the church newsletter.

"Well," Saph said, relishing the moment, "you know they wouldn't deliberately spend the night together unless they were married—"

"That's what I would have thought. The first time might have been a mistake, but again? They should know better. Which is why I was so surprised!"

Huh—more likely Mrs B was collecting fodder for her gossip cannon, than worrying about morals.

"I know people these days think nothing of that sort of behaviour, but the pastor—"

"There's something you should know, Mrs B." Saph was enjoying herself. "They *are* husband and wife. As of yesterday." Game, set and match.

After some gulping sounds, the woman continued. "They're married?" Somehow she managed to sound both incredulous and disappointed at the same time. "How come it wasn't announced at church?"

"Because even Greg and Candace themselves didn't know last Sunday—so how could they possibly announce it?" Saph didn't hide her smugness. "They only made the decision earlier this week. Then they told us and other family before telling their friends." Of which Mrs B was not one. "*We* knew they were married. And really, that's all that matters. Good-bye."

But she hesitated; it would be wise to squelch any rumours in advance. "And no, they didn't *have* to get married so fast, they chose to."

Without waiting for a response, Saph disconnected. To say the last week had been an interesting one would be a huge understatement. First there had been the accident, and then two days after that …

"Hi Candace," Saph said as her daughter entered the kitchen. She had been elusive of late, only returning home to sleep. On the odd occasion Saph had glimpsed her, she had been wearing a secretive smile. Now Candace just looked smug as she deposited some mysterious carrier-bags on the floor.

"How is Chris?" she asked before Saph could say anything.

"He's been sleeping a lot. His poor ear is still quite swollen, but he seems to be on the mend."

"How soon will he be well again?" Candace bit her lip as if pensive.

"He should be out of bed in the next day or so."

The smile returned and curiosity got the better of Saph.

"What have you got there?" she asked. But before Candace could answer, James came through the door.

"It's quite relaxing travelling home by bus," he said. "I don't have to worry about the traffic. What's going on?"

Without a word Candace reached into one of the packages and produced a pair of dainty bejewelled sandals, which she slipped onto her feet. From another bag she pulled out a simple ivory dress with a velvet bodice and lacy sleeves and skirt. Her smile broadened as she held it up to herself.

"They're nice. What's the occasion?" Saph asked.

"I'm getting married …"

"I know that … oh! Surely that's not your wedding dress?"

"… on Friday."

"Which Friday?" Saph could barely manage the words.

"This one," Candace said, her grin lighting up her face. Before Saph had a chance to recover, Candace continued. "I would have happily married Greg sooner, but it takes three working days to get the licence. Anyway we felt it would have been insensitive to do so, right after the … ah … what happened on Monday."

It took a while for Saph to find her voice. "This Friday?" She gaped. "How are we going to organise a wedding in that short a time? And so close to Christmas! Where am I going to find a dress by then? I haven't even started looking." She wailed like a steam kettle about to boil. "The shops are so busy in December, and how am I going to find the time?"

Candace gave her a dismissive wave. "Just wear any old thing. Don't worry, it's all under control. We've already organised most of it."

"But what's the rush?"

"Why wait?" Candace shrugged. "The accident made me realise that not only is life short, but also what my priorities really are. Greg and I already know we're meant for each other. And a huge flashy wedding with a full pavlova dress—it's just not us. Nor do we want to become a financial burden to anyone by spending thousands for one day. We want something casual but meaningful, held at a location which has significance to Greg and me, and witnessed by the people we love." Candace's smile was tentative. "I do hope you're both free Friday evening and that Chris will be up to it."

"I wouldn't miss it for the world." Saph's words were heartfelt.

The wedding day dawned an ominous bright scarlet before the clouds faded to dull sagging wool. Late in the morning the threatened shower arrived, causing a frantic discussion regarding a change of venue. But once the sky was freshly washed, the polished sun sparkled, promising fine weather for the rest of the day.

It was mid afternoon when Saph tapped on Candace's bedroom door.

"Come in," Candace said. Saph entered to find the bride admiring Tiff's handiwork in the mirror. Her light make-up was perfect and her hair, expertly styled into silky ringlets, was adorned with a garland of flowers.

"Even I think I look gorgeous," Candace said, turning every which way. "You're the best bridesmaid ever!" She gave her friend a hug but a cautious one so as not to undo Tiff's efforts.

"Job done then," Tiff said with obvious satisfaction. "I'm sure Greg would agree. Not that he'd care what you looked like, as long as you turn up."

"You truly look lovely," Saph said with sincerity.

Candace glowed at her. "Of course I do. I take after my beautiful mother."

At first Saph couldn't respond. Things might have been so different if Kathy hadn't saved that tiny baby from death all those years ago. "Thank the Lord you didn't die that day, the day of your birth," she murmured. "And no thanks to me."

"Oh Mum, this is a happy occasion—no morbid thoughts please."

Saph smiled around the tears that threatened. "I'd better ready Chris so we can get going. It could take a while. Understandably he's a bit wary of cars now."

"Since I'm all organised, can I come with you?" Candace grinned. "Just to comfort Chris, of course." She paused and her smile faded. "Is having the wedding so soon after the accident really such a wise idea?" Her question was tentative.

"This wedding is just what the family needs," Saph said, "as a positive distraction from all the grief we've had recently. Don't worry about Chris, he'll have to go in the car at some stage or another." Saph eyed Tiff's jeans and t-shirt. "Anyway, you can't leave without your attendants—and they clearly aren't organised. Gemma is still playing in her room."

Candace sighed. "I just can't wait to get there."

"Going with your mum wouldn't make the wedding time come around any sooner," Tiff said.

Candace poked her tongue out at her friend. "Stop being so sensible."

"You look very smart." Saph tucked Chris's best shirt into his trousers, before leading him out into the hallway. He was still a little pale and bruised, but alert and taking an interest in the happenings.

"Are you going to be okay?" she asked James. He nodded but

didn't meet her eye, instead turning to Candace who stood jiggling with impatience.

"Now are you sure you're doing the right thing?" he asked. "As the father-of-the-bride, it's my duty to ask this."

"Yes!" Candace said, nodding her head so hard she was in danger of putting her neck out.

"So I haven't taken the afternoon off work for nothing?"

"Absolutely not. As long as you're up to driving us to the venue."

He hadn't driven since the accident. Saph's heart sank when she saw his jaw harden and the colour leave his face. But when he spoke, there was steely resolve in his voice.

"I'll be fine." He clenched his jaw again.

She really wanted to believe him, but still a worm of doubt wriggled inside.

"You can do it, Dad." Candace linked her arm through his before gazing up at him so tenderly, Saph was moved. "I'm grateful and happy that you're going to be there. It just would not have been the same without you walking me down the aisle." She picked up her bouquet of roses, plucked from the bushes surrounding the deck. "Let's have a practise run along the hallway while we wait."

"I'll see you at the wedding," Saph said.

"I can't believe it's all happening at last." Candace grinned excitedly and paced with James. "God willing, we'll see you soon. I might even be a rare phenomenon—an early bride."

How they had managed to hire an arch at such short notice was something of a miracle. Praying it wouldn't fall over in the brown-sugar sand, Saph added the final touches before arranging Candace's 'ring' centre stage on the signing table amongst other shells and flowers.

She was standing back to admire her handiwork when Greg's van arrived in the car park. Soon, Greg and Karl were making their way through the gap between the small sand dunes, with the pastor close behind.

"I hope we're high enough above the tide," Saph said as they approached. "I'm not sure whether it's coming in or going out." Greg sent her a nervous looking grin and said nothing. "Candace is so excited, she can't wait to marry you," she said in an attempt to make him feel more at ease. On impulse she gave him a comforting hug, noting how tense he was. "You'll be fine."

He put his hands together and looked heavenwards. "I'm praying my bride will turn up."

"Don't worry, Greg. Tornadoes and traffic jams wouldn't stop Candace from getting here. She's that keen, she would walk if she had to." She left him fussing to his best man.

"You have got the rings haven't you?"

"Yes, for the twentieth time." Karl rolled his eyes and patted his breast pocket.

The small assortment of chairs fanned out on the beach was gradually filling up with guests. After greeting her parents and mother-in-law with hugs, Saph took the empty seat next to Chris and he reached for her hand.

She was startled to see a woman sneak up behind Greg and tap him on the shoulder. It wasn't an irate ex, was it? He spun round.

"Pen!" Greg gave her a big hug. "I didn't think you'd be able to get here."

"Mum's only just picked me up from the airport," she said. "She rang me as soon as she found out when the wedding was going to be. But we decided not to tell you in case I didn't make it. I had to rush out and buy an air ticket—which cost me a fortune by the way." She punched his arm in a sisterly fashion. "So you owe me big time. And I'm also incredibly jet lagged, so don't expect any intelligent conversation."

"No different to usual, then." Greg grinned at her and received another blow.

"It'll all be worth it to see my big bro get hitched."

Saph checked her watch. The ceremony was due to start soon, and there was no sign of the bride and her attendants. It was mildly surprising, given Candace's eagerness to get here.

By the appointed time, still only half the wedding party stood at the front, the groom fidgeting and staring intently in the direction of the car park. He was fidgeting even more after ten minutes had dragged past.

"It is normal for brides to be late," Helen said in a reassuring tone.

"True." Saph twisted round yet again to look at the gap in the sand dunes. "But Candace was ready to leave with me and that was ages ago."

"Perhaps they got held up in traffic."

"Let's hope that's all it is."

After another five minutes Saph checked her cell phone, but there were no messages. Had something gone terribly wrong? Surely there hadn't been another accident?

The small crowd was beginning to get restless. Greg looked as though he was about to be sick or faint, and the pastor kept glancing at his watch.

Saph's phone rang.

"Can you come out to the car park please?" James sounded tense.

A panicked twisting started up inside. With a sheepish grin at the worried-looking groom, she made her way to the path between the dunes, conscious of the small crowd's stares and questioning murmurs.

To her great relief, all four members of the bridal party were in the car. But Candace was in the driver's seat and James sat in the back with Gemma. As Saph neared, she could see their stress. Gemma's face was smeared with something dark.

"Is that blood?" Saph asked through the open window, horror making her voice faint.

"It's chocolate." Candace sounded a little flat. "As soon as she saw the car she had a minor meltdown. She was reluctant to get in because of what happened in the accident. I gave her the sweets to distract her." Candace lowered her voice. "Dad was even worse, and chocolate bribery didn't work on him. Which is why I ended up driving."

"I was okay until Gemma started squealing," James said. It was a humiliated murmur and perhaps his words were more for his own reassurance than anyone else's. "And I couldn't face that crossing again." He climbed out and opened the doors for Candace and Tiff. Saph gave him a hug which he received, but stiffly and with embarrassment.

"You haven't driven since the accident," Saph said, "and the first time is always the worst." He appeared mildly reassured.

By now Gemma had escaped. Like a heat-seeking missile she headed straight towards her mother, but Tiff grabbed her wrists and restrained her. As much as Saph longed to scoop the child up in her arms to comfort her, she didn't want to reward her clinginess. Nor did she want chocolate smears on her dress, even if it wasn't new.

"Can you lead her along the aisle, please Mum?" The impatience was clear in Candace's voice.

"Sure, but we can't have a chocolate-coated flower girl."

While Candace jiggled with frustrated eagerness and Tiff continued to hold Gemma, Saph used face wipes to hastily clean the child as best she could. It was like dealing with an affectionate but dirty octopus, and a miracle Saph managed not to get the sticky stuff on her own clothes.

"I'll tell you now," she said as she worked, "I refuse to bribe her every time we drive anywhere."

"Don't worry, she was fine once we got going," Candace said. "It was just the first time she's been in the car since the … please hurry up!"

Saph stood back for a quick check to see if she'd missed anything. "At least you're going to have a great story to tell your children; how you had to drive to your own wedding."

Tiff let go and the child wrapped her arms around Saph's legs.

"You're so brave," Saph said, gently but firmly disentangling Gemma and taking her hand. "And now you have to go and be a flower girl."

Chapter Thirty-Eight

The strumming of a guitar mixed with the subtle sound of the lapping waves as Saph helped Gemma scatter rose petals along the sandy aisle. Once they made it to the front, Saph sat down and pulled the child onto her lap to watch the rest of the proceedings.

Then as Tiff passed by a voice drifted into the sea air, strong enough to compete with the cry of the gulls. Saph smiled when she recognised the romantic song; the once famous Jem Stone was serenading his future daughter-in-law.

When Candace walked past, almost tugging her father along in her eagerness, Saph fished out a tissue to wipe her damp cheeks. It was hard to say who was more radiant: Candace or the late afternoon sun. James looked so proud, his earlier trauma and humiliation apparently forgotten.

"That is so Candace," Helen murmured when she saw what her granddaughter was wearing. Saph nodded before catching sight of Greg's face; his smile must surely be visible to any orbiting astronaut.

James took his place next to Saph and she reached across to squeeze his hand while she continued to swipe at her cheek with the tissue. She noticed even he surreptitiously wiped away a sneaky tear.

The ceremony was brief but meaningful and the responses, sincere. After the newly-weds had finished signing the register, Candace let out a startled shriek.

"What's wrong?" Saph asked in dismay. Surely the bride wasn't having second thoughts?

"The tide's coming in! That water is freezing."

There was a scramble to rescue the arch and table and move them to higher ground. Then the glowing couple walked along the aisle to more guitar music, their progress slow as they greeted friends and family. The music faded into soft strumming before it stopped.

The sun was casting long shadows on the beach when loud chimes from the soup kitchen van broke the peace, startling the gulls and the crowd alike.

"I didn't know it still had them," Saph said to James as they led the children over to the van.

"Ice cream!" Gemma said. Her brother lisped an echo around his sore tongue.

"Sorry kids, no ice cream," James said. "But there may be something much yummier."

Patti, followed by her husband and Kim, hurried over to them. "That man who was playing the guitar …" Patti frowned as though trying to recall something and her husband butted in.

"He did an amazing cover of one of Jem Stone's songs," he said. "Do you remember it?

"I see Greg has the same surname," Patti said. "Perhaps they're related."

Saph grinned, but said nothing. She wasn't about to blow Jerry's cover.

"I must go and talk to Candace. I see there's a gap in the crowd of well-wishers." Glad of the excuse, she moved over to her daughter where she stood gazing at the sun's dying rays on the ocean, and embraced her.

"I'm so proud of you." Saph held Candace at arm's length and smiled at her, before noticing an apparent stranger standing to one side of the crowd. "Who is that?" His hair didn't look quite natural and he was wearing tinted glasses, even though the light was fading. "A wedding crasher?"

Her daughter grinned. "It's my father-in-law."

"Oh, of course. How embarrassing. I must say it's a convincing disguise apart from the obvious wig. Where's your husband?"

"Ooh, I like that word!"

Before she could answer Saph's question, Greg, using his best pastor's voice invited everyone to gather around a picnic table. In the dim light from the van and the car park lamps, hampers were unloaded, the gas cookers were fired up and a feast was laid out. Much to the children's delight, there really was ice cream for dessert.

Long after sunset, when everyone had eaten their fill and short speeches had been made and laughed at, the hatch was closed as Candace and Greg prepared to leave.

"Good-bye Mum and Dad," Candace said as she embraced them.

"I'm so happy for you and Greg, Candace. God bless."

Saph had to wipe yet another tear from her eye as she watched her daughter and brand new son-in-law clamber into the cab, accompanied by much cheering and well-wishing from the guests. Tin cans attached to the tow bar made a racket on the gravel as they drove off.

"This wedding may have had a rough start, but it turned out to be brilliant—almost as good as ours." Saph gave a contented sigh as she and James each carried a twin, too tired and full to walk. But when they reached the car park she stopped in her tracks.

"We've both brought vehicles. Are you going to be okay to drive home?"

"Yes, I'll be fine," James said but there was a note of hesitancy in his confidence. "You take the kids in your car and I'll follow." In spite of a twinge of nervousness, she didn't query him. Instead she prayed silently for protection. After depositing their weary precious bundles in their respective booster seats, Saph kissed James on the cheek.

"There's no rush. I know you can do it."

He rolled his eyes. "Of course I can." But Saph could still hear the tension in his voice.

The journey home was at a cautious pace and it was some time before they pulled into the driveway. As they exited their respective cars, Saph glimpsed James's triumphant punch of the air. When she turned to look however, he had put his hand behind his back and was pretending to whistle a tune of indifference.

"You did it!"

"What did you expect?" But he couldn't hide a small grin of satisfaction and pride.

It was going to take time before James would be confident enough to drive to work in busy traffic. And it was going to take even longer before he would be able to bring himself to transport the children anywhere. But at least he had made a start.

"It's nice to see you two so happy and relaxed," Saph said, hugging her daughter and son-in-law. "Your honeymoon must have done you some good. Where did you go?"

"To a beach bach." Saph noticed Candace's contented smile, aimed at her husband. "We have news," she said. "Two lots, actually."

"Surely not already?" Saph said with a mischievous grin.

Candace gave her a puzzled look before the light dawned.

"No, of course not!"

"I'm just teasing."

"And not for some time yet." Candace bit her lip. "I've decided to sell the unit." She said it quietly. It had obviously been a tough decision.

"But that was your home!"

"Don't worry, I'm not taking this lightly. But it's for the best. Even with the perfect tenant, I'm still not happy about being a landlady. And any money we make on the sale can be ploughed back into Greg's mortgage." She smiled at Greg again. "Besides I now have a new home."

"And what's the second announcement?"

Candace paused for effect. "Greg's parents have given us the perfect wedding present. They're shouting us a trip to the UK and Europe. We plan to go some time in the new year. At last I will get to see all those countries I missed out on touring." She grinned at her husband and he grinned back. "This time, I'll have a trustworthy man by my side."

Epilogue

"Sorry I'm late." But Saph was talking to empty air. The house was quiet. Far too quiet. It was strange because James had asked her to be back by four and hadn't said anything about going out.

And where were the children? It was his suggestion that he take care of them for the afternoon while she made the most of some blissful Saph-time. Had it merely been a ploy to get her out of the house? He had abandoned her once before—surely he hadn't left her again?

His furtive phone calls and texts over the last week hadn't gone unnoticed. Perhaps he was having an affair—a real one this time. But he'd seemed quite content with their marriage and family life of late. So what on earth could have upset him?

Of course there had been the occasional argument, but nothing out of the ordinary. The accident was largely behind them now; the police had waived the dangerous driving charges stating James had suffered enough. There had been no major issues since.

She took some deep breaths in an effort to calm down. He had promised never to leave her again. It had taken some time, but eventually she'd learned to trust him wholeheartedly. And it was highly unlikely he would take the children with him if he was moving on with another woman. So where was he?

A rumble interrupted her musings and sent her running outside. Surely James hadn't bought another motorbike … had he?

Relief at seeing him mixed with irritation at the sight of the machine. It was a massive one this time.

"What have you done?" she asked as she approached him. After dismounting, James pulled his helmet off and ran his fingers through his hair, making it stand up in spikes. Even after all these years of marriage, her knees still went weak at the sight of her husband—hair askew, black leather-clad. He gave her that grin which always melted her heart—it was almost a puddle now and she couldn't be angry with him anymore.

The stiff leather jacket creaked as he put his gloved hand around her waist and pulled her to him.

"Pack a bag, honey," he said, sounding all masculine and strong which further jellified her legs. "We're off for a tour around the country."

"But what about our children? Where are they?"

He waved a dismissive hand. "I sold them on the internet." He grinned again, turning her heart into a warm pool. "Don't worry, I got a good price for them. Enough to pay for the bike."

It was difficult to think straight, but she managed to speak. "James, what you have done with them—seriously?"

His sigh was exaggerated. "Candace and Greg are going to have the little darlings. I thought it'd be a good idea to make the most of the babysitters before they go off to Europe. And, God give them strength, they can practice their parenting skills on the twins. Anyway I haven't bought the bike, it's a rental. As is the gear." Without letting go of her, he reached over to produce a spare helmet from the side pannier. "But it's ours for a fortnight. I've been planning this for ages."

That explained the furtive phone calls. And the subtle questions regarding her thoughts on riding around on a motorbike.

"You mean you want to go today?" She frowned at the lengthening shadows. "But it's late afternoon already."

"I thought our first stop could be Raglan which is only a couple of hours ride away—how does that sound? If we get a move on, we can sit on the beach and watch the sun set."

After some frantic packing and organising, Saph tugged on the protective gear before clambering onto the Goldwing behind James. The pillion seat was as comfortable as an armchair and once she had relaxed into it, she gave James the thumbs up and he started the machine.

The sun was already low in the sky as they left the busy Southern motorway and rumbled west towards the coast. But time didn't matter on holiday; soon they would be watching a sunset on the beach, with two whole weeks of doing nothing but pleasing themselves stretching before them. Of course she would miss the children, but she would enjoy having James all to herself.

Saph leaned forward to put her arms around her husband's waist and squeezed. Not too hard—she didn't want to distract him. He gave her gloved hand a swift gentle pat before reaching forward to grasp the handlebar once again. As the golden rays of the lowering sun gilded the clouds, Saph thanked God for this crazy, flawed, but incredibly precious man.

Acknowledgements

In memory of my dear mother, Maureen. She loved reading, was very fond of puns, could beat me at Scrabble even in her nineties, and encouraged me in my writing. Sadly, she didn't get to read this book and I miss her and her proofreading skills.

Also, in memory of my friend, Clara. Her very last text to me told of how her mother-in-law had enjoyed *Ripples in the Water*. Clara loved cats, was an accomplished violinist and musician, painted amazing pictures and owned the Cadillac that featured in *The Truth Will Out*.

A huge thank you to:

Christel Jeffs—Manuscript Assessor, editor, proofreader and good friend.

My big sister, Jen, not just for her proofreading skills, but also for checking the authenticity of my writing on parenthood, a subject I have little experience of.

Andy Mouat, for proofreading. And he is MC extraordinaire at book launches.

Vanessa—my niece who has 'been there and done that', with the parenting of twins and who was able to give me lots of helpful advice.

All the other people who encouraged and inspired me, and who showed an interest in my book.

And of course My Creator who created me to be a creator, inspired me to write, gave me wisdom and allowed me to do something I love.

So if the Son sets you free, you will be free indeed (John 8:36 NIV). Head 'into the Son Set'.

Also by Clare Matravers

The first book in the Sapphire Series ...

Ripples in the Water

Sapphire Nord, a first year university student, is in trouble—BIG trouble and doesn't know what to do.

A friend suggests a possible solution—but it's drastic and has major consequences. What will Sapphire decide?

Her life is touched by tragedy, romance, an illness and faith before she encounters a mysterious woman with a huge secret—one that involves Sapphire, and will change her life forever...

The Truth Will Out

Candace O'Brien is suspicious. Why does the whispering always stop the moment she appears?

There must be a big secret—one which involves her somehow. How can she find out the truth?

Sapphire Nord has a big secret. But when will be the right time to reveal it to her loved ones? And how will they react?

She has a mystery of her own to unlock, but is it even possible? And will the unmet desire in her life ever be fulfilled? Or will she simply have to make peace with it?